The Leopard in a Pinstripe Suit

A magical tale of everyday business folk. And a cat.

Tony Henderson

First published in Great Britain by:

Leopard Publishing Ventures Ltd
16 Woodstock Road
Begbroke
Oxfordshire
OX5 1RG

A CIP catalogue record is available from the British Library.

ISBN: 978-0-9574550-0-9

SALVETE

This is a tale of normal folk,
Who dream to lift work's tiresome yolk?
They wish for rules to help them find
A better way a clearer mind.

The leopard is the tail untold,
There is no magic to behold,
But five clear things the creatures show,
Success it brings – should no-one know?

Adapt to an environment,
Act opportune on any scent,
To hunt and kill its chosen prey,
To work at speed on every day.

Be undetected – that is five!
The one that keeps this beast alive,
Successful predator unfurled,
Who lives beside us 'cross the world.

But how these traits can help, you ask?
To clear our desks of tiresome task!
A book of thoughts in clear pursuit,
The Leopard in a Pinstripe Suit.

So read this tale – it is some fun,
When action and adventure's done.
The question at the end to see,
Are you a Leopard? Will you be?

www.theleopardinapinstripesuit.com

ACKNOWLEDGEMENTS

The Cell-Like Team
First I would like to profoundly thank:

Stephen Browne for his dedication,
humour and wonderful cover illustrations.
Tom Williams for his enthusiasm, candid advice,
editing and most of all not letting me get away with it.
Mike Smith for endlessly crafting the final drafts, creating a
brilliant website and being the absolute authority for all things digital.

The Family
I would also like to thank my family for their endless patience,
understanding and for putting up with the crazy midnight writing
shifts, air drumming and reams of paper scattered all over the house.

Help and Inspiration
I would like to thank all who have provided inspiration, feedback,
encouragement and faith in me to actually finish it! In particular:

Phil the Ranger, Kevin Bell, Ricarda Rodatus, Ed Vaizey,
Enrique Rodriguez, Janet Adam, Terri Richardson, Richard Wray,
Justin Black, David Taylor, Mike Emery, Imran Razzaq, Ken Browne,
Rob Jenkins, Jo Perry, Peter Gillman, Stacey Anklam, Fiona Petheram,
Marco Wanders, John Jeffcock, Kim Warren, Jeff Cohen, Sal Momen,
Ric Martin, James Bannerman, Sheri Margolis, Charlie Stringer,
Emma Rose, Gavin McLauchlan, and Elizabeth Greetham.

Dedication
This book is dedicated to my late father:

Ian Henderson
Author, historian and publisher.
I am pretty sure that he was a Leopard too.

CONTENTS

1

PRINCIPALS OF THE LEOPARD

The Meeting

The meeting room door opened and the participants in the meeting began to stream out into the corridor. There was some chit-chat between them as they left but the mood was subdued. Last out of the room was Alan, a fifty-something executive who had chaired the meeting. As he gathered his things and moved towards the door Jeff, who was one of the young MBA graduates, sidled over to him.

"Hi Alan – are we still good for our One-to-One-at-2?" enquired Jeff nervously.

"Yes – fine," said Alan neutrally, trying hard to remember what a "One-to-One-at-2" might actually entail.

"Shall I come to you or should we meet at the Coffee Bar downstairs?" said Jeff, more confidently.

"The Coffee Bar will be fine," said Alan firmly, immediately wondering why he had agreed to it. He hated the "coffee bar culture" of the younger members of his team, much preferring the comfortable privacy of his office.

"Cool – see you there!" and Jeff was gone, flying down the corridor, his brightly coloured backpack bouncing off his shoulder.

Alan turned slowly to head back towards his office and the

mountain of emails in his inbox and, just as he had taken his first step a bright ray of sunlight shone through the window and caused him to look up at the warm and sunny day outside. Boy – what a great day! And he hadn't even noticed.

Feeling a burst of rebellion within him, Alan turned and walked downstairs and straight out of the front door.

Alan stood for a moment as the sunlight hit him and breathed deeply. Setting down his notebook, he loosened his tie and took it off. Very deliberately, he folded it, put it in his pocket and walked down the steps and crossed the road into the park. There was so much to do waiting in his office but he desperately needed time to think. He walked into the park, found an empty bench under a tree and sat down.

This morning's meeting should have been a breeze, but it had turned into a fiasco. Worse still, Alan could not put his finger on what went wrong. He had researched each topic fully, prepared comprehensive briefing notes along with a formal agenda. He had made sure he included all the relevant people, and yet... and yet... 10 minutes into the meeting one of Jeff's colleagues – another MBA graduate called Ben – had (quite rudely) interrupted proceedings with an assertion that the briefing note on the first topic was "pure bullshit".

Even though Alan was chairing the meeting, he was totally taken aback by this interjection. A polite and mild mannered man, he was neither used to being interrupted nor having a piece of his work dismissed out of hand – especially by such a junior colleague. Before he could get the meeting back on track, another "grad" called Kate had piled in behind Ben and opened the agenda topic wide open. They were followed by several other senior people (who in Alan's view should know better), and the end result was that he had lost control of the topic and, with it, the meeting.

He had tried several times – and quite firmly too – to close down the debate but to no avail. They had got no further than the first topic, and what was left of that had been ripped to pieces. Alan was not prone to self-doubt but he wondered for a minute whether he was getting too old for all this and should look for a less stressful role.

As he sat on the bench a black cat appeared almost out of nowhere and jumped up onto the bench beside him. He was a little startled at first by this sudden interruption but relaxed.

"Hello cat. Boy, life must be good for you on a day like today," he said, reaching out to stroke the cat's ears.

"Well it's a bit hot actually," said the cat.

"Holy shit! A talking cat!" said Alan (who didn't generally swear).

He stared at the cat who was now sitting on the bench alongside him. "Tell me I am not hallucinating!"

"Not at all" said the cat. "Actually I am a Leopard."

At this, Alan threw back his head and laughed out loud.

"What's so funny?" said the cat. "Why? Don't you believe me?"

"Oh come on," said Alan, "this is pretty funny. I am sitting here talking with a cat who thinks it's a Leopard. If you really do exist then we are both pretty delusional."

"Well that may be so" said the cat, "but it's true, I am a Leopard."

"OK" said Alan. "Well in the interest of truth, I am a washed up business executive who needs to retire. A dinosaur by any other name."

"Oh I seriously doubt that," said the cat. "Looking at your suit, I can believe the business executive bit, but not for one minute that you are ready to retire."

"Hah! You haven't had the morning I have had. Trust me – the fiasco of a meeting I organised this morning has set us back about 3 months."

"Hmm, what happened exactly?" said the cat.

So Alan related the sequence of events that had led up to this morning's meeting, the work he had put in and the disruption he had experienced. "I can't believe I am sitting here telling all this to a cat on a park bench," he finished.

"Remember, I am not a cat, I am a Leopard!" said the cat. "Go and look it up when you get back."

Alan laughed. "Why? I know what a leopard is…"

"You might learn something," said the cat. "Imagine if you were a Leopard too."

"Me? A Leopard?"

"Well that shouldn't be too hard; you just described yourself as a 'Dinosaur'!"

"Yes but that was just a figure of speech."

"Just think about it," said the cat.

And with one bound the cat leapt off the bench strolled across the grass and was gone.

Alan was mesmerised. Had he fallen asleep? Was he imagining things? He stood up and looked at his watch. 1.45pm. Oh boy – he better get moving – his "One-to-One-at-2" with Jeff was coming up shortly.

Alan walked swiftly back across the road into the office and back to his desk. He didn't have much time before his meeting with Jeff, but he was curious about what the cat (was it really a cat?) had said about the Leopard. He quickly pulled up the Internet browser on his laptop and entered "leopard". Up came the summary:

> *The species' success in the wild owes in part to its opportunistic hunting behaviour, its adaptability to a variety of habitats and its ability to move at up to approximately 58 kilometres (36 miles) an hour. The leopard consumes virtually any animal it can hunt down and catch.*

Alan sat back in his chair for a moment and thought about it. As he did so, the old adage about a leopard changing its spots floated across his mind. "Am I just too old?" he wondered.

The "One-to-One-at-2"

Jeff was playing with his smartphone as he waited for Alan. Alan wondered what Jeff was actually doing as he strode up. Is he texting someone? If so who?

"Coffee, Jeff?"

"Yeah – great, thanks. Latte please."

As Alan made his way over to the counter, he bumped into one of the protagonists from the meeting, Kate. Kate was a tall, willowy blonde who, although young, exuded a calm air of authority. Alan instinctively braced himself for another acidic comment, but Kate surprised him.

"Hi Alan, I am really sorry we didn't manage to cover off that third topic this morning. I really liked your thoughts on that. Can I come and chat to you about it later?"

Alan was flabbergasted. "Uh, sure – drop me a note and we can fix a time," he said. As he collected the coffees, he smiled ruefully. Sometimes life was so unpredictable.

Alan took two lattes over to the table and sat down opposite Jeff; he became very conscious of his own formality. He could feel his craving to hold this meeting upstairs in his office, around a proper table where he could take notes. He put this out of his mind and forced himself to relax. He looked over at Jeff who had sunk back into the chair with his coffee and made a decision – the mountain would have to come to Mohammed. He got up and sat down in the chair right next to Jeff.

"So what did you want to talk to me about?"

"Ah," said Jeff. "Um, err; well you are supposed to be my mentor for the next six months. I emailed you about it last week and you agreed."

Alan was mortified. "Oh Jeff, I am so sorry," he said. "This is really important and frankly it got lost in the prep for today's meeting."

"No worries," said Jeff. "Listen if you have changed your mind, no problem, I can ask…"

"I would love to do it if you would still like me to" said Alan quietly. "That is if you can forgive me for dropping the ball so badly."

"Wow. Err, sure – I would still like you to," said Jeff.

"Really?" said Alan. "I mean after this morning, am I not a bit old hat for someone like you?"

"Oh no" said Jeff. "That was just one of those meetings. As a professional, you are the master. Everyone says so."

Alan was floored. It was a huge compliment from the young MBA graduate, but it still left this morning's problems unanswered in his own mind.

"Well that's very kind of you to say so" he said blandly. "I hope I can live up to my reputation." Alan went quiet for a moment. He knew he should ask Jeff the questions expected of a mentor but the young man's comment had confused him. He couldn't contain his growing curiosity and decided to take a risk. "Before we continue, please tell me what you mean by 'one of those' meetings?"

"Sure," said Jeff.

Post Mortem

"I guess they thought we were back at business school," said Jeff, taking a sip from his coffee.

"At business school?" asked Alan.

"Yeah," said Jeff. "We are all so used to debating the issues freely and calling things out as they are."

"Oh" said Alan. "But that wasn't the point of the meeting. The point of the meeting was to agree on the recommended next steps and actions to support them."

"I know," said Jeff. "I read your briefing note. It was really well put together. But I bet you Ben didn't."

"Why the hell not?" said Alan, who was beginning to get angry. "I spent a whole weekend preparing that. I sent it out Monday last week; he's had a whole week. He's part of the project team, he should know it thoroughly."

"Ben doesn't do email" said Jeff, beginning to wonder if he revealed too much.

"What! What? What do you mean he 'doesn't do' email!?"

"Well you asked," ventured Jeff nervously.

"I did," said Alan, feeling a little embarrassed. He took a deep breath, closed his eyes, and decided to push on.

"So please tell me what you mean by that?"

"He just doesn't read his emails. He skims them now and then but he uses Facebook and text mostly. He relies on the Coffee Bar to make sure he doesn't miss anything important."

"Well that may be, but it didn't work for him this morning."

"Actually, Alan, if you look at it, it didn't work for you this morning either," said Jeff, feeling a little more confident now.

"Well I know that, but what exactly do you mean?"

"OK. You never come to the Coffee Bar either, so you missed the opportunity to have that debate with him last week."

"I don't do coffee bar debates," replied Alan tartly.

"You are doing one right now."

"Hah! Yes you are right – so I am," Alan found himself saying.

"OK, OK – so what's the lesson here? Do I need to learn to drink lattes and hang out down here?"

"Partly," said Jeff. "But in my opinion Ben needs to adjust too. Nobody has drilled into him the need for formal meetings with agendas and a chair and notes. I'm not great at them, but without them this firm is never going to make progress. You are really great at that stuff. In fact that's why I asked for you to be my mentor."

"Do you really mean that?" Alan was surprised now. "Sometimes I think I'm a bit of a dinosaur." As he said this, his mind spun back to the surreal conversation he'd had earlier with the cat. Maybe it wasn't time to retire just yet, however it was definitely time for him to think differently.

"Jeff," said Alan. "Thank you, this has been one of the most positive conversations I have had for a long time. I would be delighted to be your mentor, and in particular with those skills you so admire. In return I am going to ask a favour from you."

"Sure," said Jeff, "fire away."

"I confess I felt rather irrelevant in that meeting this morning. I know we've discussed why things turned out the way they did, however it has convinced me that I personally need to adapt to the changes that are happening in the business, technology and culture of the firm."

"I'm not so sure about that…" began Jeff, but Alan raised his hand.

"I am going to become a Leopard," he said.

"I see," said Jeff. Now it was his turn to be puzzled.

"No really," said Alan as he left the table. "Go and look it up."

On the Way Home

Jeff pulled on his Lycra cycling shorts and slung his bag over his shoulder. He loved days like this where he could cycle the 5 miles to and from work – fitting his exercise into his daily routine was a real bonus – unlike when it rained and he caught the bus, or heaven forbid was forced to drive.

He pondered his conversation with Alan. He was astonished by the senior man's approach this afternoon. He had hoped to learn from Alan about the traditional discipline needed to grind his way to the top. He wasn't expecting Alan to reappraise his own role along the way.

Oh well, it would be fun. Or at least he hoped it would be.

Jeff walked outside to the bike rack in the yard at the back of the office, and bent over his bike to undo the lock. As he breathed in the warm summer air and grappled with cables, he became aware of a black cat walking past.

"Hey cat, how are you doing?" he said absent-mindedly as he pulled the cable through the spokes.

"Good thanks," said the cat.

"Holy shit! A talking cat!" said Jeff (who also didn't generally swear). In fact, he was so astonished that he leant back on his haunches, and then toppled over onto his back. "Oof" he grunted as the wind was knocked out of him.

"Sorry," said the cat. "I didn't mean to startle you."

"Startle me? Startle me? How about astonish me?" puffed Jeff, who generally wasn't used to being astonished by very much.

"Well you may well be astonished," said the cat, "but I am a Leopard."

Jeff felt his brain hurting. A Leopard? He had just looked it up. Was this a coincidence? "Hah!" he said, "you are just a cat."

"And you are a walking advertisement for overpriced sports equipment," said the cat crossly. "I don't know why I am wasting time talking to you."

"How in the hell would you know about my cycling gear," said Jeff, his brain still hurting – what was he missing here?

"I told you, I am a Leopard," said the cat. "Go and look it up."

"That's the point," replied Jeff. "I just have!"

"Just have what?" asked the cat.

"Just looked up the definition of Leopard," said Jeff who was more than puzzled now. What am I doing here, he asked himself? Am I really talking to a cat?

"And why did you do that?" persisted the cat.

"Because my mentor told me to." He fixed the cat with a quizzical stare. "I don't suppose you were talking to him earlier?"

"I couldn't possibly comment," said the cat, and with that he hopped up onto the wall and disappeared.

Jeff stared hard after the cat. He wasn't really sure what had just happened, but he wasn't going to dwell on it. He stood up, climbed on his bike and set off home.

Reflection

Alan sat in his office staring out of the window. The pile of emails in his Inbox remained, but it was not occupying his thoughts. Nor were the stack of reports on his desk or the scattered papers. "How would a leopard operate in today's business world?" he mused.

He pulled the browser up again and looked at the definition once more:

> *The species' success in the wild owes in part to its opportunistic hunting behaviour, its adaptability to a variety of habitats and its ability to move at up to*

approximately 58 kilometres (36 miles) an hour. The leopard consumes virtually any animal it can hunt down and catch.

He pulled out a piece of paper and looking up at the screen periodically, he wrote out five headings:

1. *Act opportunistically*
2. *Adapt to a wide variety of environments*
3. *Operate at speed*
4. *Drive any chosen activity to a successful conclusion*
5. *Remain almost undetected*

"Good start," he thought. "Let's pick this up again tomorrow." And then the phone rang.

An Unexpected Turn of Events

"Hi. Alan speaking," he said absent-mindedly.

"Oh hi Alan. Sue here. Um, I was just checking if you were still on for the quick drink this evening."

Alan's conscious thoughts flooded back. Sue who? He frantically raced for his calendar: Sue Smith, prospective programme lead for one of his projects – quick drink 6pm. What time was it? 6.20pm… Bugger! Thought Alan (who still didn't generally swear).

"Err, OK. I will be there very shortly," he said.

He cursed again as he put the phone down. He wasn't sure the project needed a programme lead yet. He hadn't really thought about it and he had agreed to the quick drink only to keep the HR Director happy as Sue was returning from maternity leave and her old job had been filled.

He left his notes from earlier strategically across the computer keyboard, grabbed his suit jacket and headed out.

Meeting Sue

Sue was very relaxed about his lateness and they took their drinks outside to a table in the pub garden. Although she was very smartly dressed, Alan was most impressed by her relaxed but forthright demeanour. He decided that rather than giving her the brush off as he had intended, he would share his dilemma about the role for which he was considering her.

"Sue, here's my dilemma. I have a possible role for you on my team. However the project I have in mind is not nearly far enough along for me to hire someone as senior as you to be programme manager."

"OK. So tell me more," said Sue. So Alan laid out the origins of the project, where he had got with it and his concern about the lack of a credible and agreed business case for what appeared to be an important project.

"Is that it?"

"Err, yes," said Alan.

"It's pretty strategic."

"I know. That's why we are having such a problem getting it signed off."

"OK well I can fix that for you."

"Oh really, how?" asked Alan, curious to know what he'd missed putting it together.

"You need a network."

"A network?"

"Yes, a network."

"Ah. So without meaning to appear a little off the pace, what exactly do you mean by that?" said Alan, his curiosity heightened by yet another new development in his day.

"A network is the informal group of people that surround the project. They share the ideals and knowledge about it and are keen supporters – including some advocates – and are dedicated to making it happen."

"Excuse me for interjecting, but isn't that the project team we put together to run it?" said Alan, trying to grasp at the logic.

"A project team is part of the network, but certainly not all of it," explained Sue. "Most of the network would include 'stakeholders' – a terrible term but one that does describe people who will be affected by or dependent on its outcome. However a network, especially a managed network, also operates behind the scenes making sure things happen smoothly."

"Huh. Really?" said Alan.

"Yes. If you established a network around the project starting now, you could probably get your business case signed off this financial year," said Sue artfully.

Alan grinned. She had backed him into a corner – not that he minded as she had really impressed him. He thought back to his notes earlier: No. 1 was Act Opportunistically and No. 3 was Operate at Speed. "OK Sue. Listen: I am going to need to clear the headcount issue, but I'm sure it won't be a problem. If I can do it this week, when can you start?"

It was Sue's turn to be surprised. Alan had a reputation for formality, and she hadn't expected him to react anything like this quickly. "Uh, OK well I would need to get up to speed, so…"

"Next week it is then," said Alan, fixing an image of the HR Director in his mental sights. "I'll send you the project briefing note."

As they stood up to leave, Alan looked at her again with a furrowed brow. "One more thing, what do you know about the Leopard?"

"The Leopard?"

"Yes, the Leopard. Go home and look it up."

"Sure. I will," said Sue, who was actually rather unsure where Alan was going with this but did not wish to dispel her good fortune.

A New Dawn

Alan had slept soundly that night for the first time in months. While he would normally have considered the circumstances bizarre, he decided that he wasn't going to worry about them rather act on the forward looking opportunity they presented. He rose early the next day and set out for the office with a new sense of purpose.

It was another stunning day, and as Alan strode up the steps to the office he paused for a last moment outside to enjoy the sunshine. The office was a magnificent building of steel and glass surrounded by trees; he could see the leaves and blue sky reflected in the building. Through the foyer was the atrium with the Coffee Bar and then the stairs and elevators to the various floors. Alan's office was on the highest floor along with most of the management offices and the meeting rooms.

Alan's first act of the day was to phone the HR Director, who was fortunately in the office. "Barbara, I had a great meeting with Sue last night. She's starting next Monday; please can you get the paperwork sorted."

"UhOhErrWhat?" said Barbara. Alan had been historically long-winded and formal about hiring decisions, and although she had hoped he might hire Sue for this role, she hadn't really thought that he would act this quickly. "But I don't have a Job Description or agreed pay grade," she back-pedalled.

"Yes you do – use last year's project – it's all there" countered Alan. "It was your suggestion. Do it for Monday please?"

"OK, alright but I am not promising" said Barbara, resigned at Alan's unexpected forcefulness. "Let me see what I can do."

Alan put the phone down and felt good about life. He looked down at his keyboard and saw the notes from the night before. No. 2 leapt out at him:

Adapt to a wide variety of environments.

He grinned, and slid his suit jacket off and hung it over the back of his chair. He picked up the piece of paper, and headed downstairs for the Coffee Bar.

A Latte Please

Sure enough there was a cabal of the MBA grads sitting in a large group – some still in cycling gear drinking coffees and smoothies – a couple had bowls of cereal. He saw Jeff and Kate amongst them, and as he walked over Ben walked in through the door. His irritation flared for a second, and then he swallowed hard. Get a grip, he told himself.

"Does anyone need a coffee?" he called out.

A dozen heads turned and the awkward silence reigned for several seconds.

"Great. Love one" said Jeff.

"A latte please," said Kate as a vague chorus of "Thanks we're fine" echoed across the floor from the rest of the group. Alan smiled to himself. "One step at a time" he thought. Jeff and Kate got up to come to the counter with him.

As they waited for the coffees, Alan decided he would grab the bull by the horns. "Kate, we are going to look at accelerating that project you said you were interested in yesterday. It's not formal yet, but can you set up a meeting with Jeff and me next Monday at 10am?"

"Sure", said Kate, "But isn't that the time we normally..."

"Yes," said Alan. "I am going to shake things up a little."

Kate's eyebrows rose several notches.

"Cancel our usual meeting," said Alan, "and please tell everyone verbally as well so that everyone is aware."

Kate's eyebrows were nearly in her hairline. "Will do," she said demurely, and turning on her heel she scuttled back to the main group.

"Wow," said Jeff. "It's all happening here this morning."

"I am glad you think so," said Alan. "Actually it's you I wanted to see but I thought it would be fun to come down. Did you look up the Leopard last night after we spoke?"

Jeff's brow furrowed at the mention of the Leopard. He recalled his bizarre experience with the cat the previous evening, but decided to put it to one side. He wasn't sure that Alan would understand, or worse still whether he had been imagining the whole thing. "Err, yes I did," he ventured, hoping Alan would pick up the conversation.

"Ah good," said Alan. He sat down and spread the piece of paper on the table. "So I have been thinking about it. I reckon there are five principles of being a Leopard. What do you think?"

Jeff sat down and peered at the piece of paper. He was now rather uncomfortable as he didn't really understand where this was going.

"I guess," Jeff replied thinly.

Alan smiled – he could sense the young man's tangible discomfort. "Do you remember our conversation yesterday?"

"About the Leopard? Yes…" said Jeff nervously.

"No, No. The one about why the meeting went off the rails," said Alan.

"Oh that. Yeah sure – but what has that got to do with Leopards?" asked Jeff, still puzzled.

"That discussion convinced me that I need to change my approach to how I do things here. I have become very fixed and inflexible in my ways, and I need to adapt and act more opportunistically."

"Perhaps I'm being thick here," said Jeff, "but I still don't understand what this has got to do with Leopards?"

Alan sat down opposite Jeff and fixed him with a firm gaze. "The Leopard is a metaphor."

"A metaphor for what?"

"The Leopard is a metaphor for the changes that I need to make – and in fact the way we all need to operate."

Jeff returned Alan's gaze, then he looked down at the piece of paper:

Principles of the Leopard

1. *Act opportunistically*
2. *Adapt to a wide variety of environments*
3. *Operate at speed*
4. *Drive any chosen activity to a successful conclusion*
5. *Remain almost undetected*

He looked up at Alan briefly and then down at the paper again. Suddenly he looked Alan straight in the eye. It was as if a light bulb had suddenly flashed into life above his head. "Got it." he said. "Wow. Interesting." He looked down at the paper once more. "You realise that this is not just you?"

It was Alan's turn to look puzzled. "What do you mean that this is not just me?"

"If I am going to be successful, I need to do this too. Especially if you are going to be my mentor."

"Absolutely fine," said Alan, "but I'm guessing that I am going to have to learn most of this from you."

Jeff shook his head. "Remember why I wanted you to mentor me? You have huge experience as well as an amazing ability to structure things and formalise them. I need to learn all that if I want to progress to and succeed in a senior role."

Alan sat back in his chair. "OK I hadn't really thought of it like that. In fact I hadn't made that leap at all. Fantastic. This will be an adventure for both of us." He thought for a moment. "The Leopard is a metaphor for the changes that we need to make." He beamed at Jeff. "We need to sit down and work out what we need to fix a time for the first session."

They agreed to meet at first in Alan's office on Monday at 5pm. The Coffee Bar was probably more appropriate, but they both wanted a bit of privacy and a white-board while they worked out their ideas.

Close of Play

Alan returned to his office re-energised. Half the morning was over and his appointment schedule had gone to pot, but he was feeling so positive about the ideas that he refused to allow himself to become stressed by them. He tore through his workload and came to a juncture at around 5pm. It was another stunning summer's day, and he found himself looking out of the window again. He stood up, loosened and took off his tie and went downstairs and out of the front door. He walked over the road and into the park, seeking out the same park bench that he had sat on just a little over a day earlier.

"The cat didn't exist," he told himself. "It was just a figment of my imagination. Never mind," he said to himself, "whatever figment it was, it sure inspired me to get things moving."

The breeze rustled through the trees, Alan felt more relaxed than he had in a long time.

"Hello, what are you doing back here?" said a voice.

Alan started and looked round to see who was speaking. There was no-one there. Then suddenly the cat jumped up from behind the bench and sat beside him. Alan laughed out loud.

"What's so funny?" said the cat.

"I thought you were a figment of my imagination," said Alan.

"Well I'm not as you can see" said the cat swishing its tail.

"You are a Leopard, aren't you?" said Alan.

"So, you remembered," said the cat. "And how about you, are you still a dinosaur?"

Alan laughed again. "No," he said, "Now I am a Leopard too."

"Aha," said the cat. "And what made you decide to become a Leopard?"

"Well you did actually," said Alan. "I looked it up."

"Well done." said the cat. "I have to tell you it's great fun, except when people think you are still a cat. But I am getting better at convincing people, aren't I?"

And with that the cat jumped down from the bench and disappeared.

Chapter Notes

Definition of the Leopard

The species' success in the wild owes in part to its opportunistic hunting behaviour, its adaptability to a variety of habitats and its ability to move at up to approximately 58 kilometres (36 miles) an hour. The leopard consumes virtually any animal it can hunt down and catch.

Principles of the Leopard

1. *Act opportunistically*
2. *Adapt to a wide variety of environments*
3. *Operate at speed*
4. *Drive any chosen activity to a successful conclusion*
5. *Remain almost undetected*

2

FIRST IDEAS

Monday Again – A New Team Member

Sue knocked nervously at the door of Alan's office. It was 10am on Monday morning and she still couldn't quite believe she was here at all. The speed of events had been quite breath-taking.

"Hello. Come in," called Alan from the office. "Ah Sue – welcome, fantastic, sit down. How was HR?" he asked anxiously.

"A little flustered frankly," said Sue. "But they have sorted out pretty much everything I need right now."

"Great," said Alan. "So I am going to take you at your word."

"My word?" said Sue.

"Yes, your word," said Alan. "You said this project needed a network," he paused. "Having thought about it carefully, I'm therefore not going to spend any time briefing you on the project today."

"Right," said Sue rather uncertainly. "So what would you like me to do?"

"I thought you might ask that," said Alan mischievously. "Here's the file. In the front you will find a list of the people who have been involved so far. Since you made that comment about how the project needed a network, I thought that they might be a better place to start than me." Alan watched Sue quizzically to see her reaction.

"OK," said Sue, leaning forward. "That's absolutely fine by me. So what have you told them about my role?" and she stared at him cautiously.

"Nothing yet," he said. "But I have spoken to each of them to let them know that you will be in touch, they are waiting to hear from you. I have also drafted an introductory email explaining that you are going to be putting together the business case for the project." Alan pulled the note out from the front of the file and passed it over. "What do you think?"

"That's fine" said Sue, "but it doesn't refer to my role or the job description that I have just signed up for at HR." She looked up at Alan, uncertain again.

"I know," said Alan. "That's because I haven't even briefed any of them about hiring you. I am very confident you will win them over, but I thought it might be easier if it wasn't a fait accompli, so to speak."

"Fair enough," said Sue. "I just don't want to mislead people."

"Somehow, I don't think you will" said Alan. He stood up. "Come on, there are a couple of other people I need you to meet."

Sue put the folder into her shoulder bag and followed him out into the corridor.

"I do like this part of the offices," she said as they reached the Coffee Bar. "It's so relaxing."

Alan's intuition was right and he immediately spotted Jeff with a couple of the younger crowd. He strode over and briefly introduced Jeff to Sue.

"Hi Jeff, this is Sue Smith who's joining the team today."

"Hi Sue, good to meet you," said Jeff.

"See you both at 5pm in my office", said Alan, wheeling round and heading back up the stairs.

"5pm?" said Sue. "What's that about?"

"Ah," said Jeff, conspiratorially. "You'll see. Should be fun."

"Right" said Sue vaguely. "Sure."

"It's the Leopard," said Jeff. "Go and look it up."

The 5pm Meeting

Jeff was unusually punctual that afternoon. Not that he was usually late, but his curiosity drove him to get the planned session off to a positive start. He was curious to find that Sue was waiting in the corridor outside Alan's office when he arrived. He was also curious as to why Alan had brought her down to introduce her to him this morning. The office grapevine had been unusually lacking in information about her or what she did.

Peering through the door they could see Alan on the phone, somewhat agitated so they waited until 5 past the hour before Sue knocked gently but firmly on the door.

Alan looked up and although still on the phone he gestured for them to come in. "Look let's cover this on Thursday. No, I will not be able to draft anything before then. We need to discuss this first. Fine. See you then." Alan put the phone down and let out a long sigh of frustration. "It's all I can do to keep my current workload moving without spurious new initiatives," he grumbled.

"Bennett?" asked Sue. Bennett was one of Alan's peers in the management team who was notorious for being difficult.

"How did you guess?" said Alan, his surprise masked by his exasperation. "No – don't tell me. Never mind let's get on with it." He paused for a second, readying himself to continue the real objective of their meeting. "Sue, if I'm correct I invited you to this session but gave you no real idea what it's about?"

"Actually Jeff, gave me a hint this morning. He said it was something about a Leopard. I didn't really understand it but I assumed you had a good reason for asking me."

"It is a serious subject and I wanted to explain it to you in person to see if you wanted to participate."

"I'm all ears," said Sue.

"I had a rare moment of lucidity," said Alan. "As you know I have been in this industry – and indeed this company – for some time. While I have had a successful career, people regard me as rather traditional –

and I suppose I am. Last week – in fact, the day we met – it all came to a head. I ran a truly awful meeting, and I mean truly awful. I prepared the agenda thoroughly and the background reading so that we could have a serious conversation, but the long and short of it was that the agenda and the running of the meeting got away from me and it was a shambles."

"Well, that happens all the time," said Sue.

"That may be," said Alan. "But not in my meetings. Particularly as I had done a huge amount of preparation for the meeting. I was just not expecting it. In fact, it really made me question the value that I was bringing the organisation. I began to wonder if I was becoming out of touch and off the pace." Alan paused to let this sink in. "I had a long discussion with Jeff, who I think represents the best of the next generation." Alan waved away Jeff's embarrassment. "And the conclusion we came to is that we – collectively – need to change our personal approach to how we work in order to be successful going forward."

"Jeff and I spoke about it this morning briefly. So what have leopards got to do with it?" asked Sue, who was leaning forward, and listening intently.

"Ah, glad you asked" said Alan. "Have you managed to look it up?"

"Not yet," said Sue. "I assumed you would explain."

"And I shall," said Alan, standing up and moving across to his desk. "This is what you will find if you look it up," he said handing over a piece of paper on which was printed:

The species' success in the wild owes in part to its opportunistic hunting behaviour, its adaptability to a variety of habitats and its ability to move at up to approximately 58 kilometres (36 miles) an hour. The leopard consumes virtually any animal it can hunt down and catch.

"What inspired you to look up the Leopard?" said Sue.

Alan sighed and pushed back his chair. "Well," he said, "to be honest with you I was becoming very disillusioned with the way in which I was able to handle day to day business." He paused.

"Even 10 years ago, there was so much more structure and hierarchy than there is today. Frankly it didn't make for better business but it made life much less stressful."

He looked Sue directly in the eye. "I guess the truth is that I was seriously questioning my relevance in today's world and in particular my role here." He looked a little sheepish. "As for the Leopard idea, I suppose you could say that it came to me in a moment of deep thought." At that Alan smiled warmly, "I think it provides a great metaphor for defining a new approach to day to day business. Talking to Jeff I realised that the formality and structure I use from my experience is still valuable, but it's no longer agile or flexible enough to deal with today's business environment. Jeff gave me some great insight into how informality can make some things and people work really well. At the same time he values – or at least I think he does – the experience and insight that I have gained over my career." Finishing, Alan pulled out a second piece of paper from his desk and passed it to Sue. "This is how the Leopard definition could translate into the business environment:"

Principles of the Leopard

1. *Act opportunistically*
2. *Adapt to a wide variety of environments*
3. *Operate at speed*
4. *Drive any chosen activity to a successful conclusion*
5. *Remain almost undetected*

"I suggested to Jeff that he and I meet regularly to put together a plan on how we could do this – so this is the first session. Sue, I asked you to join us because I value your insight and thought it might appeal to you." Alan smiled at Sue and she eased back in her chair peering intently at the sheet. "I also thought that if you found it interesting you could explain to us your whole networking concept – if you want to, of course."

"I would love to participate," she said. "I really love the idea although I don't yet have the first clue as to how we can make it into something tangible. By the way how are we all going to find the time?"

"Let's work out when we can meet at the end of today's session. By the way – how are you both for time right now?"

"Fine," said Jeff.

"Yes. I'm OK," said Sue.

"Great", said Alan. "I don't want to make this a lengthy session but I do want to get the discussion flowing before we leave. Will you both please take a longer look at 'The Principles of the Leopard' as a starting point, and let me know if you think we should change them, add to them or delete anything? If it's OK with you," Alan continued, "I would like to pick No. 1 'Act Opportunistically' as a starting point for today, so as a starter what would you think this means, and what's stopping us?"

"Well I can tell you what's stopping us," said Jeff. "Existing commitments and time for starters."

"OK good," said Alan. "Sue?"

"Hmm… Alan as an example I'd say you were very opportunistic in taking me on" said Sue. "Quite how I would define that is another story." She paused for a second. "OK try this. I think it's mainly about priorities. You clearly had quite a lot on your plate last week when we spoke, and yet once you understood – or rather had a vision of how things could work out, you shifted your priorities and made things happen." Sue became very self-conscious at this point, suddenly aware that Jeff, who she barely knew, had no idea of the possible politics behind her appointment.

"Interesting," said Alan. "Thank you Sue, that was very forthright." Alan had noted Sue's sudden nervousness and, partly to reassure her, he added: "Let's be clear. For now, anything that we discuss in these sessions stays in these sessions. I would like it that we make our findings public at some point, but we must speak frankly and openly if this is going to work. Sue, I really appreciate your candour."

Jeff stirred himself "Well, I have five major projects at the moment, and these I regard as my commitments, but I don't have them broken down any more than that. Listening to you talk, I am not sure that these really are my priorities. I mean, I think this has just become a major priority for me, and I don't have anything planned for the personal development we discussed last week Alan."

Alan got up again and walked over to his desk. He lifted a piece of paper from the desk and showed it to them both from a distance. "My priorities are all on here – both at a detail level and a major project level he said. This is my weekly task list, which along with my diary is how I plan everything." Alan paused for second. "Therein lies the problem," he said. "I can see everything I need to do – which is great – but I guess my scope for 'Acting Opportunistically' is always limited by the stuff that piles up here and in my diary."

"Please can I have a look at your list?" asked Sue tentatively.

"Oh well, I ah…" stalled Alan.

"Come on Alan", said Jeff. "Everything stays in the room remember? You said it!"

"Oh all right then" said Alan reluctantly. "I am not sure what value it has…"

"I had a thought," said Sue. "Humour me for a minute."

Alan brought his Priorities list over to the table.

"Show me how it works for you," said Sue.

"OK" said Alan, "here goes:"

To Do or Not To Do

"I type everything I need to do onto a single side of A4 paper, that way everything I need to worry about is in one place. I put domestic stuff on here too – a little embarrassing to admit, but does mean less angst when I get home. I break the page up into blocks, and generally assign one for every project and put the detail items within each block.

The projects should line up with my Annual Performance Goals, but the day to day reality is that not all of these make it onto here although they probably should. I also have a block for my peers in our management team that I work with regularly, that way I can ensure when I give them a commitment, or ask them for something I remember to follow it up."

"Everything I need to do today I mark with an asterisk, I cross it out with a pen when it's been done, and once a week I transfer all my markings back into the computer. Everything that is in progress, and does not need action, I put in italics."

Alan sat back for a second. "The reality is that it works pretty well," he said. "But I never run out of things to do. Ever! I would really love to find a way of making the process more agile. I love having everything on one side of paper, but there is always too much to do."

Creative Versus Functional

"Alan" said Sue. "How many of those things on your list do you just need to do and how many of them do you really need to think about?"

"I am not sure I understand what you mean?" said Alan.

"OK looking at your list, it seems to me that some of these things you just need to get done. For example on your personal list you have 'Car Service.' Surely you just need to book it in then you can put it in the diary and take it off your list."

"That's right" replied Alan. "But I don't understand what you are driving at"

"OK, what if you compare it to some of the other entries. For example on my project you have 'Market Entry Strategy.' Surely that is something that needs some in depth discussion, meetings and a plan to be written before it's complete?"

"Well yes. That is different," admitted Alan.

"Exactly," said Sue. "The Car Service just needs executing. It's what I would call a 'Functional' item and will have a pretty defined amount of time attached to it. You book it in, take it in and then collect it. Job done. While you could call the other project a variety of things, it would be hard to define the amount of time it will need. It requires some thinking first which will then break down into more of a plan."

"That's really interesting," said Alan. "I never think of it like that. I'm just getting my list of things down on a page. So assuming my Car Service is not an emergency – and it was a work thing rather than personal – how could I prioritise in principle between these two items if it's not a stupid question?"

"Well," said Sue, "it's not a stupid question. To be honest, I am just thinking this through, but it really depends on when you want to do them. Take the Car Service, which could just as easily be a piece of admin for your computer or trip to the dry cleaner. There are times of the day when you are between clearly defined events such as meetings which have deadlines and preparation. I guess you use these for catching up on email, or making calls, that sort of thing. The point is that you rarely do something meaningful during this time because you are getting ready for the next meeting." Alan nodded, so Sue continued. "You need to actively separate these types of activity on your list from the more strategic ones, and either use existing slots or even schedule additional time to do them."

"OK. Well that makes sense", said Alan. "But that's rather simplistic, isn't it?"

Sue shook her head. "No" she said firmly. "It all sounds simplistic, but in practice I suspect it is quite hard. The reason is that hidden in all your project level activities are a range of smaller Functional Tasks which may well not be visible to you. I think that if you could get all your Functional Tasks out in the clear so to speak, you could really cut down your list significantly."

"I get it," said Jeff. "What you are saying is that there is lots of 'noise' hidden in Alan's list that prevents him from cutting it down and acting opportunistically."

"Noise?" said Alan in a puzzled voice. "What exactly do you mean by that?"

"Noise," said Jeff "is lots of little stuff which is keeping you from thinking about the big important stuff."

"Right," said Alan. "So what you are saying is that I need to break out the – what do you call them – 'Functional' items out of my list? Right?"

"Exactly," said Sue.

"So should I keep them separate on my list so that I can get them done in shorter, defined periods of time in between other things?"

"That's what I'm suggesting," said Sue.

"I guess that's what I need to do too then," said Jeff.

"What do you do now?" said Sue.

"I just do stuff as it comes along," Jeff explained. "If I run out of time during the day I just do it in between other things."

"What do you mean?" said Sue.

"Well if I go out with friends after work, and I haven't finished what you call 'Functional' stuff I just send texts or posts from the pub or wherever I am at the time. Sometimes I miss stuff off but generally it works for me I guess."

"Don't your friends get annoyed with you?" asked Alan. "I know mine do if I start looking at my BlackBerry."

"I have an iPhone," said Jeff. "We are all posting stuff to Facebook so I guess it's no big deal to my friends." He frowned though as he said this. "Actually I have never really thought about it. I wonder whether things would be different if I didn't play with my phone?" He paused and looked up. "I wonder whether we would all enjoy ourselves more if we all switched our phones off and put them away? Then again I wonder if everyone would turn up if we did that?"

"What do you mean by that?" asked Alan. "I mean if you planned to meet for the evening surely everyone who agrees to come will turn up?"

"Gee, I don't know," said Jeff. "Most of them operate pretty much like me. They take calls and do email and texts throughout the evening. Some of them are social but I know several people who do work stuff after hours and if we cut it off they might not come."

"Would that be a big loss?" asked Sue. "I mean if they are not contributing to the social interaction between you, will you really miss them?"

"Well now you are asking," said Jeff. His brow furrowed, and he paused for several moments. Alan and Sue waited patiently for his next comment. "There are two aspects to that," he said eventually. "Yes you are absolutely right, the social interaction can be very poor, and frankly if those that are disrupting it didn't come then it would be better." He relaxed and sat back with a half-smile on his face. "If we organised a no-phone session, that would be just so much better. However, there are occasions when it's a really informal gathering and it just doesn't matter when people slip away to make a call or answer a text or email. On those occasions, it's great to get people coming who otherwise wouldn't turn out."

"I get that completely," said Sue. "But what is it that wrecks your formal gatherings? Is it just people using phones?"

"Yes, to an extent," said Jeff. "But actually I'm wondering if it isn't the attitude of the people attending. I mean there are a couple of people who make such a performance of taking a call or looking at their email." Jeff looked directly at Alan and Sue.

"Go on," said Alan. "This is a really interesting area."

"OK well there are a couple of people who have quite ordinary jobs. Sure their work is important, but when their phone, or whatever device, goes off – and boy does it go off – they interrupt the entire conversation to announce the fact that they have to 'take this call, because it's so vital.' On the other hand, there is one guy who is pretty senior. His phone vibrates rather than ringing and he just slips away and nobody notices until he has been gone for a few minutes."

"Interesting," said Alan. "So you could say that he remains almost undetected?"

"Yeah," said Jeff. "Oh – you mean just like the Leopard. Well, yes – I guess so. He never makes a big deal about it."

"So how would he react," enquired Sue, "if you all agreed to switch off your phones when you get together?"

"Funnily enough," said Jeff, "I think he would be fine about it. He would just quietly take a view on whether he needed to skip the session to get stuff done or whether he could just wait a few hours."

"So actually what are you saying?" said Sue. "Is it that a phone ban would probably be beneficial?"

"Probably," said Jeff. "But do you think that should mean a ban on playing with all devices?" He grinned at Sue, curious to see her reaction.

"I don't know," said Sue. "I mean yes in terms of doing things like email, but if you are looking at photos and posting things to Facebook then does that stifle what you all enjoy doing together?"

"So what are you are saying here?" said Jeff.

"I guess what I am saying here," said Sue, "is that if you as a group of individuals have taken the time and trouble to gather in person, you shouldn't allow yourselves to be interrupted in a random fashion by someone external to the gathering."

"Boy, would I agree with that," said Jeff. "But much as I would love us to get together without being interrupted, I don't know if I could persuade everyone to redirect calls, texts and email for several hours."

"Surely," said Sue, "there is more value in being together in person than being connected to other people electronically?"

"I'm with you," said Jeff. He sighed. "We never talk about this stuff, we are just too busy getting on with our lives."

Be Where You Are

"Let me give you my perspective," said Sue. "I have three small children at home. The youngest is just three months old, and generally only notices if she doesn't get fed or her nappy changed," Sue looked up wistfully. "But my two oldest are five and seven, and I can tell you if I am doing something with them, and I get interrupted by a call – especially a work call – they don't understand it and get frustrated. I have tried distracting them, but it rarely works. Generally when I take a work call, and I'm on duty with them, it leaves all of us feeling very dissatisfied about life." She paused for a moment, feeling rather emotional. "But I guess that's just the way it is."

"I am not sure that it has to be like that," said Alan. He leaned forward in his chair.

"I have the same issue at home," he said. "I regularly get calls in the evening and occasionally at the weekends. I have taken them when I am with my children, but frankly it doesn't work." He turned to Sue. "Mine are a little older," he said, "but the issue is the same. I travel a lot and work late most weekdays, so when I get home the time is precious. The children are OK when I'm away but they really resent it when I take a call in the middle of their time."

"So what do we do?" said Sue, letting her frustration get the better of her. "The projects that I have typically run demand really good communications and the ability to get information first hand and make decisions quickly."

"Absolutely," said Alan. "But the trick is managing expectations, especially around your responsiveness. Email has taught people to expect an instant response. However if people know that you will get back to them, then they will adapt their expectations. Now I switch off my phone when I am with the children – I really do. But in order to do that I have to be ruthless about returning messages," he smiled. "I also have to update my voicemail message regularly too. If you try and return morning messages by lunchtime – say 2pm, and make sure that you return all messages by the end of the day, you will be fine," he said. "There are occasions when I have to leave my phone on when I'm with the family. The deal I have with them is that I keep the discussion short and re-schedule it whenever possible. That way they know that I will make the most of my time that I spend with them."

"So, you are actually engaged with them wherever you are," asked Sue.

"I hadn't thought about it like that," said Alan. "I am where I am."

"Be where you are," said Jeff, "I like that. That's a great mantra."

"Well, it's a great mantra if you can make it work," said Alan.

"You are making it work, aren't you?" said Jeff.

"I mostly make it work at home," said Alan. "I can't say I do the same at work."

"What do you mean?" said Sue.

"Well, if I am truthful, I'm not so good about applying the same discipline in the office. I attend meetings where I get distracted either by something that's on my mind or something on my BlackBerry." Alan put his hand up sheepishly. "I know, I know, I'm not a technology geek, but I find it very addictive to try and keep on top of my email. So when we get a lull in a meeting, I sometimes check my email or let my mind wander. It's not good."

"But you are usually the chair," said Jeff in astonishment. "I mean you are Mr Meeting Discipline, Mr Focus and Mr Agenda… all rolled into one!"

"You are absolutely right Jeff," said Alan. "And that makes it worse. I am really embarrassed about it, but recently I have found it hard to keep things on track."

"Well if people interrupt like Ben did last week, I can see why," said Jeff.

"There is no excuse," said Alan. "The truth is that I have attached much less relevance to meetings recently, and I have prepared badly for them." He smiled ironically. "The one exception was the meeting I did last week. I thought I had that one covered before we went in. So as my penance I will put together 'Alan's Guide to Meetings' at another one of these sessions."

After this, Alan shifted in his seat and looked at his watch. "Let's get back to the time topic again – I want to take this a little further today." He looked down at his To Do list and then up at Sue. "How do you deal with stuff Sue?"

More To Do and the Hierarchy of Time

"Well I must say I'm not as strategic as you are with your single page," said Sue. "It's pretty simple really, I just have a small pocket book which I write action items into, and then I schedule time at the beginning and end of most days to go through them. Anything that I put on my list that needs more time than that, I schedule additional diary slots to deal with it. In terms of what we were talking about, you could call this Functional Time." Sue's brow furrowed for a second. "Actually that's not entirely true," she said. "I do a certain amount of these on my commute into work in the morning. If I come on the bus, I send emails and mark things off. What sort of time am I using there – I mean it's Functional for sure – but if I'm driving in, it's effectively 'Dead Time?'"

"OK so what are we saying?" said Jeff. "We have Functional Time, Dead Time – and what do you call everything else?"

"Well, Free Time I suppose," said Alan. "But that doesn't separate time that is Unallocated and time that is used for Creative stuff like brainstorming."

"Creative it is then," said Jeff.

"So is there some kind of hierarchy here?" asked Sue, pulling out a pen and some paper. "If Dead Time is the least valuable, then Functional must be the next level up. Free or Unallocated Time is clearly the most valuable which leaves Creative Time in second place behind Free Time."

"Interesting," said Alan. "But Dead Time can also be Creative as well as Functional. I mean I often have some of my best ideas in the shower for example."

"I think we need to put down definitions for each of them," said Jeff. "That way we can understand if we are going up a blind alley."

"OK," said Sue. "Let's start with Dead Time. How should we define that?"

"Well," said Alan, "it's dedicated time allocated to a specific function that cannot normally be reallocated. For example booking my car in for a service may be Functional Time, taking the car to the garage and picking it up would be dead time."

"I'm not sure," said Sue, "You could run another errand on the way there – or the way back?"

"That's true," said Alan, "But in practical terms I can't allocate additional tasks or time to these, or I risk impacting the purpose of the appointment. I mean, if I'm late the garage might not be able to complete the service. Or if I am late back in the evening, they might have closed. Let's change it slightly: Dead Time is time allocated to a single task that cannot have additional tasks assigned to it or planned within it. That way any reallocation is opportunistic – which is after all what we are trying to do!"

"That's great," said Jeff. "I like that. OK let me try Functional Time." He furrowed his brow. "Functional Time is dedicated to a list of defined tasks, which just require execution."

"Almost," said Sue. "I would add one more tweak. Functional Time is dedicated to the management and execution of a list of defined tasks, both personal and work related."

"Personal and work related?" queried Jeff.

"Yes," said Sue. "This is really important. If you separate the personal tasks and put them on a different list, you just store up trouble. Remember when I was talking about managing time with the children at home? If I didn't juggle what needs to be done at home with my work list, my home life would be chaos. That helps no-one, so I manage things as one list and using the planning system I described earlier – at the beginning and the end of the day – I try to make sure that work doesn't impact home and vice-versa."

"For what it's worth, I think you are absolutely right" said Alan. "The professional lives we used to live have traditionally dictated a separation between the two. But now our professional life is much more demanding. I mean we have just been talking about the disruption we tolerate in our personal lives. I suggest we encompass the principle that all the definitions cover both home and professional lives. That means that we should shorten the Functional definition to: 'Functional Time is dedicated to the management and execution of a list of defined tasks'."

Alan leaned back: "So that just leaves us Creative Time. Thoughts?"

"I'll take a stab again," said Jeff. "Creative Time is not constrained by time or agenda constraints and is used for brainstorming, meeting people or having fun." He laughed, "I am sorry, I'm being a little facetious – but that's what it seems like to me – especially if you put it across into the personal domain."

"Don't laugh Jeff," said Alan. "That may work. I think the whole idea of unconstrained thinking or activity is really useful and productive. We are always weighed down by things we have to do or by deadlines." He put his hands together and leaned back in his chair. "Try this: Creative Time is not constrained by time or agenda constraints and is used for brainstorming, unstructured ideas, relationship building or entertainment. It's pretty much the same but now it covers both worlds, I think." He paused.

"However there is one caveat, even though it is unconstrained, it will have some time limits. I mean it will start and end, and it will have to fit in with our Functional activities."

"I have a suggestion," said Sue. "Why don't you add a second sentence? For Creative Time to work, it needs to be allocated sufficient time in the diary with Dead Time either side."

"Why Dead Time?" queried Jeff.

"That way if you are late starting or overrun, you don't impact the creativity. I mean if the start time is rigid and people are late they are going to be stressed. Far better to allow extra 'arrival time' like many corporate events do. Or if you find that things are in full flow, you don't cut off the end unless you really need to. I mean if you are having a really productive and interesting debate at the end of an event, you don't want to cut it short because of scheduling."

"That makes good sense," said Alan. He stood up and walked across to his computer. "Sue – did you capture all those?"

"Yes, got them here", said Sue proffering the page to Alan.

"Just read them back to me if you wouldn't mind," said Alan. As Sue read, Alan typed them into his computer using his rather noisy but effective two-finger style.

He typed up a short document and printed it out:

The Leopard's Hierarchy of Time

- *Unallocated Time is just that and is the most valuable type of time.*

- *Creative Time is not constrained by time or agenda constraints and is used for brainstorming, unstructured ideas, relationship building or entertainment. For Creative Time to work, it must be allocated sufficient time in the diary with Dead Time as a buffer either side.*

- *Functional Time is dedicated to the management and execution of a list of defined tasks.*

- *Dead Time is time allocated to a single task that cannot have additional tasks assigned to it or planned within it.*

- *The Hierarchy of Time applies to both personal and professional worlds.*

Alan handed a copy to Sue and Jeff. "I have to say I am rather excited and inspired," he said. "That was a really insightful session. I think we are onto something here. What do you think?"

"I'm really keen to take it out and see if it really works," said Jeff. "I'm going to think about that idea of removing mobiles from the next meeting with my friends. Hey can I pitch the Creative Time definition to them? That would really help."

"Sure," said Alan, "but if you don't mind, please don't tell them what we are doing here just yet."

"No problem," said Jeff, "I'll let you know how I get on."

"Sue?" asked Alan.

"I cannot tell you how refreshing this has been," said Sue. "It really resonates with me and although I'm instinctively aware of the issues, I have never been able to put structure on them before. Thank you Alan." She looked up at Alan and smiled warmly.

"No – thank you both," said Alan, "Great insight. So when are we going to meet again?" he asked.

"How does Friday morning work for you both? 10am?"

"Have you put some Dead Time around that?" quipped Jeff.

"No, good point," said Alan. "I will run it until 12 noon and then leave an hour afterwards. Does that work?" He peered at the screen again.

"I have an appointment that runs until 10am this week, I can't shift it, so I will make sure it's finished on the dot of 10am."

"Great – see you then if not before." Jeff got up and moved to the door.

Sue gathered her things and stood up also. "Thanks Alan, see you then."

As they closed the door behind them, Alan sat back down at his desk and pulled his To Do list up on the screen of his computer. "Right," he said to himself, "here goes."

"Creative versus Functional…"

Chapter Notes

Reminder of the Principles of the Leopard

1. *Act opportunistically*
2. *Adapt to a wide variety of environments*
3. *Operate at speed*
4. *Drive any chosen activity to a successful conclusion*
5. *Remain almost undetected*

The Leopard's Hierarchy of Time

- *Unallocated Time is just that and is the most valuable type of time.*

- *Creative Time is not constrained by time or agenda constraints and is used for brainstorming, unstructured ideas, relationship building or entertainment. For Creative Time to work, it must be allocated sufficient time in the diary with Dead Time as a buffer either side.*

- *Functional Time is dedicated to the management and execution of a list of defined tasks.*

- *Dead Time is time allocated to a single task that cannot have additional tasks assigned to it or planned within it.*

- *The Hierarchy of Time applies to both personal and professional worlds.*

3

THE HIERARCHY OF COMMUNICATIONS

Out With the Gang

Jeff made a final check on his appearance in the mirror before heading for the front door. He was meeting three of his friends tonight including the two people he had called out as examples in the meeting on Monday. He picked up his iPhone and keys and set out to walk to the bistro where they were meeting. It was a grey but warm evening and Jeff strode purposefully along the street.

"Where's your cycling gear then?" called a voice.

Jeff stopped dead in his tracks and looked around. The black cat was sitting on a branch of a tree just a few feet away. "How did you get here?" said Jeff, "I mean the office is 5 miles from here. Seriously, how did you manage it?"

"I am a Leopard," said the cat simply.

"Ah yes exactly," said Jeff knowingly. He thought for a second. "And how do you generally spend your time?"

"Well you know that I have to eat," said the cat. "But beyond that it's up to you to find out." And the cat hopped off the branch and was gone.

"Huh! No answers there then," muttered Jeff. "I guess it's up to me." He walked on towards the Trattoria.

When he arrived two of his friends were there already, including Kate from work, who he already known quite well from business school. Kate smiled warmly at Jeff and rose to kiss him gently on the cheek, which Jeff acknowledged but didn't consciously register. Although he didn't know it, Kate had had a crush on him from business school, which she worked hard to conceal as she wasn't entirely sure what his feelings were.

Rufus was also there. He was tall, serious and dark haired. He had been the intellect at business school with Jeff and had been rewarded with a director level role at a venture capital firm. Jeff could have been jealous of his success but the truth was Rufus was brilliant with numbers, and Jeff loved the operational cut and thrust he was now experiencing in his own role.

"Hey guys, how are you?" asked Jeff as he sat down. "Where's Peter?" He asked innocently as if he didn't know.

Rufus smiled thinly at Jeff. "Waiting to make his entrance I am sure," he said ironically.

The Arrival of Peter

Peter hadn't actually been to business school with them and it really rankled him. He was shorter than Jeff and Rufus, slightly overweight and had an inferiority complex for which he made up by making his role as a regional manager for a retail chain sound desperately important. Sure enough just as Rufus had predicted they could hear Peter approaching, mobile phone clamped to his ear.

"Yup, yup – well we can do that out of cash flow… no that one needs to go to the board… OK I'll come and see you first thing… all right? Bye!" he snapped the phone shut.

"God what a disaster," he said slumping into a chair. "The CEO is all over me this week."

"Really?" said Rufus drily with a hint of irony. Peter either didn't notice or he wasn't put off.

"Oh we have this great new store format. Well, I say great…

I thought it would be but the first three stores we rolled out have been a disaster."

"In what sense?" asked Jeff. He was mildly curious but shared Rufus' sense of irritation with Peter.

"Well we wrote this mega plan for it. And invested heaps in the design and the build. But the research and assumptions we made look like they are nearly all wrong."

"Are you on the hook for this?" said Jeff leaning forward, now a little concerned.

"I guess so," said Peter, looking sheepish and somewhat self-conscious. "I mean it was a great plan. Tell you what I'll show you." He turned and rummaged in his shoulder bag and pulled out a weighty document an inch thick. He passed it to Jeff. "You can check all the numbers and tables. I mean we did heaps of studies and projections."

"Doesn't matter how many you do if your thinking is flawed," said Rufus. Peter began to bristle.

"Hang on a minute," said Jeff, wanting to defuse the tension. He lowered the document. "How did you go about putting this together?" he said. "I mean how did you get started?"

"Well the CEO hauled me in and told me what he wanted us to do."

"So really he is on the hook for this not you?" said Rufus, now listening quite intently.

"I suppose so but I did all the legwork," said Peter, and it began to dawn on him that it might become just his problem alone. "But I guess it will be me that takes the rap if it gets any worse." His normal bluster had evaporated and he looked very crestfallen. "I really wish I had chatted to you chaps beforehand."

"Never mind," said Kate, who had been listening quietly up to this point. "What's done is done. The question is what you can do to fix it?"

"You know Kate, I'm just about all out of ideas," Peter said. Just then his mobile went off.

As he went to reach for it Jeff put his hand over Peter's and shook his head. "Let it go to voicemail," he said looking Peter directly in the eye. Peter looked at him for a second while the phone rang and then pulled his hand away from the phone.

"Thanks Peter," said Jeff. "Let me explain."

Jeff to the Rescue

"I'm doing a project with some people at work and we are looking at how we all use our time."

"Oh god, time management," Rufus rolled his eyes sardonically. "Been there, done that."

"Me too," said Jeff. "At least I thought so. The truth is that despite the training we get, we all have our own way of doing things which means that we all think about time in a different way."

"What has this got to do with my plan?" said Peter looking confused.

"Bear with me Peter," replied Jeff. He straightened himself in his chair and looked at the other three to see if he had their attention. "We talked about these sessions I have with you guys and the others every week. Mainly because I often use these occasions to catch up on my admin via this thing," Jeff picked up and waved his iPhone. He looked at them intently. "I didn't realise until I thought about it how much phones and smartphones disrupt the time we spend together. Actually one of the things I was going to suggest was that we switch off devices when we meet anyway. So the reason I asked Peter not to answer his phone was because we are in the middle of a serious conversation about his plan and the problems he is now dealing with."

"So what has this got to do with your time project?" asked Rufus. "Not that I disagree with you by the way." Rufus grinned at Jeff's furrowed brow.

"We are trying to find ways to act more opportunistically," said Jeff. "So we have ended up dividing up our time into four basic types."

Jeff reached into his pocket and pulled out the sheet that Alan had given them. He had scribbled over "The Leopard" part of the header to keep it out of the discussion.

The Hierarchy of Time

- *Unallocated Time is just that and is the most valuable type of time.*

- *Creative Time is not constrained by time or agenda constraints and is used for brainstorming, unstructured ideas, relationship building or entertainment. For Creative Time to work, it must be allocated sufficient time in the diary with Dead Time as a buffer either side.*

- *Functional Time is dedicated to the management and execution of a list of defined tasks.*

- *Dead Time is time allocated to a single task that cannot have additional tasks assigned to it or planned within it.*

- *The Hierarchy of Time applies to both personal and professional worlds.*

"Here it is," he said. He spread it out on the table and then with one hand holding it down, he looked up at them. "At the bottom of the hierarchy is Dead Time," he said. "You all know what this is: taking a shower, sleeping, catching a bus etc."

"Oh I'm not sure about that," piped up Kate. "I mean you can do other things while you are doing some of those."

"Hear me out," said Jeff. "Our definition is that Dead Time is time allocated to a single task that cannot have additional tasks assigned to it or planned within it." He sat back and looked directly at Kate. "I mean I suppose you can use the time in the shower or on the bus for doing something, but you can't rely or plan to use that time, it's already allocated."

"I have some of my best idea in the bath," added Rufus, somewhat ironically.

"OK Jeff – continue," said Kate.

"The next level up is what we call Functional Time," said Jeff, "basically this is for planning and getting stuff done," he looked down and read from the sheet. "Functional Time is dedicated to the management and execution of a list of defined tasks."

"OK get that," said Kate. "And?"

"Finally there is Creative Time," said Jeff reading from the sheet again. "This should not be limited by time or agenda constraints and is used for brainstorming, unstructured ideas, relationship building or entertainment." He looked back at the group. "In a long winded way what I am saying is that I think these sessions are Creative Time. That's why I think we should can the devices."

"Wow!" said Rufus. "There are some neat ideas there." He looked at Jeff quizzically. "I still think Kate and I are right though. You can have Creative ideas in Dead Time. Actually you can have Creative ideas at any time."

"I think I agree Rufus," said Jeff. "But I still don't think you can plan to do so. You need to create the right conditions for thinking."

"Well you may well plan Creative Time," said Rufus. "But who's to say you will actually end up being creative?"

"That's true," said Jeff. "But if you don't create space to think properly, I think it's unlikely you ever will."

"I guess you may well be right," said Rufus, turning to Peter.

"So, picking up the baton: Peter, how much Creative Time did you spend on this project?"

"Err, what?" said Peter, who had begun to think that they had forgotten all about him.

"If you look back at the planning process, how much of the time you spent on it would you say was Creative? Under Jeff's definition?"

The Inquisition

"Boy. Hard to say," Peter replied. "I met with the CEO weekly for an hour for two months. I suppose that was the Creative Time." He looked up at Jeff. "Frankly I wouldn't call it Creative though. I did most of the listening. I mean he just briefed me on what he wanted to see in the plan. I then went ahead and commissioned the research and wrote the plan."

"Pah!" snorted Rufus. "No wonder you are in trouble."

Peter reddened in the face. "Well what would you have done?" he asked indignantly. "No, actually don't tell me. You are so clever with all that business school stuff."

"Bollocks Peter!" said Rufus who was starting to get angry. "Just because I have an MBA doesn't make me any smarter than you. Yes, you get lots of benefits from doing an MBA, but there are plenty of smart people who didn't so don't give me that crap!"

"OK, OK, I'm sorry Rufus," said Peter trying to mollify his friend. "But I'm really frustrated as I still don't understand where I went wrong."

"Where you went wrong, Peter, is that you assumed that the CEO knew what he was doing," said Jeff quietly.

"But he's the CEO!" yelled Peter. "He's supposed to know what he's doing. That's what he gets paid the big money for, isn't it?"

"Well – yes, but he's only human," said Rufus, who was still a little upset but was starting to think more clearly. "Look – he's backed you to deliver because you are good at getting stuff done, right?"

"Right!" said Peter.

"So this project is really strategic – right?"

"Yes, correct. It's probably the most important one we're doing for the next two years."

"So how much time did you two spend discussing strategy?"

"Well as I said, we met for at least an hour every week for two months. Sometimes we met for the whole morning," said Peter weakly, now beginning to see some light at the end of the tunnel.

"So in these meetings, you didn't really debate any of the key issues with him did you?" asked Kate gently.

"No. I did what I normally do. I listened carefully, took notes and delivered against my action points." Peter smiled. "It's the skills that have got me where I am," he said. "I am good at getting stuff done." He gave a lopsided grin.

"You are good at getting stuff done," said Kate.

"In this case, if you think back to what Jeff was saying, both of you were acting 'Functionally'. You were getting stuff done rather than thinking about what you really needed to do. At no point did either of you stop to think 'Creatively' about what you were doing. I'll bet that there is a raft of assumptions in your plan that weren't properly tested."

"But I did a proper risk assessment," protested Peter. "It was done by the book."

"Peter, it doesn't matter that you do it by the book," said Jeff. "What matters is that you get it as near to right as possible. I'll tell you what, let's go through the plan right now and see if we can find something that will help you."

"Before we do that there's something I would really like to say", said Rufus, who had calmed down and was now back to his usual languid self. "Jeff – I think you have brought some real insight to the table this evening. I think your project has some real promise. On your one point earlier I absolutely agree with you – when we meet from now on, we will keep the phones switched off. Having said that I think you should take some of our comments back with you." Rufus pulled out a pencil from his jacket, leaned forward and scribbled on the "Hierarchy of Time" note that Jeff had been reading from. "Firstly you need some kind of communication hierarchy," he said, scribbling down on the paper. "Whilst people attach huge weight to emails or phone calls, actually face to face gatherings like this are the most important and everything else is really secondary."

Jeff laughed at this point. "Be where you are", he said.

"What?" said Rufus.

"Be where you are", repeated Jeff. "When you are in a group you should be fully focused on the people there and then. It's a mantra that one of my colleagues uses."

"I like that," said Rufus. "Me too," said Kate. "That's spot on".

"Anyway," said Rufus, "think about the communication hierarchy. My other point for you to consider on the same vein is interruptions. I find I get interrupted frequently during my day, and to follow your mantra it's hard to know whether to be 'Creative' about it. By that I mean latch on to it and deal with it. Or 'Functional' which is to reschedule it or deflect it." Rufus grinned. "Lots to think about but I'm really curious to know if you have any answers."

"Thanks Rufus, much appreciated," said Jeff, he grabbed Rufus' pencil from him and scribbled a couple more notes on the sheet. Jeff looked at it one more time carefully before folding it and putting it into his hip pocket. "Right Peter," he said, "let's get back to your plan – talk us through it from the beginning."

Friday 10am

At the Friday meeting in Alan's office, Jeff arrived in really inspired form. The session with Rufus, Peter and Kate had been really productive and they had given Peter a list of ideas to consider and action points to try out. From the state of flustered depression he arrived in, Peter had departed in a haze of optimism and energy. All of them had really enjoyed the session and were really looking forward to the next one on Monday. Jeff was so keen to relay Rufus' comments to Alan and Sue that he had nearly picked up the phone to call Alan several times over the last few days, however now that his moment had arrived he had to get in first. "You'll never guess what happened to me?" he opened.

"What was that then?" said Alan cautiously. He was used to receiving "good news" from others that later turned out to be bad news.

"Well, you know I meet with a group of friends from business school after work?"

47

Alan nodded and Sue looked at him quizzically.

"Well we were trying to help one of the guys with a rather serious crisis he had got himself into."

"And?" said Alan.

"Well without giving away exactly what we are doing here, I explained the Hierarchy of Time to them. It was really useful, and it turns out that it's not just Time that is Creative and Functional – people are too. And that was the basic cause of my friend's problem." He finished, suddenly conscious that he had been holding the stage for rather too long.

"What was?" said Sue.

"Well can you supress disbelief for a moment and agree with my hypothesis that people can be either Creative or Functional?"

"OK – shoot!" said Sue.

"The basic problem was that the two people working on the project are both Functional – they are good at getting stuff done."

"So how would that cause a problem?" asked Sue.

Jeff grinned. "Look you have to keep this under your hats – as one of them is really senior. But basically they didn't think it through properly. They hadn't spent any proper 'Creative' time thinking it through or debating the issues and let's say they made a number of incorrect assumptions. I mean they dotted all the 'i's and crossed all the 't's but simply hadn't thought it through properly."

Alan stirred and shook his head. "Why am I amazed but not really surprised?" he asked rhetorically. He leaned back and looked directly at Jeff. "Are you completely sure of your basis for all this?" he asked carefully.

Jeff waved his hand emphatically. "Yup! Let's just say I have seen the paper trail and interrogated one of the co-conspirators. Seriously though, I am sure of my facts and what's more I am also sure that this isn't the first time that this kind of thing has happened."

"Don't they do all the usual team personality matching tests when they set up a project?" asked Sue.

"You have got to be joking," said Jeff. "I mean this had to be done fast and the two people know each other really well. Why would they waste time formalising it?"

"Well it would have been time well spent!" bristled Sue.

"No kidding," said Jeff. "I'm not pooh-poohing it. It's just that formal project processes are cumbersome and time consuming, and they work in a pretty informal environment. Which is why they have been very successful to date."

"OK, OK," said Alan. "So if I understand you correctly people are naturally either Creative or Functional – yes?"

"Yes," said Jeff. "Think about it. It makes sense and follows the hierarchy of time."

"Which gives them both a problem," said Alan. "How does each of these types deal with their need to operate in the opposing mode, so to speak? I mean, what types do we think we are?" He looked at each of them carefully.

"Functional – definitely," said Sue firmly.

"Good question." said Jeff, "Creative, I think." He shifted in his seat. "What's more I think I can explain why. All my life I have really enjoyed problem solving, but have really struggled to get everything I need done and dusted. You know the Functional stuff. Even at business school I really cut my deadlines to the last minute and even now I struggle to get through my workload." He looked at Alan directly. "To answer one of your questions Alan, when Creative types have to operate in Functional mode, I would call it 'The Struggle for Discipline'."

"The discipline to remove the Functional tasks that prevent them from being Creative?" mused Alan.

"Exactly," said Jeff. "Conversely, if you think about the example I quoted just now, when Functional types have to operate in Creative mode, you could call it the 'Search for Lateral Thinking'." He laughed out loud. "I'm not joking but that is a pretty accurate description of what went wrong."

Alan clasped his chin between his thumb and forefinger, a gesture he often used when thinking. "Jeff, thank you. That's really excellent.

I think that summarises it brilliantly. I will write it up for next time."

"Not quite finished," said Jeff. "There were two other ideas that we touched on during the session that I wanted to feed back to you. They are both interrelated. One is around interruptions and the second is whether there is a Hierarchy of Communications that sits alongside the Hierarchy of Time?"

Reportus Interruptus

"Basically we have agreed that when we meet up, our sessions are Creative Time and should not be interrupted. So basically we are going to switch off our mobiles from now on."

"Good idea," said Sue. Then, suddenly understanding where Jeff was heading, "Ooh interesting! Interruptions, how do you handle them, Creatively or Functionally?"

Jeff laughed. "Exactly. We asked ourselves the same question. Seriously though I think there are two separate issues here as even without mobile phones, interruptions are a real problem."

"I agree absolutely", said Alan. "In fact if we look at the opportunistic principle of the Leopard, interruptions could be a major issue."

"Oh boy and we are all guilty," said Sue. "I mean we really are!"

"What do you mean exactly?" said Alan.

"Well we are all guilty of randomly interrupting people every day. Funnily enough it's usually Functional behaviour that drives it – but not always. You know exactly what I mean. You need a number or a document from someone or you need to ask them a question. And often your need to get it quickly overrides any sensitivity about whether they are in a position to help you at that moment."

"Give me an example," said Alan.

"OK. Last night you were looking for Kate for this week's key account report," said Sue.

"Yes. I found her and she sent what I needed over about half an hour later."

"Well thanks for that. As a result I had to stay an hour later." Sue grinned good-naturedly although she recalled she had been furious with Alan when she found out what he had done.

"Sorry – I don't understand. It's her responsibility, as I understand it anyway. It should have been absolutely no problem for her," said Alan, more curious than defensive.

"And there is the root cause of the problem," said Sue. "Let me explain. My whole team including Kate had spent the whole of yesterday writing up a financial analysis for the project. In fact we had rescheduled the day around it, and Kate had agreed to finalise the report after we had finished."

"Oh," said Alan, feeling a little sheepish.

"Well because you got hold of Kate personally and asked her on an urgent basis, she felt she couldn't refuse. As a result, she had to drop what she was doing and we all had to wait behind until she had completed the key account report."

"Sue, I am so sorry," said Alan, feeling more foolish now.

"No hear me out – apology accepted – but only if we can do something with the learning," said Sue who was now fully in her stride. "The issue is a combination of an interruption, and the urgent request for something completely unconnected with what she was doing."

"OK so what happened at your end?" said Alan quietly.

"Well she had been in the middle of completing quite a complex spreadsheet, and the end result of the interruption is that even though it only took 30 minutes to complete the report for you, it took us another hour to get Kate back into the mind-set for the analysis and get it completed."

"Oh boy," sighed Alan. "Sorry."

"Alan, apology accepted, and you know what: we need to help Kate to manage her side of the equation too."

"Sounds like you 'randomised' her completely," said Jeff cheekily.

Alan glared at him and Jeff put up his hand in (mock) apology.

"I like that," said Sue, "'randomised' – yes that describes it perfectly. By the way I have now met Bennett."

Alan sighed. "Oh yes?" he said heavily.

"Well he has a well-known but untamed habit of striding up to people's desks and doing just that to them. For the record he's much worse than you."

"Thanks for that," said Alan ironically but it was lost on Sue.

"We have to do something to help Kate next time as well as Bennett and his victims."

"You won't change Bennett – ever," said Alan grimly. "But for those of us who should know better, I think a little help with self-awareness is in order."

"Which funnily enough brings me back to the Hierarchy of Communications," grinned Jeff. "If we park all forms of electronic interruption under that heading for now, it comes down to just two things: self-awareness about what is a necessary interruption and how to handle it on the receiving end, especially if it's from someone senior."

Alan looked at Jeff curiously. "OK so if you were Kate, how would you have handled me yesterday?"

"Well Kate doesn't know you so well which would have helped, but she could have done two things. Firstly she should have taken the request down and explained that it would be delayed until she had completed the analysis. If you had pushed back and told her you needed it immediately, she could have then spoken to you, Sue, and asked you to phone Alan and ask for an extension."

"Well why do you think she didn't?" asked Alan thoughtfully.

"I think, in part, because she is a little nervous around you Alan. But mainly because she didn't understand how important it was to stick with the Creative process she was working on," said Sue wistfully.

"Oh, right," said Alan.

"I have one other comment on this," said Jeff. "It's one of the benefits of the Coffee Bar downstairs."

"Go on", said Sue.

"Well it's really a neat way of making yourself actively available for interruptions," said Jeff.

"Sorry I don't get it?" said Alan.

"Well it's a really useful place for meeting people, but because it's informal, no-one can expect you to have the information or be able to answer the request there and then."

"So?" said Alan.

"It enables you to ask the person interrupting to formalise the request in a follow-up email or set up a time to discuss. Also because we meet there and do informal meetings there at regular times in the morning and after lunch, people actively seek us out there – as you first did a few days ago – and it makes the process more manageable."

"So if I get what you are saying, manage your interruptions by making yourself available at certain times of the day and certain locations?"

"Well it works for me on the receiving end, now all we have to do is work out how to stop interrupting other people," finished Jeff.

"Well, I think this has been an excellent – if somewhat humbling session," said Alan. "Let's work on the Hierarchy of Communication next week."

"Not so fast," said Sue. "Just before we leave you have to answer a question you successfully dodged earlier."

"What do you mean?" asked Alan quizzically.

"We both answered your question about whether we are more naturally Functional or Creative, so really you need to answer the question too."

Alan smiled. "I have a good idea but to tell you the truth I'm not entirely sure. Let me know what you think next week and I will tell you then."

Sue looked at Alan sharply but he had retreated to his desk and wasn't going to be drawn any further on the topic.

"Thanks – see you next week."

Chapter Notes

The Leopard's Hierarchy of Time

- *Unallocated Time is just that and is the most valuable type of time.*

- *Creative Time is not constrained by time or agenda constraints and is used for brainstorming, unstructured ideas, relationship building or entertainment. For Creative Time to work, it must be allocated sufficient time in the diary with Dead Time as a buffer either side.*

- *Functional Time is dedicated to the management and execution of a list of defined tasks.*

- *Dead Time is time allocated to a single task that cannot have additional tasks assigned to it or planned within it. It should be the realistic but the minimum amount of time that can be allocated.*

- *The Hierarchy of Time applies to both personal and professional worlds.*

Be Where You Are

- *Be where you are: concentrate on the environment you are in and don't take calls or read emails when you should be doing something else.*

Creativity Versus Functionality

People who are naturally Functional in behaviour:

- *are brilliant at bringing structure and order to things, making plans and executing tasks – Getting Things Done.*

- *struggle to making the leap and approaching something from an alternative perspective – The Search for Lateral Thinking.*

People who are naturally Creative in behaviour:

- *are able to look at things differently and solve problems that seem simple with hindsight but need inspiration – Great Ideas and Problems Solved.*

- *struggle to prioritise their creativity and often don't have the patience to work through tasks thoroughly – The Struggle for Discipline.*

4

THE ELEVEN RULES OF EMAIL

The Hierarchy of Communications

Alan was right in the middle of summing up in the weekly management meeting when his mobile went off. He cursed silently for forgetting to put it in silent mode and switched the call to his voice messaging service. He was so preoccupied that afternoon that he didn't even check his voicemail until the following morning, which was the Friday of the Leopard meeting. The call was from Jeff.

"Hi Alan, I need to speak to you, please call me back as soon as possible."

Alan suddenly felt remorse at his carelessness, and although he was due to see Jeff in under an hour, he picked up his mobile and called him immediately.

"Hi Jeff – it's Alan here. My apologies, you called me yesterday."

"Oh, hi Alan – thanks for calling back. Look no problem; I will explain when I see you shortly."

Feeling slightly puzzled, Alan hung up the call and went back to his computer for finish up his preparations for the meeting at 10am. He was really pleased with the progress they had made since last time, and as an exercise had been considering what the Hierarchy of Communications should look like.

He looked at his notes and typed out the list:

The Leopard's Hierarchy of Communications

1. *Face to face meeting*
   - *For: offers best opportunity for verbal and non-verbal communication; real time.*
   - *Against: not everyone pays full attention*

2. *Video Conference*
   - *For: next best thing to being there; real time.*
   - *Against: stilted conversation, hard to set up, inconsistent quality.*

3. *Phone Call*
   - *For: flexible; real time.*
   - *Against: timing; no visual communication; not everyone pays full attention.*

4. *Instant Messaging*
   - *For: real time; can conference in other people.*
   - *Against: too easy to type the wrong thing in a hurry.*

5. *Text Message*
   - *For: one to one communication; near real time.*
   - *Against: too quick to have value; easy to misconstrue.*

6. *Email*
   - *For: generic, fast to use tool; offline (not real time).*
   - *Against: too much noise, too quick to have value; easy to misconstrue.*

He then added at the bottom without any ranking:

Written Letter
- *For: unusual, personal; stands out in today's world.*
- *Against: more complex to write and send; relatively slow compared to electronic format.*

Social Networks
- *For: quick, relatively personal*
- *Against: Against: too public?*

He considered the page for a minute and then printed three copies for the meeting.

The 10am Leopard Meeting

As Jeff and Sue sat down in Alan's office, Alan passed his notes across. "So I spent some time thinking about the Hierarchy of Communications," he added. "Here are my thoughts though I'm not sure how much they add to the discussion."

"Interesting," said Jeff, scanning the notes. "You have missed a couple that I would have added, but flagged one that I wouldn't have expected you to," he grinned enthusiastically.

"Oh, you mean social media?" asked Alan.

"Yup, thought you would definitely skip that one," said Jeff jovially.

"Why?"

"I just figured you wouldn't have bothered with it."

"To be frank with you, it's pretty new for me," said Alan. "But you will now find my up to date profile on LinkedIn, and I also have a Facebook page."

"Now you are really starting to scare me," said Sue and all three laughed.

"Actually, I don't disagree, it's definitely the domain of the younger generation," said Alan. "But then again if I want to communicate with them on their terms, it's something I have to learn about."

"Good for you," said Jeff approvingly. "You have got to use it though, you can't just ignore it."

"I know. In fact I sent you a friend request just now. I will be honest with you, I am not going to do much with it for now, but I do have a niece and nephew who have pages, so I will use it to keep up with them."

"OK hold that thought for now," said Jeff. "I want to add some context later, but I think we need to go back to another picture right now."

Do You Return Your Calls?

"I have spent the last few days doing an informal research into people's responsiveness, and it's been an interesting exercise, even if it the results are a little rough."

Alan angled his head as he looked at Jeff. "Was that the phone call yesterday?"

"Exactly. I have called everyone on the Board plus the management team and the next reporting layer down."

"I am sorry, you did what exactly?"

"I called them to see how they responded."

"You are not serious? Especially after all our discussions about interruptions last week?" Alan was suddenly quite anxious, while he very much believed in what they were doing; he really didn't want the career-sky to fall until he had at least completed the process.

"Hey Alan, don't worry. I put together a plan with Kate."

"Oh well that's OK then. It'll just be you two who are in trouble."

"Seriously, Alan – it will be fine. Hear me out."

In truth Jeff hadn't really anticipated the consequences of what he had set out to do until he had had a rather short conversation with Bennett, who had been very rude.

"I made it look like I needed some input and guidance for the project I'm working on, and when people objected I apologised for being naïve. They were mostly OK about it."

"I'm guessing Bennett, amongst others, wasn't," said Alan carelessly, noticing that Jeff had reddened slightly in the face.

"Well he wasn't very pleased, but to be honest with you, all I did was call them," said Jeff. "I mean I didn't interrupt them personally. They get called by people all day every week and weekends too."

"So let's park the rights and wrongs for a moment. What exactly did you set out to achieve?" asked Sue.

"I wanted to understand how responsive people were to phone calls, and whether they responded to voicemail. It's a pretty small sample – we called 75 people in total but the results were fascinating."

"Did anyone actually rumble what you were up to?" said Alan hopefully.

"As it turns out, no." said Jeff. "The closest I came to it was with Bennett who really didn't want to talk to me at all and jumped to the conclusion that it was something you had put me up to."

"Huh?" said Alan, still concerned.

"Here's my sheet of notes," said Jeff, pulling out several pages of printed spreadsheet with handwritten notes on it. "It's interesting to see how many still haven't responded to voicemail, especially at a senior level. See here… and here." He said indicating several people on the list.

"I am not surprised really," said Alan. "I mean how many of them know you personally?"

"Well, quite a few. But that's not the point," said Jeff. "The point is that a number of the voicemail messages promised me that they would call me back. If that isn't true, why bother putting it in your message?"

"Interestingly of the people I actually spoke to, many of them actually did follow up or pointed me at other sources of information."

"OK Jeff," said Sue. "So what do you really think about all this?"

"I think there are a handful of standard rules about phone and mobile use that everyone should observe – especially if they want to be Leopards," said Jeff. "How long has the mobile phone been around?

By my count well over 20 years and yet there doesn't seem to be any standard guidance for people. So here's what I put together:"

Basic Rules of Responsiveness

1. *Personalise your voicemail so that people know it's you. Set an expectation of what information you are looking for and when you are likely respond to a message, and give alternative contact methods such as other phone numbers, email address, or how to contact an assistant or department administrator.*

2. *Check your voicemail daily or more often if possible.*

3. *You should return every call unless there is a compelling reason not to. Return your messages received in the morning by lunchtime and afternoon calls by the end of the working day.*

4. *If you are going into a meeting, especially a Creative meeting, switch the mobile off. Or at the very least to silent.*

5. *If you know someone wants to speak to you, try and schedule calls as you would a meeting so that you can focus on the conversation. It's much more productive than allowing someone to call you at a random time in the middle of something else that may also be important.*

6. *Always remember that a phone call is an exclusive use of a caller's time, so it's much more important than most other ways of communicating.*

"What do you think?" asked Jeff hopefully. "Am I miles off base?"

"Not at all," said Sue. "In fact I think you have done a great job of capturing it."

"Surely most people do this already," said Alan in a puzzled voice. "I mean this is common sense, right?"

"You would think so," said Jeff, "and that's exactly why I did the research this week It's not from lack of thought or intelligence that people miss out on doing this, it's simply a lack of discipline."

"Do you think it's a Creative / Functional divide?" asked Sue. "I mean do you think Functional people are better at doing this?"

"Possibly," mused Jeff, "but frankly it doesn't matter. Everyone needs to do this, it's, how do you say, 'Hygiene' and management should insist on it. Anyone who wants to follow the Principles of the Leopard has to do so at the very least."

"Jeff, last week you were talking about applying some of this to your business school group. How is that going to work?"

"That's in rule number 4. We agreed we are going to turn our mobiles off when we meet, especially as they are pretty much all smartphones and have email and other stuff that can distract us. Oh I nearly forgot – there's one more." Jeff reached out for the list, and scribbled another short sentence underneath.

"Be where you are," read Sue aloud. She grinned. "So glad you like that."

"I have to say I regularly watch people answering their email in meetings. I do have some sympathy and understand why they do it," added Sue. "Too many routine and poorly run meetings mean that people cannot resist the temptation to catch up on their workload."

"Well we need to do a session on meetings," added Alan. "So while that doesn't solve the problem, at the individual level what we are saying is that it's a matter of personal discipline. Discipline – there we go again. Another one for the list?"

He leant forward in his chair.

Back to the Hierarchy

"Returning to my Hierarchy of Communications list, I think that phone calls only fall behind face to face meetings and video conferences. Thoughts?"

"Can't disagree with you," said Sue. "Depending on the people present, face to face meetings pretty much always trump a call. But I'm not sure about video conferences. They are really hard to set up and usually involve quite a few people so I can't see that a phone call should trump them."

"What do you guys think about texting?" asked Jeff.

"Well I put it just below phone calls on the basis that it although it is personal it's not real time," added Alan.

"Makes sense," commented Sue. "But there's one more piece of context that is worth adding here." She looked up. "Don't get me wrong, I think text is an important tool. But you need to know someone reasonably well for it to have any impact. But, on top of that," she paused for effect, "I think it's mostly a tactical tool." She looked directly at Alan. "I think you have to consider which of these methods is tactical and strategic. By that I mean which one holds its value over the longer term. I see you added 'Written Letter' to the bottom of the list without ranking it. Well I would say that was probably one of the most strategic forms of communication, despite being somewhat old fashioned."

Alan smiled. "I know," he said. "And you are right; it is very old fashioned, although ironically it makes a huge impact today – especially if you write it by hand. I guess we need to rank these methods for day-to-day communications as well as strategic communication."

"And on that note," added Jeff, "can we return to social networking? I would suggest that it succeeds as both a tactical and a strategic method. You may disagree, but unlike email or texts, most social networking tools retain everything that is uploaded to them which means that there is both a permanent record and the ability to search them."

"Interesting," said Alan. "So where do you think it sits in my list?"

"Tactically? Pretty low, maybe just above email. Strategically, though, I'd place it very high, probably above phone calls." Jeff stated firmly.

"You are kidding Jeff," said Alan. "I mean... seriously?"

"I am very serious Alan," said Jeff drily. "Especially if you consider purely social networks like Facebook, I mean if you get someone's attention on there, you have it on an on-going basis." Jeff leaned back in his chair. "If you think about it, all the other forms of communication we have been talking about are 'transactional.' I mean, they are one-off events. But, when you communicate using social networking tools like Facebook, it's much more like a conversation. For example someone posts a comment about their favourite football team and then everyone piles in with comments. That's really very powerful."

"What about those short messaging networks?" asked Sue.

"Oh you mean Twitter?" asked Jeff. "Well they don't have as much content or detail. They are only short messages. But they are really fast to use, and can get a message out very quickly. I use it quite a bit but not as much as Facebook, but my Twitter feed has a different audience that's much more interested in real time information than in building a close relationship."

Alan looked up at Jeff with a serious expression. "Jeff, I must say I think I am beginning to understand this now. I am not sure how we include tactical and strategic importance in the same list though. Let's all of us have a think about it." He got a "Fine – no worries" from Jeff and an "OK sure from Sue".

"There's one more thing I want to talk about today, and after Jeff's really excellent piece on phones I think we also need to do some informal research before next week. The topic is email." As Alan finished the sentence both Sue and Jeff groaned.

"What? What?" he asked in confusion.

"Oh I'm not groaning because of the topic," said Sue. "I guess we are both groaning because it's the bane of our lives. I am getting up to two hundred emails some days, and even with the help of my BlackBerry it's almost impossible to keep on top of it. I confess I miss the occasional email and people get so cross when I do."

"All the more reason for us to try and do something about it," said Alan. "I work to some informal guidelines which I can add to the debate. However what we need is a good idea of the top issues that bother everyone."

"OK sure, well let's ask people over the next week." added Sue.

"Well if we are going to learn from my research, then I guess we should ask them face to face," laughed Jeff.

"Actually you're right," said Alan. "Can you both ask everyone verbally and make it very informal? That way we can perhaps get some insight from people who don't like using it."

Sue's Research

Later that evening Sue sank gratefully into an armchair at home with a glass of wine. The children were in bed and her husband Barry was watching the TV through half closed eyes. Barry was a senior manager at an NGO involved in healthcare. It was a world that was very alien to Sue although she had huge empathy with him and tried to keep up with his issues.

"How was your day then?" she asked quietly, not fully expecting an answer as Barry looked shattered.

"Complete bloody chaos to be frank," he answered. "I guess we have made some progress this week but frankly I would have to dig hard to find it right now." He lifted his head and smiled ironically at Sue. "How about you?" he enquired, suddenly livening up.

"Well I'm pretty exhausted but I think I have made progress on a couple of fronts this week. Listen," said Sue, changing the subject, "can I ask you a question?"

"Go right ahead. No promises of any kind of sense from me at this time of night though." Barry smiled.

"If I asked you how well you felt you were able to manage your email, what would you say?"

"My email? God my bloody email," Barry chuckled. "It's an unremitting nightmare which I am learning to ignore."

"In what way?" Sue was energised by his response.

"Oh boy, where do I start? OK let's start with volume. You know I have a public profile, right?" he asked and Sue nodded. "Well I get so much stuff through that you wouldn't believe. A lot of it is junk, but let's face it pretty much all of it could come from potential sponsors or donors so I really can't afford to ignore it."

"So what do you do with it?"

"My assistant Gloria helps me sort it. She also sends out standard responses wherever she can, but I still have to reply individually to a lot of them, and then track the follow ups."

"Do you have a customer database?" Sue began. "No, scrap that."

"A what? Oh you mean a marketing database? Our marketing folks have one but it's not much help to me." Barry grinned ironically. "And I haven't even mentioned all the email crap from the Advisory Board."

"Why, what do they send you?"

"It varies hugely. From simple questions that they should know the answer to – or could even look up, to the more serious members of the board who send me massively long articles and links daily and then phone me to ask me what I think of them."

By now Sue had grabbed the telephone pad off the side table and was scribbling furiously.

"Oh and finally there are 'disaster zone' emails that people send internally. Usually a joke or a rude comment about another member of staff that, if I don't catch it, can create a crisis."

Sue pulled a face "You mean what we might call an HR Violation?"

"Exactly. Some of them are pretty funny actually if they didn't have the potential to land us in serious hot water. We got such a hard time in the papers for that fundraising mix up last year. I really wince when I imagine what they would say if they got hold of even one of them."

Sue scribbled again.

"So if I could find a way to help you with some of these issues that would be pretty useful to you?"

"Oh, wow, any help gratefully received," said Barry sinking back into his sofa. "The truth is that even if you could help me personally, there are more than a few people I work with who need help too," he muttered darkly.

"Well I will see what we can do. It's something I'm working on," said Sue. She pulled out two pages from the phone notepad and stood up to put them in her briefcase. "Thanks, darling, that's more helpful than you can know. I really appreciate it."

"Don't know how listening to me rant can be helpful at all. But I feel better now." He smiled back at her.

Alan

Alan had excused himself from family duties that Saturday to play golf with John who was an old friend and mentor. Following a stellar career as a financier, John was currently Chairman of a major global firm and a non-executive Director of several more. Although they had known each other for a long time, Alan often wondered why John kept up with him as he spent so much time with powers that be.

"Oh God old boy, they are such a bunch of stuffed shirts, I would rather go on an adventure with you any day," was all John would ever say when Alan gently chided him about it.

They chatted informally around the golf course. It was pretty general: family, holiday and the usual heated debates on sport. At the 17th hole, Alan sliced his tee shot deep into the trees. John of course was right in the middle of the fairway, as always. Alan found his ball without too much trouble, and was just about to take his shot when a familiar voice rang out.

"What is a Leopard doing playing in these trees?" asked the cat. "I mean that was a bit of a rubbish shot if you ask me."

"Huh!" jumped Alan, who was just able to prevent himself from swearing (which he didn't generally do). "No-one's asking you!" he said crossly.

"Your friend, is he a Leopard too?" asked the cat.

"I have no idea," said Alan. "Why?" he asked and then peering round, he saw that the cat had vanished again. Alan shrugged and played his shot out of the trees and turned his thoughts towards the clubhouse and the 19th hole.

When they sat down to lunch, John opened the conversation with a bombshell. "Alan, I have to tell you I am thinking of packing it all in and retiring," he opened as they took their seats.

"You are joking," Alan spluttered. "How can you say that, you are the same age as me?"

"I have had a great career, made my pile and frankly would love to get out at the top while I can."

Alan directed a hard stare at John. Under the usual polished demeanour, he detected something else. "All good reasons, but that's not what's driving this is it?" he said boldly.

John returned Alan's steely gaze. "What do you mean?" he asked flatly.

"You and I have known each other a long time," began Alan firmly. "And one thing I have always known about you is that you are one of the toughest competitors I have ever met, whether on the golf course or the boardroom."

"Kind of you to say so Alan," John's smile warmed.

"I mean it. If you had sold the firm and handed over the reins, then I would understand." John shook his head. "So then what is it that's driving this?" Alan persisted.

John sighed. He tried a smile but it didn't quite work. "Alan, you are right, we have known each other a long time and I trust you implicitly." He paused. "The truth is that I think I am losing my cutting edge in the modern world. There are a number of new people I work with – both at the Firm and at my other directorships. These people are smart, well informed. But brash and arrogant too. They steamroller through everything without a second thought, and I'm finding I have my work cut out just to keep things on track. I am also beginning to wonder if they aren't right and I am wrong," he finished.

Alan smiled. He thought back to his own experiences a few weeks ago. "Would it surprise you to know that I have just been through something very similar to this?"

"You? Surely not you – the consummate professional?"

Alan waved his hand in an embarrassed fashion. "Thanks John. That's kind of you to say but I had a moment very similar to this one you are having now. I reached the crossroads, so to speak."

"And clearly you decided to continue. Why?" John asked.

"It was a little bit of inspiration, along with the discovery that the next generation are actually just as keen to learn and contribute as we are." Alan looked at John directly. "The world has changed radically over the last few years, and the truth is that we have to deal with it. Not only do we have to deal with it today but also tomorrow and beyond tomorrow. In fact I'm running a separate project to help us do this, and I have to tell you that I know that I can contribute to it and still make a difference." He paused. "I don't know all the details of your situation, but frankly my view is that you can still make a difference too." Alan leant back to see the effect of his monologue.

"Well you never cease to astonish me Alan." John smiled warmly. "I can't remember the last time I saw you so fired up about something."

"So what should I do?"

"Well you can start by not resigning!" Alan started to laugh and they both chuckled for several seconds.

John was the first to recover. "I am serious," he said. "If it's firing you with that much enthusiasm, I would love to understand why. What do you think I should do?"

Alan's brow furrowed as he was suddenly reminded of the question that the cat had asked him out on the course, about whether John was a Leopard or not.

"I think you and I should sit down together in the next week or two and I will show you what we have so far," responded Alan. "It's quite limited to date but what have is very helpful – to me anyway. In return, I have what is probably quite a curious question to run past you right now."

"Go ahead."

"How do you use email to communicate?"

"Email, well good question. Firstly I have to tell you that I really hate all this new technology." John reached into his pocket and pulled out a BlackBerry. "However, I use one of these things to read pretty much all my email. It works fine."

"That's fascinating." said Alan. "To be honest I have never seen you with one of these before."

"And I would like it to stay that way," finished John. "If everyone knew I had one of these I would be deluged. I am really careful what I reply to, at what time of day I reply to it and how long I leave a message before I respond."

"Go on," said Alan.

"I get such a lot of rubbish it's not true. Some of it is generic traffic, but even people I know well send me emails and I have to confess that I have no idea what they want me to do."

"By that I assume that you mean there is no definite action or request?"

"Worse than that, it's usually on notes that are sent to a long list of people, and I am guessing that they are mainly taking pretty much the same response." He laughed.

"What's so funny?" asked Alan.

"The ones that really amuse me are where someone has copied me by mistake. They are obviously going through their email address list and accidentally add my name. And then don't check it. I have had some real clangers, I can tell you." John laughed again.

"John, thank you so much, that's fantastic insight," said Alan. "In fact I can't really relate it back to the first conversation we had."

John shrugged. "I guess you do what you have to do," he added.

"I think you will make an excellent Leopard," said Alan. "I'll explain next time we play golf," he added, somewhat enigmatically, as he got up from lunch and left John to puzzle over what he meant.

Jeff's Team

Jeff was on time for the meeting with his friends the following Monday, and was surprised to find that everyone else had made it on time too.

"Hey guys," he hailed the team. "Peter, how's things with you?" Jeff managed to get the question out first before anyone else could.

Peter was a changed man. A lot more subdued than the previous week, he also looked somewhat healthier and slightly more relaxed. "Jeff, Rufus, Kate, I simply cannot thank you enough for last week. We are not out of the woods yet, but the project is being reviewed and I think there might just be a way to turn things around."

"How are you and the CEO getting on?" asked Rufus.

"OK, I guess," responded Peter. "I mean he's still pretty angry that it's not going according to plan. But I think he is relieved that we caught it before it became a total fiasco." He stood up. "So as a thank you, dinner is on me tonight guys. What would you like?"

As they looked over the menus, Rufus raised his gaze to Jeff and asked quietly. "Hey Jeff – how did you get on with all the communications ideas we were talking about last time? By the way here's my phone – please note that it's switched off!" Rufus produced his phone and placed it on the table face down.

"Pretty well thanks. Actually after our meeting Kate and I did a piece of informal research about phone habits across our firm which was really interesting. It turns out that people are pretty inconsistent in their approach to using them. It doesn't seem to matter about age, sex or seniority. Everyone does their own thing. So we put together this list of basic rules."

Jeff unfolded the Rules of Responsiveness they had drafted for last Friday's meeting and placed them in the middle of the table. Peter and Rufus lowered their menus and leaned over the table to look.

Basic Rules of Responsiveness

1. *Personalise your voicemail so that people know it's you. Set an expectation of what information you are looking for and when you are likely respond to a message, and give alternative contact methods such as other phone numbers, email address, or how to contact an assistant or department administrator.*

2. *Check your voicemail daily or more often if possible.*

3. *You should return every call unless there is a compelling reason not to. Return your messages received in the morning by lunchtime and afternoon calls by the end of the working day.*

4. *If you are going into a meeting, especially a Creative meeting, switch the mobile off. Or at the very least to silent.*

5. *If you know someone wants to speak to you, try and schedule calls as you would a meeting so that you can focus on the conversation. It's much more productive than allowing someone to call you at a random time in the middle of something else that may also be important.*

6. *Always remember that a phone call is an exclusive use of a caller's time, so it's much more important than most other ways of communicating.*

7. *Be where you are — concentrate on the environment you are in and don't take calls when you should be doing something else.*

Rufus was the first to comment. "Well to be honest, there should be no surprises for me there but No. 3 about calling people back the same day is a really good principle and something I simply don't do right now. I just don't have a consistent rule for when I call people back. It all depends on who they are."

Jeff was making notes: "OK thanks, I think that's a good point also. We haven't talked about managing relationships in detail yet."

"No. 6 about the exclusive use of a caller's time is interesting to me," added Peter. "You know what I'm like, always in a hurry to get onto the next thing. I find it quite easy to create a short reply to an email but I am guessing that some people may find me a bit rude on the phone." He grinned ironically. "I guess I might not have admitted that a week ago."

"Thanks Peter. I'm glad you mentioned email, as that's what we are researching this week," said Jeff. "I have asked Kate this already: how do you guys manage your email, and what do you struggle with?"

Peter on Inboxes

"Well without wishing to boast, I have started doing something that has made a hugely positive impact on my email workload," Peter chipped in. "I have a pretty big inbox every day, and I used to stay late to try and reply to it all every night. I used to find that I ended up responding several times to the same email chain as updates came through before I had responded to the original email. I also used to respond to pretty much every email I was sent." He grinned sheepishly. "Eventually I learnt as my inbox got bigger and bigger!"

"So what do you do now?" asked Jeff.

"I have set up a folder for each of the groups I work with, and every time I start a major new project I also add a folder for that project. I file ruthlessly, several times a day. Even if I haven't read the email, I leave the last email on a topic in my inbox as an action reminder." Peter leaned forward with a serious expression on his face. "The truth is that if your inbox goes over the page, you lose visibility of the emails on the second page. You have to make decisions about email: do I need to do something, do I need to read it, file it or bin it?" He looked around the group, who were looking at him intently. "I hope I'm not boring you." Jeff indicated to him to continue.

"The last one is really hard by the way as people are nervous about deleting stuff – but I digress. The truth is that email will take over your life if you allow it to. It's pretty easy to send an email without thinking about it and absolute trivia can completely distract you if you are not careful. But, if you file your emails along the lines as I suggest, you can go back to each topic folder in turn and read through the email chains in your own time. You know where they all are, and unless there is something urgent that needs doing, you can clear them out of your mind until later." Peter grinned. "Especially to make way for some Creative Time!" to which Jeff laughed.

"Thanks Peter, that's really useful. I have to say that I do file some of my emails but my inbox is huge. By the way do you have a smartphone or a BlackBerry?"

"Yes, but I only use it for keeping track of things when I'm mobile," responded Peter. "My laptop is much better for organising and managing email, and that's what I use every day. I always aim to finish every day with fewer than 30 emails left in my inbox."

"What about you Rufus?"

Rufus on Rules

"I must admit I also have a big inbox," added Rufus. "Although I do one thing that does help clear out the noise. I'm signed up to whole heap of industry newsletters, none of them are very urgent topics but they are interesting and useful to read. So like Peter I have several topic folders to file them, but I have set up automatic rules on my inbox to route the email straight to the topic folder." He laughed.

"What's so funny?" asked Kate.

"Well I set them up for my newsletters, but there are a couple of people who send me so many news links and stories with comments attached that I route all their email to the topic folders too. So I also have to check and make sure they don't send me something important." Rufus shook his head ruefully, "I really wish they would learn. I mean I guess I should say something."

Kate's Bulletins

"Maybe you should gently suggest that they hang onto all their links and ideas and send them out on Fridays as a weekly bulletin?" ventured Kate. Rufus laughed.

"Kate, that's brilliant! It's exactly what I will do," he replied.

Peter was burrowing in his briefcase and pulled out his laptop. "Rufus, this might be useful as well," he turned his laptop round. "I have this program on my laptop called OneNote," he said. "It's brilliant for taking notes and dumping all your ideas including photos, other documents and web links. I use if for gathering all the data and content for my weekly reports."

"I also have something very similar called Evernote on my Mac," added Jeff. "It's really useful."

"Thanks you guys. I really appreciate it," replied Rufus.

"Me too," said Jeff who was busy scribbling in his notebook. "That's some really useful input. Kate I know we have talked already, what are your thoughts?"

Arguments You Cannot Win

"Well I saw a great example of email gone wrong last week for one," started Kate. "David who works in my section sent out a meeting summary, and one of the other people in the meeting replied that she disagreed with his summary of events. Instead of getting hold of her to clarify her perspective, he argued back and it turned into a public squabble – argh!" Kate screwed up her face in distaste at the memory. "Oh, and the other thing I discovered last week on our phone survey was that one of the management team who never – I mean never –

responds to any email was really friendly to me on the phone. I mean he hardly knows me and we chatted for 20 minutes," Kate smiled.

"You know what you were saying earlier Rufus about the relative importance of who it is on the phone?" Rufus nodded back at her.

"People naturally turn to their own preferred method of communication, and I guess if you want to reach them you need to understand and approach them using that method," continued Kate.

"Hmm. I wonder if that varies by whether people are naturally Creative or Functional?" offered Jeff.

Peter piped up: "Well I'm naturally Functional as we discovered last week and email is definitely my thing. I'm thinking that's because it's very efficient, which really suits me for getting things done."

Rufus stirred. "I have been thinking about this whole Creative versus Functional question," he looked at Jeff quizzically. "I believe I am naturally Creative and yet on the surface, my primary role in finance would seem to be Functional. Absolutely my preferred method of communication is definitely face to face, and if I look at most of my electronic communication, it's used to set up and manage face to face meetings. Does that make sense?"

"Not entirely," responded Jeff. "I mean surely a major part of your role is doing all the financial modelling and analysis. I know you are really good at it, which rather confuses me if you say you are naturally Creative?"

"I agree with you – and to be truthful I really hate the Functional part of doing all that," said Rufus. "But once that part's done, all the strategic issues really fascinate me. So when I started the role I spent the first three months building a set of modelling tools in Excel that automate lots of the Functional work that needs to be done. I still have to check them and update them, but basically I have managed to significantly reduce the amount of Functional work that I have to do."

Jeff was riveted. "Wow – that's very smart."

"I don't think of it as smart," countered Rufus. "I think of it as eliminating the repetitive, dull and tedious work that either I or another team member would have to do anyway."

"I guess you could say that you took a Creative approach to it," laughed Kate.

"I'm thinking that I need to do something similar," ventured Peter. "If I worked with finance to agree and create standard financial models from our business planning processes that would halve the review time window."

Jeff grinned and shook his head. "Thank you all. Ah great. The food is here."

Putting it All Together

When Sue and Jeff arrived at Alan's office on Friday, they found him standing at a flipchart writing with a magic marker. As they walked in, he tore off the top sheet and handed the pen to Sue.

"Hi how are you?" he greeted them breezily.

"What do you want me to do with this?" asked Sue blankly.

"Oh sorry," said Alan. "I was miles away. So you've been talking to friends and colleagues about email – can you put your top issues on the flipchart? Thanks. If you can space them apart so we can fill them in that would be great." Alan picked up some adhesive tape from the desk, walked over to the window and taped his sheet to the glass. He waited patiently as Sue and Jeff finished their sheets and helped them tape them alongside his on the window.

"I really wanted us to crack this email thing. I'm not sure if it's what we are going to be using in 5 years' time but it's causing all kinds of issues for people right now. Sue, why don't you go first?"

"Sure. Well three big ones for me. I think volume management is my biggest issue, followed by what I will call 'organisational risk' which means inappropriate emails that, if they get into the wrong hands, can cause a disaster. Finally expectation management is the last issue I have which is all about people not wasting your time with unproductive email requests."

"Have you got any good examples?" asked Alan.

"Well you know Barry my husband." Alan nodded and Sue

continued. "He is a senior manager at a healthcare NGO with a public facing profile. He simply cannot afford not to respond to a large proportion of his emails because lots of them are from donors and stakeholders. As a result he has a massive inbox. He gets some help from an assistant but frankly it keeps him late at work pretty much every night. He also has to manage the expectations of his Advisory Board, who ask him simple questions that they already know the answer to. Otherwise he is being bombarded with long articles which he is expected to read instantly. And the final one is the 'organisational risk' issue – HR violations or inappropriate emails, whatever you want to call it." She looked up. "I have coined a term for this one – the Daily Mail test:"

> *Never write anything in an email that you would not be*
> *happy for your mother to read on the front page of the*
> *Daily Mail.*

Alan fell back in his chair laughing, "I love it!" he chortled. Jeff grinned.

"But it's so true," commented Sue. "Every time I see someone in the papers for sending an inappropriate email – or even a text – they are pictured having to explain what they have done to their nearest and dearest in front of the world's media. It's only a moment's indiscretion but it can have life changing consequences."

"Barbara's going to love this one," said Alan. "You know, Barbara, our HR director?" They all nodded. "OK great," Alan continued. "That's the first of the rules of email. Can you write it up on your page in the window?"

"On your second point – expectation management, I got some good insight from a friend of mine who is a city financier. He's one of the old-school who on the surface doesn't 'do' technology, but right in the middle of lunch he produced a BlackBerry which he uses to keep across everything. In fact I have his comments right here. He said,

'If everyone knew I had one of these I would be deluged. I am really careful what I reply to, at what time of day I reply to it and how long I leave a message before I respond.'"

Alan paused to let this sink in and then continued, "I think he is dead right. So I translated his thoughts into two simple ideas – what do you think?"

> *Responding – Don't be too quick to respond to email requests – emails are very easy to send, and it is often hard and time consuming to respond.*

> *Expectations – Get people to call you if they want something urgently so that you know whether they are really serious and why they need a response.*

"Sue – does that help you at all?"

"Yes. That makes sense for the Board type issues. I need a way of dealing with the volume of emails though; even if the responses are delayed they still need to be responded to."

Jeff stirred at this point and pulled out his notes. "I think I can help you there. The first of my issues was also around inbox volume – or rather overload. In the first instance they always ended up responding several times to the same email chain as updates came through before they had responded to the original email. The answer is to set up a topic folder for each of the groups that you work with, and every time you start a major new project, add a topic folder for that project."

"Oh and you absolutely have to file ruthlessly even if you have not yet read the email, leaving the last email on a topic in the inbox as an action reminder. The insight is that if your inbox goes over the page, you lose visibility of the emails on the second page. You have to make decisions about email: Do I need to do something? Do I need to read it, file it or bin it?"

"Hear, hear," muttered Alan as Sue nodded.

"Anyway I wrote this up as follows," continued Jeff.

> *Inbox Management – Clear your inbox every day to less than 30 emails (so the list does not reach the bottom of the inbox page). Set up folders covering each area you work on – or groups you deal with – and file religiously. Even if you have not always read them. You can then go back and review by topic and avoid the stress of an overfull inbox.*

"Oh that's excellent. Please add it to the window," said Sue. "That's also going to really help Barry. Thank you Jeff!" She scribbled furiously on her pad.

"Jeff, I want to pick up with you on the comment about making decisions," added Alan.

"Another key piece of feedback that came back to me was about emails that are circulated to a group of people without a clear indication what action is required. I have had a long think about it and I think it breaks down into two parts. The first is in the subject of the email. It needs to have 'Action Required' contained in it so that everyone who it's copied to actually reads it. The second part is that when a specific action is required, there must be a note to call this out and assign it to someone. For example 'Action: Alan to send out the notes.'"

Alan leapt out his chair, really quite energised by now, picked up a magic marker pen and walked over to the window.

"So if I write this out in full – it looks like this,"

> *Getting Something Actioned – if you are sending an email looking for someone to act:*
>
> *1. Flag that action is required by putting ACTION REQUIRED in the title which will mean that everyone who the email is copied to will read it.*

2. To make it really clear who and what you are asking you must highlight specific requests e.g.: "Action: Alan to check this issue and confirm." This approach works well with people you know, but may be ignored by people who you don't. It's a good idea to get verbal agreement first.

"I added that last bit because I think there is a significant risk that people will assume that an action they called out in an email will just get done. It's never as easy as that." He grinned.

"As you know only too well Sue."

"Indeed I do," said Sue. "I am going to tweak my approach to follow that next time and see where we get to. But while I think that will help with specific actions, I can't help thinking that there must be better ways of getting an email to make more impact – especially with senior people."

"That was a complaint I had also. Which was directly related to the action rule above, far too many vague and directionless messages."

"What's the easiest type of message that you get?" asked Jeff.

"Easy. One that sets up the proposition in the title, gets the message across in three short paragraphs or less and makes it dead easy to respond to."

"OK well maybe we need to write this up."

Jeff picked up the pen and walked over to the window.

Getting Your Message Across – If you need to get an email response from senior people who are busy or don't know you very well:

1. Construct your title carefully (perhaps write it as a proposition such as – "Getting final approval for Project X").

2. *Get the message over in three short and punchy paragraphs – no more.*

3. *If you want approval, ask for it by asking them to merely reply to that email and type 'yes'. This works very well as it makes it so easy for them to respond!*

4. *Remember that people are all really pressured by email but generally always scan the title and first few lines.*

"Good, thanks again Jeff," said Alan. "I have one more minor item to finish off which I have tagged 'copying by mistake'. The feedback I have had is similar in vein to Sue's around inappropriate emails but it focuses on genuine mistakes which are hard to catch and reverse. I haven't any ideas on this apart from being more careful. But people will make mistakes. Any ideas?"

"Oh that's an easy one," proposed Jeff. "You always have to check the address list on an email because it's too easy to accidentally click on the wrong address that Outlook or your mail programme suggests. But the killer tool is in the rules section. I'm sure you can probably do this on other email clients too. The key is to set a delay on your outbox. Normally if you hit send by mistake it's gone and you cannot retrieve it. But, you can set up a delay for all messages, specific emails or even specific organisations with the same email suffix. 2 minutes is normally fine." Jeff rose again. "Here, I'll write it out."

Avoiding Inevitable Email Accidents – the speed and simplicity of email will always lead to some mistakes; many of them can be rectified by adopting two simple principles:

1. Set a Delay: Set a sending delay of at least 2 minutes on your Outbox. It gives you just enough time to delete that accidental email. Better still you can set it for specific addresses such as clients.

2. Double Check Addresses: Double check your address lines in email before you send. Outlook auto insert often puts odd names in there.

"There is another related rule which is having arguments by email," Jeff looked at Sue. "Without giving too much away I think we know why that's a very bad thing."

"Why's that?" asked Alan.

"Oh you mean the David email?" said Sue. "Yes that is a bit close to home. Have you and Kate come up with something then?" Sue artfully avoided further enquiry by Alan.

"Yes here it is – pretty simple I think," Jeff handed over a note with the copy of the rule written out on it:

Arguments – Never, ever have an argument by email – everyone loses and it is recorded for posterity. If you sense a disagreement coming, make a call or organise a face to face meeting and then circulate the conclusions by email.

"Would you like me to give a copy of this to David?" Sue asked Jeff.

"Up to you – I would give him the whole list if and when we publish it."

They looked at Alan for guidance.

"I have been thinking about all this," he responded slowly. "I think we almost have enough ideas shaped up and written down to test on a wider group." He rose from his chair and pulled on his jacket.

"Come on it's nearly lunchtime – let me buy you both lunch and let's mull it over together."

The Bistro Over the Road

As they settled into a booth in the Bistro over the road, Alan leaned forward. "Firstly I have to say I have really enjoyed working on this with you both; you have been great contributors and have kept the debate pretty sharp. I would love to continue as we are but I am conscious that despite our research, we'll become too insular and comfortable with our own opinions over time."

"What are you saying?" enquired Jeff cautiously.

"Firstly, I think we need to pull more people into our group on Friday morning, and secondly I think we need to publish what we are doing," stated Alan bluntly. "The first point is to ensure the health of what we are doing, the second part is a necessity because the company pays us and they need to see a return on their investment – we need to share our work with everyone."

Jeff thought for a moment. "I have an additional suggestion," he ventured. "What about opening it up to people outside the company?"

"I think that is a definite possibility," replied Alan. "Actually I have been thinking about it quite a lot. It would bring in some significant value to the program, but we need to square away our internal people first."

"Who were you thinking of?" asked Sue.

"Barbara for one. She will need to approve anything we do, but if she agrees I'm going to have a quiet word with the Chairman."

"What about Bill?" asked Jeff. The CEO's name hung over the table like a cloud.

"He will support it if he can see it makes sense, but frankly until we have something more to show, he won't appreciate the discussion. It needs to be wrapped up in a parcel ready to go. The chairman is a bit of a lateral thinker. He will love the innovation it will unleash. I also have some help available to persuade him!"

"OK. So what's the first step?" asked Sue, ever keen to be pragmatic.

"Firstly I think we need to finish off the rules of email. Could you guys make an hour later this afternoon?" They each checked their calendars on their phones and agreed 4.30pm. Sue knew Barry would be cross at another late evening, but she could probably console him with the email rules they had created.

"The next step is to add one or two more people to the group, and I would like to do that next week – any ideas? Kate for one. And Barbara, if she is available," said Alan.

"I think you should include Ben," said Jeff carefully. "I know you think he is precocious and prickly but I think we could get him onside and he would be a fantastic contributor."

"I'll think about it," said Alan, suddenly uncomfortable about the idea of someone from Bennett's team being involved.

"On second thoughts Jeff, can you and I have a separate discussion about it later?"

Jeff nodded. "Fine."

Alan turned to Sue. "So here's my little bombshell for you. Next week could you put together the training session for all of us on the networking principles we discussed."

"Are you serious?" she asked.

"Very, and although I have the week from hell next week, I will make time to help you prepare it if you want."

"If it was just the three of us it would be fine," she ventured nervously.

"Well Kate works for you and – seriously – Barbara doesn't bite."

"Well I guess it will be OK then," Sue finished cautiously.

"You will be fine. I have seen you in the project reviews," Alan smiled.

The Finish Post at 4.30pm

Sue turned up promptly at 4.30pm; Jeff however was nowhere to be found. Despite all the insight she had provided in the morning Sue was unexpectedly quiet until Alan eventually said to her.

"Sue, what's wrong – are you still anxious after our conversation at lunch?"

"Frankly – yes I am. I can't think where to start. I know the topic so well but..." she left her sentence hanging.

"Well if I were you I would use your time here as a case study. How long have you been here now? A month?"

"Just completing 3 weeks – why?"

"Well if you look back to your outline plan you made when you joined – and I know we talked about if your first day here. How far have you got? What hasn't worked?"

"Well that makes some things easier and some more difficult."

"Why? What's more difficult?"

"Well some things have not worked out exactly as I expected and if I call them out, it may get back to the people involved."

Anonymising a Case Study

"OK well there's an easy way to fix that," volunteered Alan. "All you have to do is anonymise the situation."

"Anonymise it?"

"Basically you write out the example and then take out the details so that the audience can't distinguish who was involved. For example, 'Alan disagreed with Sue and blocked approval for the project' translates to 'we were unable to gain agreement for the project to be approved.' It gets the point across without the need to detail who was responsible for what. It's a great technique for writing case studies."

"OK fine. I'll give it a go." Sue was looking more cheerful now.

"Sure. Give me a call or send me your notes if you want some help. By the way I am planning to do the presentation on Meetings that I promised the following week."

"Don't you want to have the honour of kicking off next week?" Sue ventured ironically as she knew Alan wouldn't have asked her if he hadn't had a good reason.

"No, I need you to do the first one rather than me." He looked at her seriously. "If we are to really make this initiative work, it cannot be seen as something that I am driving alone. You joined us quite recently and that means you have a different perspective – which, by the way, you do – and we need this initiative to be seen as something new and fresh." He smiled warmly at her. "I hope that makes sense. I have great faith in both you and Jeff."

Sue's confidence began to return. "Oh well I can always haul him in to help me prep if I need to," she thought.

At that moment there was a knock at the door and Jeff came in. "I am really sorry to be so late," he began, somewhat flustered.

"No matter," Alan waved nonchalantly. "Let's crack on with the email issues and finish them off. Jeff, I think you had several left."

"We had an interesting debate the other night about whether Creative or Functional people tend to use different forms of communication. By the way we think they do. Anyway, one thing is clear: email is certainly not everyone's favourite form of communication. Some people are better in person. Others are better on the phone. And there are others who like formal hardcopy. I think its key to find out which one people like."

"Over to you then," said Alan, handing the inevitable magic marker pen back to Jeff.

"OK here goes," he started writing at the window.

> *Favourite Form of Communication – Email is not everyone's favourite form of communication. Some people are better "live", others like to use the phone, and others respond to formal letters or memos. Try and find out which form your key people like and use it for important communications.*

"I like that," said Sue. "That works. I would like to spend some time on the link between Creative and Functional people later."

"I have one more," said Jeff. "And then my last note is around interruptions which I think we should re-visit because I think email can really help."

"But first I want to go back to inbox volumes again. I went back to my laptop and looked at where I had multiple repeats of the same email thread. Frankly this is nonsense. People are spraying emails to all and sundry without thinking about who they need to go to and whether they need to be involved."

He edged off his seat and picked up the pen again. "I am proposing we add a rule called Circulation List – here goes:"

Circulation List – When you need to respond to an email with a wide circulation on it, you need to stop and think. Do I need to send this to everyone? Is this 'thread' wasting a lot of people's time? (You can be sure that it is).

Jeff dropped the pen back onto Alan's desk and sank back into his chair with a sigh.

"Not quite, Jeff," said Alan. "We still have 'interruptions' to do."

"Oh right. Well you know we were talking about interruptions last time?" Alan and Sue acknowledged, so Jeff continued.

"Well often if I chat to someone at the coffee area and they have an idea they would like some input from me on, I ask them to send me an email note as a reminder. So it occurs to me that even if you could interrupt someone physically, or by phoning them, you could just send them a note with a simple request. Or just ask them when you see them at lunchtime." He stood up to write it out.

Interruptions – While internal emails can be a huge waste of time they can also avoid unnecessary interruptions. After you have interrupted someone at their desk it can take up to 30 minutes for them to get back to their original task.

"So," Jeff continued, "while talk is best, email may be a useful method to log a question or thought. Equally making a note and saving it for a lunchtime chat is also a good option."

Alan and Sue stood up to join him as he finished and look at their output. "Any more ideas?" asked Alan.

"No I think that's it for now."

"Nothing more from me."

"Well thank you both – a marathon session," Alan counted almost inaudibly. "That's eleven in total. The Eleven Rules of Email: it has a definite a ring to it," he pronounced. "OK I will write these up for next week," he volunteered. "In the meantime let me know who you think should come and let me know by Monday so we can invite them?"

Chapter Notes

The Leopard's Hierarchy of Communications

1. *Face to face meeting*
   - *For: offers best opportunity for verbal and non-verbal communication; real time.*
   - *Against: not everyone pays full attention*

2. *Video Conference*
   - *For: next best thing to being there; real time.*
   - *Against: stilted conversation, hard to set up, inconsistent quality.*

3. *Phone Call*
   - *For: flexible; real time.*
   - *Against: timing; no visual communication; not everyone pays full attention.*

4. *Instant Messaging*
   - *For: real time; can conference in other people.*
   - *Against: too easy to type the wrong thing in a hurry.*

5. *Text Message*
   - *For: one to one communication; near real time.*
   - *Against: too quick to have value; easy to misconstrue.*

6. *Email*
   - *For: generic, fast to use tool; offline (not real time).*
   - *Against: too much noise, too quick to have value; easy to misconstrue.*

Written Letter
- *For: unusual, personal; stands out in today's world.*
- *Against: more complex to write and send; relatively slow compared to electronic format.*

Social Networks
- *For: quick, relatively personal*
- *Against: Against: too public?*

Basic Rules of Responsiveness

1. *Personalise your voicemail so that people know it's you. Set an expectation of what information you are looking for and when you are likely respond to a message, and give alternative contact methods such as other phone numbers, email address, or how to contact an assistant or department administrator.*

2. *Check your voicemail daily or more often if possible.*

3. *You should return every call unless there is a compelling reason not to. Return your messages received in the morning by lunchtime and afternoon calls by the end of the working day.*

4. *If you are going into a meeting, especially a Creative meeting, switch the mobile off. Or at the very least to silent.*

5. *If you know someone wants to speak to you, try and schedule calls as you would a meeting so that you can focus on the conversation. It's much more productive than allowing someone to call you at a random time in the middle of something else that may also be important.*

6. *Always remember that a phone call is an exclusive use of a caller's time, so it's much more important than most other ways of communicating.*

7. *Be where you are – concentrate on the environment you are in and don't take calls when you should be doing something else.*

The 11 Rules of Email

1. *Daily Mail Test – "Never write anything in an email that you would not be happy for your mother to read on the front page of the Daily Mail."*

2. *Responding – Don't be too quick to respond to email requests – emails are very easy to send, and it is often hard and time consuming to respond.*

3. *Expectations – Get people to call you if they want something urgently so that you know whether they are really serious and why they need a response.*

4. *Inbox management – Clear your inbox every day to less than 30 emails (so the list does not reach the bottom of outlook page). Set up folders covering each area you work on – or groups you deal with – and file religiously – even if you have not always read. That way you can go back and review by topic and avoid the stress of an overfull inbox.*

5. *Getting Things Actioned – if you are sending an email looking for someone to act:*

   a. *flag that action is required by putting* ACTION REQUIRED *in the title which will mean that everyone who the email is copied will read it.*

   b. *To make it really clear who and what you are asking you must highlight specific requests e.g.: "Action: Alan to check this issue and confirm." This approach works well with people you know, but may be ignored by people who you don't – a good idea to get verbal agreement first.*

6. *Getting Your Message Across – If you need to get an email response from senior people who are busy or don't know you very well.*

   a. *Construct your title carefully (perhaps write it as a proposition such as – "Getting final approval for Project X").*

   b. *Get the message over in three short and punchy paragraphs – no more.*

   c. *If you want approval, ask for it by asking them to merely reply to that email and type "yes". This works very well as it makes it so easy for them to respond!*

   d. *Remember that people are all really pressured by email but generally always scan the title and first few lines.*

7. *Avoiding Inevitable Email Accidents* – *the speed and simplicity of email will always lead to some mistakes; many of them can be rectified by adopting two simple principles.*

    a. *Set a Delay* – *Set a sending delay of at least 2 minutes on your Outbox* – *it gives you just enough time to delete that accidental email. Better still you can set it for specific addresses such as clients.*

    b. *Double Check Addresses* – *Double check your address lines in email before you send* – *Outlook auto insert often puts odd names in there.*

8. *Arguments* – *Never, ever have an argument by email* – *everyone loses and it is recoded for posterity. If you sense a disagreement coming, make a call or organise a face to face meeting and then circulate the conclusions by email.*

9. *Favourite Form of Communication* – *Email is not everyone's favourite form of communication. Some people are better "live", others like to use the phone, and others respond to formal letters or memos. Try and find out which form your key people like and use it for important communications.*

10. *Circulation List* – *When you need to respond to an email with a wide circulation on it, you need to stop and think. Do I need to send this to everyone? Is this "thread" wasting a lot of people's time? (You can be sure that it is).*

11. *Interruptions – While internal emails can be a huge waste of time they can also avoid unnecessary interruptions. After you have interrupted someone at their desk it can take up to 30 minutes for them to get back to their original task.*

   So while talk is best, email may be a useful method to log a question or thought. Equally making a note and saving it for a lunchtime chat is also a good option.

5

BUILDING A NETWORK

Alan Meets Ben for Coffee

As Jeff ran down the stairs towards the lobby on his way home that Friday night, his iPhone went off. Jeff cursed and slowed down to reach for it. He was late for a night out with some friends and he could have done without the interruption.

"Hi Jeff. It's Alan. Sorry one more thing, please could you see if Ben would be around for a coffee on Monday morning first thing. Say 8.30am?"

"No problem," puffed Jeff, "I'll send you a text." And with that he hurled his phone back into his bag and took off again.

Ben had no problem with meeting them at 8.30am, but was rather curious about what the meeting was for. "What does he want with me then? Blood?" he texted back ironically. "Just be there," advised Jeff.

Sure enough Ben was there on Monday morning. "Hi Ben," Alan strode up to Ben and shook him by the hand warmly. Ben was rather taken aback by Alan's friendliness. While he didn't have any regret about crossing swords with him on previous occasions, he was smart enough to know that Alan was not going to be a big supporter of his. Ironically Ben had found a rather unique source of support in Bennett, Alan's prickly and rude counterpart on the management team.

Although Ben worked for Bennett, he had also managed to get through to Bennett the first time they had met and they had become friends, which, Ben gathered, was pretty unusual as Bennett didn't "do" friends.

"Err, good to see you," replied Ben warily.

"Coffee?"

"Thanks. A latte would be good."

"Me too," said Jeff.

They all queued together for few minutes, and much to Ben's surprise Alan started some banter with one of the coffee baristas, a large and rotund lady with long black pony tails

"Hi Suzanne, I trust we are all suitably cheerful this morning?"

"Oh we are all fine, Alan." Suzanne replied shyly, "Especially as you are here to cheer us up."

When they had sat down at a table a little way away from the main crowd, Alan began. "Ben: Jeff and I are working on the planning stage for a new project," he said. "It's pre-budget and pre-approval right now, but it's something we think could have major impact in the company moving forward. It will also be a lot of fun. The reason I wanted to meet with you was to see if you would be interested in contributing to the work we are doing now. It is pre-budget so you would have to clear some space alongside your existing commitments, and it won't count formally towards your appraisal."

"OK. I'm intrigued," said Ben. "Tell me more."

"The project is all around best practice in the day to day working environment. Communications, social networking, that type of thing," Alan was being deliberately vague about the background as he didn't want it to leak out just yet.

"Anyway, we want to do a session on technology next week and I would love it if you could work with Jeff to help put that together." Jeff's eyebrows had shot up with surprise at this point, but he just about managed to control himself.

"OK. It certainly sounds interesting. Can I think about it and discuss with Jeff?"

"No problem," said Alan. "But I need confirmation by this

Wednesday morning otherwise there won't be enough time for you to do the prep."

"Oh. When would the session be?" asked Ben.

"Friday week," responded Alan. "I can send you details on Wednesday, and we can talk about timings, audience and anything else you need to know." He looked directly at Ben. "One last point," he said firmly, "as this project is pre-planning you must keep it confidential for now. If you decide you want to participate, I will cover for you, but you must keep the content and nature under wraps until we have finished the planning."

"That's fine," said Ben who was excited to be included in the project but already wondering what he was going to say to Bennett.

"Thanks for your time," said Alan, shaking Ben's hand again. He turned and walked away.

"Wow, that's just not the same guy we did that meeting with the other week," breathed Ben as he watched Alan walk away.

"Oh man. I really hope you can do this with me," said Jeff. "It's quite a tough assignment, but I really like working with him."

"If you say so," said Ben. "But I mean I'm not that into technology. I'm really just a data guy, so why the hell did he pick me?"

"Two reasons," responded Jeff. "First because I recommended you. And second because he knows that I am really into technology and he wants someone who isn't as a counterpart."

"Well that's smart thinking."

"That's what he's like."

"What are you going to tell Bennett?" Jeff knew of the relationship and was curious to see how Ben would handle it.

"Oh, I can get past him fine," Ben waived breezily.

"You know they don't get on. And that's putting it mildly," said Jeff.

"Yeah. I know. Don't worry I'll handle it."

"OK, so when do you want to meet up and get started?"

Twenty minutes later, Alan's mobile went off. He was in the management meeting and had fortunately remembered to set it to vibrate. He could see it was Jeff and he smiled. At the next break in the meeting, he darted outside and called Jeff back.

"Hi Jeff, thanks again for setting up the meeting earlier."

"Well you have just gone and set me up, so thanks for that!"

Alan could hear just a whiff of sarcasm in Jeff's tone. "Oh come on!" he said, "it's your favourite subject and you did want to include Ben."

"Well you hadn't said anything to me about it. And hey, weren't you supposed to be doing next week?"

"I changed my mind. Anyway you're a grown up, I knew you could work it out."

"OK so can I invite Ben to this week's session?" asked Jeff.

"Tell him to ring me and agree to sign up and then you can invite him," countered Alan.

"Alright, I will do. I am sure he is going to shortly. We're planning to meet tomorrow to start the prep work."

"Please make sure he does before you share anything with him."

"Good point. What should I share with him?"

"Well really you need a briefing note. I will try and write you something this evening," said Alan, looking at his already crowded schedule. "Leave it with me."

The Briefing Note

After dinner that evening Alan sat down to clear his remaining emails. Following the fourth "Rule of Email" he was still setting up folders and clearing a backlog of emails in his inbox. It was refreshing to feel that he could now control something that had been the bane of his life for the last few years.

He reached into his briefcase and pulled out his file of notes from all the previous sessions and spread them out on the desk. Where to begin?

Confidential – Presentation Briefing

As such the project described below is informal and pre-budget; therefore it is internally confidential at this stage. Please assist any successful outcome by keeping it so until the business case is formalised. Please refer any queries directly to me.

Background

We have put together a small informal team to look at how individual skills could contribute to a significant increase in operational performance. If our initial findings carry enough promise a formal business case will be created for an induction and training programme that would be rolled out across the company.

Our first phase of the work is almost complete and from this we have established five key principles to examine, which are the ability of an individual to:

1. *Act opportunistically*
2. *Adapt to a wide variety of environments*
3. *Operate at speed*
4. *Drive any chosen activity to a successful conclusion*
5. *Remain almost undetected*

Session Briefing

Subject: Technology
Duration: A 1 hour presentation followed by Q&A.
Time: To be confirmed

Objective: The presentation should consider the five principles outlined above and how the topic can contribute to each principle.

Notes:

1. *At no stage should the presentation suggest that the company is required to carry out an action. The background is the status quo in terms of the tools and systems that the company already provides and anything that an individual could reasonably acquire on their own behalf.*

2. *The emphasis should be to provide guidance that an individual can use on their own to improve their capability.*

3. *You should assume that the output applies to all pay grades across the company.*

Alan looked back over the text and smiled. This was really starting to take shape. He dropped the text into an email to Jeff with a note:

Jeff, please use this for your meeting but retain any copies at this stage – thanks Alan.

He paused for a moment and then sent a version with slightly revised topic to Sue.

Sue, please use this as a briefing note for Friday – hope it's useful – thanks Alan.

He was just about to close his laptop when he remembered the last thing he needed to do; he looked up Barbara's mobile number and rang her quickly.

"Barbara – sorry for bothering you so late, I need to ask a big favour. Well two actually."

Despite the hour, Barbara was quite affable.

"Hi Alan – no problem, comes with the territory."

"One, can I borrow you for an hour on Friday at 10am. If you could just block it out that would be brilliant."

"Friday morning. I may have to shift stuff. Can you leave it with me? Is something wrong?" a note of caution entered Barbara's voice.

"Not if you can make it on Friday," laughed Alan. "Seriously though, I also wanted to see you before Friday to tell you what it's all about."

"I can do tomorrow at 5.30pm, but I have to be gone by 6pm, and, Alan, I do mean 6!"

Getting Barbara On Board

Much as he liked Barbara, Alan was uncharacteristically nervous when 5.30pm rolled around the next day. He knew that she was no pushover and her friendly demeanour masked a rapier like intellect. He wondered briefly whether she was a Creative or a Functional type but quickly scrubbed the thoughts from his mind. "Concentrate and remain calm," he told himself.

"Come in," she called when Alan knocked on her door.

Alan found her busily typing on her keyboard and looking somewhat harassed. "Hi Barbara. Everything OK?" he asked breezily.

"Oh about as good as it ever gets," she responded wearily. "Email hell today."

"Really? Why's that?" Alan's curiosity was heightened. "Or can't you tell me?" he smiled.

"Some of your colleagues are a real pain to be frank," responded Barbara crossly. "They don't read what's sent to them and ask questions to which they already have the answers. Worse still, we end up with these massive email chains with everyone copied. It does my head in frankly. I should be spending my time with our people rather than writing emails."

"It's rather ironic. But that's what I have come to see you about," he replied.

Barbara went white. "Oh please tell me we don't have another email violation. That's all I need!" she said tartly.

Alan smiled and waved his hand affably. "Relax, Relax! Nothing like that. In fact just the opposite," he said.

"Oh really. Well that would make a great change," she said peering at him carefully. "You're not about to resign are you? That would finish me off today, it really would!"

"No. No. In fact I think what I have to say is very good news for you. But I do need your advice about how to take it forward," he paused. "A small group of us have been meeting for three weeks now to consider some very important issues," he began. "It all started because I – or rather we – became very aware how very different everyone's approach is to their day to day interactions with each other. I don't think that this is just an internal issue. In fact the more research I do I think this is universal, and goes way beyond the company. We live in a very different world than we did even a few years ago. The pace of change is huge. In fact change is probably the only certainty in today's world. Along with Death and Taxes of course," he grinned.

"You have my full attention," replied Barbara. "Go on."

"Advances in technology have changed social attitudes and working practices hugely, but there is so little guidance or formality about how to interact with them or manage them." He held up his hand as Barbara began to interrupt. "Yes, I do know you have policies for all these things. But what I am talking about is discretionary behaviour here. This is not stuff you can make policy for. It's day-to-day working interaction. For example, you know me: formal and old fashioned right? The new graduates are completely casual and think completely differently. Tradition says that they are supposed to learn from us but actually I think am learning as much from them. I'm serious Barbara, I really am." Alan leaned forward earnestly. "If I can get everyone together I think we could make this a much better and more professional place to work," he said simply. "It could help people right now – and for the rest of their careers for that matter. But it could really get this company moving," he finished with a flourish.

Barbara was silent for a few moments. "Alan, I like that, I really do," she started slowly. "From my perspective it's really hard to put my finger on what I can actually do about it. What do you suggest?"

"I'm suggesting that we put together an internal programme to help everyone get started. We have done quite a bit of work informally, and it's been very positive so far. I cannot continue on this basis though because it's growing fast and we have to either formalise it or draw a line underneath it," Alan said neutrally, hoping that Barbara wasn't going to use the way out he had just opened for her.

"I think what you are suggesting is very worthwhile in any circumstances, but especially if we can show benefit back to the company," responded Barbara.

Alan felt relief flood through him as Barbara took the route he had hoped she would.

"Can you summarise what you have done so far?"

"Well we have identified five principles:"

1. *Act opportunistically*
2. *Adapt to a wide variety of environments*
3. *Operate at speed*
4. *Drive any chosen activity to a successful conclusion*
5. *Remain almost undetected*

"That's very interesting – why did you choose these in particular," asked Barbara

"These are the main characteristics of a leopard."

"A leopard? I'm sorry I don't understand."

"When you have a minute, go and look it up. The characteristics of a leopard provide an ideal metaphor for how we need to operate in today's world."

"You are joking."

"No I am dead serious. Here let me show you." He stood up and moved over to Barbara's computer, waited briefly for her to pull up her browser and then typed quickly. "Here you go."

The species' success in the wild owes in part to its opportunistic hunting behaviour, its adaptability to a variety of habitats and its ability to move at up to approximately 58 kilometres (36 miles) an hour. The leopard consumes virtually any animal it can hunt down and catch.

There was a long pause while Barbara looked in turn at the screen and then looked at Alan. "Alan I am stunned frankly. I am struggling to work out whether you are a genius or you have gone completely bonkers." She pushed the computer keyboard away. "As I have known you for a while," she said slowly, "I have to bet that you haven't gone mad. But this is quite a departure from what we normally cover in any type of training or development programme. Do you understand my dilemma?"

"I do indeed," responded Alan, "which is why I asked you to attend the session on Friday. Sue is going to do a presentation on networking – which, by the way, she is very good at – as the first part of our next sessions. If you don't think what we have is worthwhile, then fine, we'll call it a day."

"So what happens if I like it," asked Barbara. "What happens then?"

Alan paused for a moment. "I want get Robin [the Chairman] involved and have him come to the next one."

"God you don't want much do you?" breathed Barbara. "What about Bill [the CEO]?"

"It's too early. He won't get it and it will probably end there and then if we speak to him about it."

"Much as it disappoints me to agree with you, I think you are probably right on that count," murmured Barbara. "But we need to be really careful if he finds out in the meantime." She looked up at him.

"OK here's the plan, I need you to email me a short summary with a request to attend on Friday. I will email you back accepting and suggesting that we need to speak to Robin and Bill if it goes well," she raised her hand to stop Alan interrupting. "I will then set up a meeting for you and me to see Robin first and discuss with him how we brief Bill. Frankly if I'm on board with it, and we position it as a pilot stage, Bill won't have a problem as he is a big supporter of development activity. Where it can come unstuck is if it looks like some unauthorised attempt to bypass existing systems and re-invent the wheel."

"That's my concern also Barbara. I think that makes good sense," Alan began to feel a sense of elation that he had felt in the early days of putting the idea together. "I really want to thank you for your support, and for listening to me."

"On the subject of your email issue, you may find that this helps." Alan reached into his bag and pulled out a copy of the Eleven Rules of Email which he had printed just in case.

"What's this for?"

"This is the output of the work we have already been doing on communications. There is more to come but this is a good start I think," he replied. "By the way have a look at Rule 1, I thought that might appeal."

"The Daily Mail test," she began, pausing to read it in full. "Oh Alan I like that! I can't tell you how many thousands we have spent developing online courses to try and nip this particular issue in the bud. You've managed to get it in one sentence – it's so simple!" Barbara looked directly at him. "If this is what the Leopard can do, then I'm with you 110%," she exclaimed. "I'm really looking forward to Friday."

Sue's Big Session

Alan had spoken to Sue on the phone several times before the Friday session, but beyond thanking him for the briefing note, she had not asked him for further help. He had let her know that there would be a couple of new faces attending but not told her that Barbara was now coming or that Ben would also attend. He had also reminded Jeff to ask Kate to join as well. He had booked a larger meeting room with a screen and projector for the Friday session, and moved the start time for the new attendees back by 15 minutes so that Sue, Jeff and he could get together first for an update.

He was waiting in the meeting room when they arrived and was pleased to see that Sue was looking calm and relaxed. "Good news for you both," he said as Sue and Jeff found their seats. "I spoke to Barbara on Wednesday." He saw Sue tense slightly out of the corner of his eye. "She is fully on board and is coming today," Alan grinned. "She loved the Daily Mail test, as we thought! Anyway if she likes it, she and I are going to see Robin and then brief Bill."

"Wow!" said Jeff. "That's great news."

"Well we are not done yet. I am sure today will be good, but at least we have a route to formalise all this. Anyway, enough of that. Sue – let's get set up – do you have some slides?"

"Just a few. Where's the projector cable?"

Alan helped her connect the laptop, while Jeff set up camp in his own corner of the room. The door opened and Ben and Kate peered round the door.

"Hi guys," said Jeff. "Come on in."

Sue seemed unconcerned about the visitors, and even when Barbara arrived a few minutes later and was introduced, she managed to remain surprisingly calm.

Networking

"Before we start – can I ask you each what you understand by the term networking?" Sue began.

"I guess – getting to know people," said Jeff slowly.

"Meeting people at events," added Kate.

"Building a range of industry contacts," said Barbara.

"Hanging out with people like me," said Ben, not wanting to be outdone.

"Establishing key relationships internally and across the industry that can help you strategically," said Alan carefully.

"That's pretty close," Sue responded. "You are all on the right line, however with networking it's important to be precise about what you are doing. My personal definition is:"

The ability to build influence through acquiring, building and maintaining the right relationships.

She paused. "I have spent a lot of time honing and thinking about that definition, as in previous roles I have really needed my networking skills to rescue projects that were doomed and manage hugely disparate groups." She looked up at them intently. "When everything else has gone south, the quality of the relationships you build through networking skills can be all that remain to prevent a disaster."

"Can you give me an example?" interrupted Ben forcefully.

"Sure. Two years ago, the systems architect on a project I was working on quit two weeks before we were due to go live. He had a lot of stress at home and a routine disagreement at a team meeting got blown out of all proportion. He stormed out saying he was never going to work for us again." She paused for slight dramatic effect. "Through my network I happened to know his old boss from his previous role, so I called him up and asked him to intervene. He kindly rang the architect, and then went over to see him personally, and from that meeting the architect was back on site 24 hours later."

"Wow, I bet that cost you!" commented Ben.

"It did. I bought him a case of champagne. It was a lot cheaper than missing the deadline." There was a sudden hush in the room; Sue now had their complete and full attention. "Any other questions?" she ventured. "OK, I will move on."

She flashed up the definition again on the first slide:

The Purpose of Networking

To grow your personal influence by knowing and finding the right people, and maintaining your relationship with them.

"Why is this important?" she asked rhetorically. "In the previous world, people only worked for one or two organisations throughout their careers, so once they had built a network they knew everyone. Their networks rarely required any additions and they were easy to maintain. In today's world, we work in much more transitory roles, deadlines are much shorter and people move around a lot more. So even if you remain in a role – or on a project for a period of time – knowing the right people is much, much harder to achieve. You have to get much, much better at finding the right people, building relationships and maintaining links; in an uncertain world, this has become vital for your career. In addition all the new forms of electronic communication – email, text, social networking and instant messaging – mean that we have to deal with many more people and relationships than we are used to." She moved onto the next slide:

The Three Objectives of Networking

1. Knowing the right people to get things done.

2. If you don't know the right people, finding them and getting to know them (so you can get things done).

3. Maintaining links with people once you know them – even if you no longer work with them or see them – so that you can continue to get things done.

"How many people do you think you should have in a network? I'm curious," asked Barbara.

"Well between 100 - 150 people is reckoned to be ideal in terms of people you can get to know well, and yet if you look at how many contacts people have in their Outlook it isn't unusual to find 500 to 1000 people in there. And often that's just work contacts."

"Interesting. Thanks," replied Barbara.

"I think we can assume that in today's world – Objective 1 – Knowing the right people to get things done – is always a moving target. In other words we always need to be working hard to get there. So we are mainly faced with two key challenges of Objectives 2 and 3," continued Sue. "Any questions or comments so far?"

"Fine. Thanks," said Alan and no one else demurred.

Practical Networking

"So going back to the beginning. Kate and Barbara respectively mentioned going to events and making industry contacts. This really works and there are some neat things you can do to maximise the benefit of this approach. I will come back to this later if that's OK."

"Why's that? I'm curious but I thought that was really the whole point of networking," countered Ben again. Alan was beginning to wonder if it was a good move to bring him into the group.

"It is useful but it's generally not focused enough," countered Sue. "The most useful networking you can do is much more focused than that. If you really want to be successful you have to target very specific groups of people. When I take on a new project or programme I make it my business to build a really good network around that project."

"What's the point in that?" Ben interjected again. Alan sighed; he wished Ben would just let Sue continue.

Sue smiled broadly "Have you ever had complete responsibility for a project or part of a project?"

"I'm a senior analyst so yes I do take responsibility for my part of the project."

"And as such you deliver part of that personally, right?"

"Right!"

"And everything beyond this is someone else's responsibility, correct?"

"Correct again. And they screw that up far more often if you ask me." In his arrogance Ben had overreached but was completely unaware of the hole he was digging himself into.

"OK, well try and imagine this. I don't deliver any part of the project personally. Nada. Nil. I have one single role which is to deliver a successful project as a whole," said Sue quietly. "To do this I have to know what's going on, who's doing what, where the problems are going to come from and where I can find help," she stared at Ben.

Barbara leaned forward. "I think before we get too off the agenda here it's worth mentioning that Sue was the successful program lead for the Orpheus platform project two years ago."

"Oh," said Ben. Even he was aware of the success of Orpheus. He sat back in his chair, chastened.

"Let's continue," said Alan, smiling inwardly to himself.

"Project networks are quite small, focused and in the short term. The same principles apply to any network."

"Like what sort of network?" asked Barbara.

"Well a good example is if someone wants to move into a different role or industry in their career, they build a network to understand more about the role or industry and often find a new position that way. Contractors or freelancers do this as a matter of course."

"Thanks Sue." said Barbara.

"Remember Objective 1 – Knowing the right people to get things done. Firstly you need to build a list of everyone who is working on the project, along with their contact details. If you are me, you will need to spend some time with most of the list in the shortest time possible. When I took on the role with Alan's team I spent the first three weeks just seeing people that I would need to work with. You need to be aware of everyone that is relevant but first you need to pick out the key people to focus on." Now, Sue decided to throw out a question to the group. "OK, so if you were starting out, where would you begin?" Sue looked round at Jeff, Alan, Ben, Kate and Barbara.

"Easy. The decision makers!" ventured Kate.

"Good. Any others?"

"Troublemakers," added Ben, somewhat ironically.

Jeff laughed.

"Not exactly," responded Sue coolly. "There are always people who raise difficult issues but they shouldn't be labelled as a Troublemaker."

Jeff grinned. "Touché," he muttered.

"Influencers?" enquired Barbara.

"Thank you Barbara," beamed Sue.

"An Influencer is someone who a Decision Maker will rely on for their opinion," she added, tuning back to look at Ben.

"Returning to your suggestion, if someone who is not in a position of influence raises a difficult issue, then sometimes it may be taken on its merits or it may be discarded. If either a Decision Maker or an Influencer raises a difficult issue then you have a problem, and that's why the quality of your relationship with them is vital. Are there any other types?" Sue ventured quickly, before they got too much off topic.

"What about Gatekeepers?" ventured Alan.

"Ah, yes Alan. Well spotted! These are the people who have to be onside otherwise they will block things. They are not necessarily Decision Makers or Influencers, but can stop things dead if they want to."

"Any more?" she enquired. "In that case let me summarise:"

Identifying Who's Who:

There are four key types to identify:

1. *Decision Makers – key stakeholders, should be obvious but not always.*

2. *Influencers – those who Decision Makers rely on for their opinion.*

3. *Gatekeepers – those who you have to keep onside for anything to happen, often the Decision Makers but not always, they are the decision blockers if they are not onside.*

4. *Good for Branding – people who others look to and recommend for involvement but not necessarily a Gatekeeper, Influencer or Decision Maker.*

"There is one more type, which I have called 'Good for Branding'. These people are either senior or a rising star, and are someone people look to for approval on a wide range of topics. You could think of them as an Influencer type, but in fact they are generally well respected 'thought leaders' you can bring in to support, 'bless' or approve a project or decision."

"OK. So, if I meet someone at an Event or informally, how do I know which type they are?" interrupted Ben again.

"It is unlikely that you will find out from meeting them initially, but as you talk to them and other people you will start to get a picture of what they do." Sue paused and looked up at the group. "I can't tell you how important this is," she added. "If you get it right, you can achieve an enormous amount with seemingly little effort."

"The old adage 'It's who you know' is exactly right," added Alan.

"If you don't get it right you will spend huge amounts of energy setting things up, only to watch them fall apart without understanding why," Sue summarised.

"Isn't this just about playing office politics?" asked Ben.

"Oh, I wish it was," answered Sue. "But this is actually about life. We always like to think everything is up to us as individuals – and that is certainly true to some extent. The truth is we always need other people to help us at some stage along the way."

"OK let's take a quick break for 5 minutes and get some coffees." Sue was aware that she needed to let this first part sink in.

Why a Troublemaker Isn't a Troublemaker?

As Sue poured herself a glass of water at the back of the room, Alan wandered over. "I am curious about your comment on Troublemakers," he said. "I agree it matters where they are Influencers also, but surely aren't they a breed in their own right?"

"I don't agree with that view. And never have," she looked at him directly. "Are you thinking about Bennett?" she asked curiously.

Alan laughed. "I couldn't possibly comment," he returned. "So why don't you agree with that view?"

"Two reasons. Firstly if you label everyone who disagrees with you a Troublemaker, you immediately discount their point of view by labelling them. It's vital to have dissenting voices in the ranks. If there is a better way of doing something we need to know about it and have the debate. Secondly, it lets you off the hook for not managing your relationships properly. If you have someone awkward – like Bennett for example – the temptation is just to label him a Troublemaker. Am I right?"

"Well, say you were right hypothetically," Alan wasn't going to acknowledge the myriad of problems that Bennett had caused him in the past, "how would you deal with him?"

"If you step back and label him as a Troublemaker, you mentally absolve yourself of responsibility for dealing with him. You will then end up allowing him to run riot on important projects instead of managing him properly, which is exactly what you need to do."

At this point Alan held his hand up to stop her. "OK I hear you. Rather than explain to me can you share this with the group?" he asked.

"Sure, no problem. I have a slide on this anyway."

As Barbara, Ben and Kate wandered in and sat down, Sue marched back to the front of the room and fiddled with her laptop briefly before looking up expectantly to start again. "Alan and I have just been discussing the issue of Troublemakers that Ben raised earlier," she began. "I want to round this off. There are two really good reasons for not labelling someone a Troublemaker," she continued. "Firstly if someone disagrees with something and you label him or her a Troublemaker, it glosses over a point of view that, while it might be dissenting, could be very important. Secondly if you label them a Troublemaker, you mentally absolve yourself of the need to manage them properly," she finished.

"So how do you manage them properly?" asked Barbara curiously.

Managing the Troublemakers

"Firstly it depends if they are Influencers, Decision Makers or Gatekeepers" said Sue.

"If they fit in with any of these categories you need to spend time with them to understand how they think. They will have definite views about certain things and they can influence the outcome of your project so you need to appreciate in what areas you need to convince them of your point of view. You must at least understand where they will be coming from. Your objective is to avoid surprises, and depersonalise any debate to a more objective level. Above all you need to listen to them, recognise when they are adding value and understand how you can influence them."

"But what if they are not Influencers or Decision Makers?" asked Ben.

"Much the same approach applies," responded Sue. "However in this instance it's sensible to use a friend or colleague to help you influence them."

"Oh OK," said Ben, unaware that Alan had used exactly that approach with him by using Jeff to help.

"I have a summary slide for this," said Sue, putting it up on the projector.

Managing the Opposing Viewpoint

1. *Understand if they are Influencers, Decision Makers or Gatekeepers.*
   - *If Yes then you must deal with them directly.*
   - *If No then you can enlist a friend or colleague to help you.*

2. *Spend time necessary with them to establish a good working relationship as possible.*

3. *Above all you need to:*
   a. *Listen to them.*
   b. *Recognise when they are adding value.*
   c. *Understand how you can influence them.*

4. *Your objective is to understand where they are coming from and avoid surprises.*

5. *"Better to have him inside the tent pissing out, than outside pissing in." – Lynden Johnson, of J. Edgar Hoover*

Barbara started giggling.
"What's so funny?" asked Sue.
"I'm sorry I am being childish!" exclaimed Barbara.
"Well he did say it," responded Sue. "And anyway it's true, isn't it?"
"Absolutely," grinned Barbara. "If you say so!"

Building Your Network

"Well if we assume that you have worked out who you need to actively target," continued Sue, "you need to get to know them. And here's the next challenge. Any ideas?" she added after a pause.

"Well you could just go and see them I suppose," said Jeff.

"What if they don't want to see you?" countered Sue. "I mean they don't know you, they're busy people. Why would they make the time?"

Jeff stirred himself. As the architect of the maverick phone survey, he was confident enough to tackle any executive or VIP. "That's easy. You just need a good reason," he added. "I mean if you have a plausible reason and you approach them in the right way, it shouldn't be a problem."

"OK so how would you go about seeing Bennett?" shot back Sue. She knew that this was a very difficult area for people, and she didn't want Jeff to make it appear trivial.

"Oh. That's a little harder than most," responded Jeff. "He doesn't come to the Coffee Bar at all, so no chance of grabbing him there." He thought for a moment. "Two approaches. I could ask him at the end of a formal meeting if he could spare me 20 minutes for a short discussion on a topic he likes. People like giving advice and if I asked him for a bit of advice about business models, which I happen to know he is really interested in, I could definitely engage him. I know it's not the direct topic but sometimes it's easier to get in that way. The other way is to mail him a short outline about the project, clearly marked DRAFT, and ask for a conversation to get his input. It's riskier because if he is not aware of the project, it might irritate him. But he does have an ego and always loves to have his say," he finished.

"Thanks Jeff," said Sue slowly, feeling a mixture of remorse at giving him such a hard challenge, and pleased that he had returned with such a good answer. "The great secret here is that whoever your target is needs to get some benefit out of the meeting, otherwise it just becomes a favour or what I call an 'Ask'."

"One additional approach is to send people interesting content or articles or links from the web. It's a great way of starting a dialogue, especially of you can find things you know they will be interested in. Senior people rarely spend much time reading, and appreciate receiving well targeted knowledge and information."

"Ben and I do a lot of business at the Coffee Bar also," added Jeff.

"Aside from Bennett, lots of the internal folks we need to see come through there."

"That's a good idea," said Sue. "And for external people, industry events, such as conferences, are great ways to target people. Especially if they are speaking. You do need to pick your moment though. It's no use grabbing them if they are in a big hurry or distracted by someone else." She put up the slide:

Getting a meeting

- *Getting to see people on a one-to-one basis is hard.*

- *You need a specific reason to meet such as asking for advice or input for a project.*

- *Research them on LinkedIn or on the web generally to see if they have an interest you can ask them about or someone you know in common.*

- *Try to understand what is interesting from them.*

- *Another method is to email relevant articles or web-links to key people on an individual basis to start a conversation, which can then either lead to a meeting or provide ammunition if you later meet them informally.*

- *You can also find a public way of introducing yourself – in our case departmental events or at the coffee bar. For external people trade shows, conferences or events work. Timing is the key.*

- *Finally you can have someone who knows them well introduce you.*

"Last point – but not least – see if you can get someone who knows them well to introduce you. It's much harder for them to say no!"

Making a First Impression More Than Once

"People say that making a good first impression is vital," said Sue. "In fact I think it's more important than that. As an individual you need to make a consistent first impression every time."

"What do you mean by that?" asked Kate.

"Well aside from doing your homework, you need to set up and attend each meeting as yourself, and not someone you want them to think you are."

"Sorry, I'm not with you," said Kate with a puzzled frown.

"I have watched people put on their 'best face' when they come to see me only to find out later that they aren't really like that. As I said, you need to be professional and do your homework. But you need to present yourself as you are in pretty much the same way at every meeting. That's how you build a reputation."

"Do you mean you have to dress the same?" asked Barbara.

"Not exactly the same, but you need to follow a consistent approach. Your consistent approach. And wear what you are comfortable with."

"I'm sorry Sue," said Jeff, who ironically was probably the most fashion conscious. "But why is this so important?"

"Well Jeff I will start with you. I have noticed that while you mostly dress very casually, your appearance is always tidy and carefully thought through."

"Wow!" said Jeff. "I suppose I asked for that."

"As for Alan," continued Sue, noting that she had just made Alan jump in his chair, "he is nearly always formally dressed in a suit and tie."

"Years of habit," drawled Alan, very relieved that he hadn't been singled out further.

"I think you all understand what I mean now," said Sue. "So having said that, can anyone tell me what they think the objective of any first meeting would be?"

"To get them to like you? Or perhaps respect you?" ventured Ben hopefully.

"Either of those would be good outcomes," said Sue. "But that's a lot to ask for what may be quite a short meeting."

"How short exactly?" asked Barbara, furiously scribbling notes while she peered at Sue intently.

"30 minutes is fine," responded Sue. "More or less should be at their discretion."

"So what should be the outcome?"

"To remember me?" asked Alan tentatively.

"Thanks Alan, that's exactly right." Sue looked up. "Getting them to remember you is the key outcome. They may decide they like you, they may decide they respect you. Or not. As long as you make a positive connection with them they remember you, that's all you need."

"I threw coffee all over my interviewer's desk," confessed Ben. "I don't suppose he will forget me in a hurry."

"Well did you get the job?" asked Barbara.

"Err, yes – it was actually for this job." Ben's face brightened up as he realised what he had just said.

"I guess it worked then!"

"What exactly happened when you spilt it?" asked Sue.

"Oh I was mortified," said Ben. "I mean if someone did that to me I would be mad with them. So I apologised profusely and ran back down the corridor to get some paper towels from the kitchen I had just passed. It took a few minutes to clear up, but by the time I was finished, we were laughing and joking about it."

"So I'm not recommending that approach," said Sue ironically. "But clearly you came across as empathetic and a man of action."

"I guess so," said Ben, wondering what Sue really meant by the word empathetic, a word with which he was not that familiar.

"What I generally recommend," said Sue now with a grin on her face (and an image of a coffee stained Ben in her mind), "is to prepare some good insightful questions as well as some good background on yourself. Think of it like a well-planned date," she ventured.

"A date?" asked Alan incredulously.

"Precisely. If you were inviting someone out for a romantic dinner, this is all the sort of preparation you would normally do."

"That was all rather a long time ago," muttered Alan.

"Oh I get it," said Kate. "You are planning how you are to going to entertain your dinner partner."

"Thanks Kate," said Sue. "I guess it's been a while for me too!"

Jeff and Ben nodded, grinning to one another. Barbara, however, was inscrutable.

"One final caveat," added Sue. "You do need to think through your personal background or story, what you might call an 'Elevator Pitch.' It needs to be short and to the point. Unlike on a date."

"Elevator Pitch? What's that then?" asked Barbara, much to everyone's surprise.

"It's an old expression from the Advertising industry," said Alan. "It's the ability to sell or 'pitch' an Idea to a senior executive between floors in the lift or elevator."

"Well I have never come across it before," said Barbara. "Sorry for being a bit dim."

Making your meeting work

1. *Time: plan for 30 minutes maximum, short or longer at their discretion. If you can't get a formal time a short chat in the corridor can work well.*

2. *Key objective: to have them remember you.*

3. *Planning: You have no previous record, so making a positive impression is vital – appearance, attitude and focus on the target person.*

    a. *Research them on LinkedIn or on the web generally. See if they have an interest you can ask them about or someone you know in common.*

    b. *Prepare a list of insightful questions. Especially if you are asking for advice or input.*

    c. *Prepare a short description of you, your background and role. This should be an "elevator pitch."*

4. *Follow ups: work out if there is anything you can do which would be of immediate value for or interest to them. Volunteer to send them an article or introduction if appropriate.*

"Here are my notes on this," said Sue putting up the next slide. "Now the last piece before we finish today – the Follow Up! All of this effort is wasted unless you can do a good follow up properly. If you see an opportunity to add value when you are in the meeting – by making an introduction, sending an article or web-link – then offer it and take it as an action item to compete afterwards. That makes it very easy for you to send a follow up note or email after the meeting. My personal favourite is sending people books."

"Books?" asked Alan.

"If you go onto Amazon, you can very easily send people a book with an attached message. They are rarely expensive, certainly no more than a few coffees and you can be sure that if you select the right title, you are onto a winner. I mean how can you ever forget someone who sends you a book?"

Alan laughed. "How indeed?" He added. "That's very clever Sue."

Sue shrugged. "It's worked for me," she said. "You can send people music too, but that's quite personal."

"Any other rules for the Follow Up?" asked Barbara.

"Yes – sorry getting off track." Sue pulled up the next slide.

The Meeting Follow Up

1. *Send your first follow up immediately thanking them for their time.*

2. *Send a further follow up a few days later with an additional article.*

3. *Response to either or both of these will tell you whether you have made an impact. Or not.*

4. *Lack of response does not indicate failure. There are myriad of reasons why people do not respond, even if they have been friendly.*

5. *One of them may be that they do not like email, and if so a hand written note or phone call may be a better follow up.*

"You need to get your first note out the door as soon as possible after the meeting," she added. "Unless I get a response from doing this – which I often do – I plan a further follow up one to two weeks later. As per our discussion on Communications, you need to pick your form of communication although email or a handwritten note is the best."

"I am sorry – but a handwritten note in this day and age?" Countered Ben sarcastically.

"As a result of its scarcity," responded Sue, "it tends to have rather more impact that an email."

"Huh, really?" said Ben, not convinced.

"Anyway – thanks for all your time and comments," said Sue looking at her watch. "It's time to wrap up. Any questions?"

"Just one. You talked about maintaining relationships," said Barbara. "We haven't covered that yet."

"I have the notes on it but we are out of time. I can do an hour at 4pm today if everyone can make it?"

"I'll have to shuffle my diary but I'll make it," said Alan.

"Yes fine here," said Barbara. "I can make that."

Ben was about to take the opportunity to duck out, when Jeff interrupted him. "We'll all be there," he said, bundling Ben out of the door.

"Oh man – what did you do that for?" asked Ben when they got in the corridor. "I got things to do this afternoon."

"Did you learn anything today?"

"Yes but…"

Jeff interrupted him. "Did you learn anything today?" He was angry now.

Ben sighed and swallowed hard. He was conscious of Kate listening to them. "I did. I know I shot my mouth off, but your networking lady really knows her stuff."

"Thank you."

"Actually I should thank you," started Ben. "I just don't know where it's all leading to." He smiled and wheeled around.

"I'm starving, let's go and get something to eat."

Chapter Notes

The Purpose of Networking

The ability to build influence through acquiring, building and maintaining the right relationships.

The Three Objectives of Networking

1. *Knowing the right people to get things done.*

2. *If you don't know the right people, finding them and getting to know them (so you can get things done).*

3. *Maintaining links with people once you know them – even if you no longer work with them or see them – so that you can continue to get things done.*

Identifying Who's Who

There are four key types to identify:

1. *Decision makers – key stakeholders, should be obvious but not always.*

2. *Influencers – those who decision makers rely on for their opinion.*

3. *Gatekeepers – those who you have to keep onside for anything to happen, often the Decision Makers but not always, they are the decision blockers if they are not onside.*

4. *Good for Branding – people who others look to and recommend for involvement but not necessarily a Gatekeeper, Influencer or Decision Maker.*

Managing the Opposing Viewpoint

1. *Understand if they are Influencers, Decision Makers or Gatekeepers.*
   - *If YES then you must deal with them directly.*
   - *If NO then you can enlist a friend or colleague to help you.*

2. *Spend time necessary with them to establish a good working relationship as possible.*

3. *Above all you need to:*
   a. *Listen to them,*
   b. *Recognise when they are adding value*
   c. *Understand how you can influence them*

4. *Your objective is to understand where they are coming from and avoid surprises.*

5. *"Better to have him inside the tent pissing out, than outside pissing in."*

Getting a Meeting

- *Getting to see people on a one-to-one basis is hard.*

- *You need a specific reason to meet such as asking for advice or input for a project.*

- *Research them on LinkedIn or on the web generally to*

see if they have an interest you can ask them about or someone you know in common.

- *Try to understand what is interesting from them.*

- *Another method is to email relevant articles or web-links to key people on an individual basis to start a conversation, which can then either lead to a meeting or provide ammunition if you later meet them informally.*

- *You can also find a public way of introducing yourself – in our case departmental events or at the coffee bar. For external people trade shows, conferences or events work. Timing is the key.*

- *Finally you can have someone who knows them well introduce you.*

Making Your Meeting Work

- *Time: plan for 30 minutes maximum, short or longer at their discretion. If you can't get a formal time a short chat in the corridor can work well.*

- *Key objective: to have them remember you.*

- *Planning: You have no previous record, so making a positive impression is vital – appearance, attitude and focus on the target person.*

  - *Prepare a list of insightful questions, especially if you are asking for advice or input.*

- *Prepare a short description of you, your background and role. This should be an "elevator pitch."*

- *Follow ups: work out if there is anything you can do which would be of immediate value for or interest to them. Volunteer to send them an article or introduction if appropriate.*

The Meeting Follow Up

1. *Send your first follow up immediately thanking them for their time.*

2. *Send a further follow up a few days later with an additional article.*

3. *Response to either or both of these will tell you whether you have made an impact. Or not.*

4. *Lack of response does not indicate failure. There are myriad of reasons why people do not respond, even if they have been friendly.*

5. *One of them may be that they do not like email, and if so a hand written note or phone call may be a better follow up.*

6

ALL THE PEOPLE YOU EVER KNEW: NETWORKS AND RELATIONSHIPS

Lunch With Noodles

Ben had wanted to visit his favourite sandwich bar for lunch but as they walked down the road they spotted a well-known noodle bar and Jeff prevailed on them to try somewhere new. "It will be better for you. No bread," he announced.

"But I like bread!" complained Ben.

"We'll do sandwiches next time, OK?" said Jeff.

"I love noodles!" said Kate enthusiastically.

"That settles it," said Jeff so they went in and sat down on one of the long communal benches.

"I have got to hand it to you, on reflection that was a very interesting session," began Ben just as they finished placing their order with the waiter.

"I told you it would be useful," said Jeff. "What did you think Kate?"

"Oh I learnt a lot this morning," said Kate looking directly at Jeff.

"I know you are really good at networking, but that's because you have the chutzpah to barge straight in on people," she added.

"I do not barge straight in," replied Jeff in mock indignation.

"You know what I mean Jeff," replied Kate with a smile. "I have no idea what he thinks about me," she thought to herself. "Or whether he thinks about me at all," she continued, "what the hell am I going to do about it? Come on get a grip!"

She gathered herself together.

"Jeff, I have to say that you do have the confidence to approach people directly. It's absolutely second nature to you. Personally, I find some people easy, but I have to say others I really struggle with."

"But you were fine with the phone survey I put together," said Jeff. "In fact I overheard you, you were really excellent!"

"That's because I was working from a script, which you had written, and I knew what we were trying to do."

"Well it's no more difficult than that!"

"I know, but I still find it hard."

How Do You Deal With Bennett?

"Hey Jeff I got another question for you," said Ben, poking curiously at his noodles which had just arrived.

"They're noodles. They won't kill you," said Jeff ironically.

Ben grunted acknowledgement and finally ate some noodles. "Not bad at all. So my question is how do you really deal with Bennett? You answered Sue with some neat approaches, but I have seen how he talks to you. I mean I don't know if I could take that if I was you."

Jeff sighed and lowered his chopsticks. "To tell you the truth, I decided to hate Bennett straight away," he said. "I thought it would save time later." Kate burst out laughing.

"Well I'm not surprised," said Ben. "But it never shows."

Jeff shook his head. "I'm kidding," he said. "I would not spend time with him socially but I can't afford the luxury of hating him. Sue is right. If you label someone a troublemaker, you will fail to deal with them."

"So how do you deal with him?" asked Kate earnestly. "He's horrid to me too, and it takes me ages to recover after an encounter."

"I have to deal with him regularly," said Jeff. "So I need a consistent approach. I take everything I know about Bennett – past conversations, behaviour traits, arguments and incidents – and mentally I divide them into two groups: a bad group and a good group. The bad group is really important, because it's all the hard things you have to deal with, the aggression, the rudeness and the paranoia to name a few. Every time I have to deal with Bennett, I take these bad traits as a given, and try and imagine which one I am going to encounter. That way when I inevitably do encounter it, it's no surprise and I have prepared a response to diffuse him."

"Well that makes good sense," said Kate. "I will try and see if that helps me next time I have to confront him."

"You need to be very unemotional with him," said Jeff. "It's not personal, and you need to treat him dispassionately."

"But I can't," burst out Kate. "He's so horrid to me!"

"Kate," said Jeff. "That's exactly what I mean. You allow him to get to you. He knows it and that makes his behaviour worse. That's why you have to mentally separate out all the bad things he is likely to do and prepare for them."

"How does that really help me?" asked Kate.

"Well you can start by trying to predict what he is going to do; that will distract you from what he might or might not do. The important thing to do is not to react. It's very hard, I know."

"I guess I should give it a try it then," said Kate tentatively.

"The other part of the approach is to think about all the good things," said Jeff moving on to a different tack. "In other words all the things that he likes, does well and puts him into a positive frame of mind. A good example of this with Bennett is business models, which I mentioned in the earlier session."

"That was one of my worst subjects at business school," said Kate.

"It doesn't matter," responded Jeff. "The point is that it's his favourite topic. The reason for bringing it up is to get him to talk about it. In fact if you weren't very good at it all the better. He will probably give you a tutorial." Jeff paused. "Does this make sense Kate?"

"I think so," she answered slowly. "If I understand you correctly, what you are saying is prepare to endure the worst of his behaviour while looking for opportunities to trigger his best behaviour."

"Exactly," said Jeff.

"Oh wow," I get it said Ben. "Thanks guys that's really helpful." He laughed.

"What's so funny?" asked Kate.

"Well it's almost the reverse for me. Bennett and I get on really well and he is rarely bad tempered in my direction," ventured Ben. "But I know it's unusual, and that he does have a reputation."

"You should share that with Sue and the Group at 4pm," he finished.

"I agree," said Kate. "I'm feeling a little more confident about dealing with Bennett now."

Barbara Does Her Stuff

Alan hid in his office over lunchtime. He tended to use Fridays to catch up with people and do meetings for which he had run out of time earlier in the week. But today he was trying to clear his desk so that he could make the 4pm meeting without any distractions. Just as he was tidying up his Inbox, the phone rang.

"Hi. Alan speaking," he answered almost absentmindedly.

"It's Barbara here." Alan instantly steeled himself for Barbara to cancel her attendance at the 4pm session.

"Hi."

"Alan, I have to tell you that was a really good session this morning," continued Barbara. "Sue is not only a great asset to your team, but to the whole company frankly."

"Thank you Barbara. I am so glad you found it useful," responded Alan, very relieved.

"I think you are onto something here," said Barbara, "so I have just got off the phone with Robin."

"Oh?" said Alan, who had not really thought that things would move this quickly.

"He wants to see both of us on Monday at 2pm. Can you make that?"

"Oh. Hang on. Not at the moment but give me 10 minutes to confirm. I'm sure I can swing things around. What does he want to talk about particularly?" queried Alan, his mind racing to work out what prep work he would need to do.

"He wants you to go through the whole concept with him from start to finish. Think of it as short training seminar."

"OK, fine," said Alan. "I can get organised over the weekend. I have most of the material but it needs sorting out."

"Do you want any help?" asked Barbara.

"I may do," said Alan. "I'll call you if I need you to look at something."

"OK – fine, see you at 4pm," finished Barbara.

Back at 4pm

As they arrived back at the meeting room at 4pm, Kate sought out Sue. She knew Jeff would need prompting to share his insight from lunchtime so she primed Sue to ask him at the beginning. "Before we start has anyone got something they would like to share? Jeff?" Sue honed straight in on him.

Jeff looked unsure for a second, and then Kate leaned over.

"Come on," she said, "she's talking about what we discussed at lunchtime."

"Oh thanks guys," said Jeff in mock indignation, but secretly feeling pleased that Kate had put him on the spot. He looked at Kate and smiled, she was a real brick.

"It goes back to what you were saying about dealing with difficult people and not calling them Troublemakers," he began. "I have a method that I use to help me."

"Go on," said Sue. Barbara leaned forward, listening intently.

"When I have to deal with someone difficult, I take all their bad traits as a given, and try and imagine which one I am going to encounter. That way when I inevitably do encounter it, it's no surprise and I have prepared a response to diffuse the situation. It's a really hard thing to do but it is really critical to be totally unemotional with whoever it is," said Jeff. "Whatever they say or do is very rarely personal, and needs to be treated dispassionately. At lunchtime we talked about a specific example, where an emotional response actually worsens the situation, giving rise to further provocation and worse behaviour."

"So how does that work?" asked Barbara intently.

"Well if you can start to predict what he or she is going to do it will distract you from what actually might happen. The second half of my approach is to think about all the good things. In other words all the things that the person likes, does well and puts them into a more positive frame of mind."

Jeff looked up and around at everyone. "Kate did a great summary of this," he said glancing down at a scribbled note on his pad. "What was it you said?"

"Prepare to endure the worst of his behaviour while looking for opportunities to trigger his best behaviour," said Kate firmly.

"I wonder who you were talking about," said Barbara neutrally. Kate's face reddened as she realised that she had given the game away.

Jeff gave her a reassuring look. "Forget it!" he mouthed silently.

"Jeff, Kate, thank you both," said Sue who was scribbling furiously. She finished with a flourish and stood up.

Who Loves Ya?

"So the main point of this afternoon was to finish off by talking about maintaining relationships," she began. "However all of us already have a large number of personal and professional relationships. Before we can understand how to maintain them we have to understand the quality of the relationships we have already."

"Oh that's easy!" said Ben, "Facebook, LinkedIn and I'm done."

"Really?" said Sue, who had mentally prepared herself for Ben this afternoon, coincidentally in a similar way to Jeff's approach. "How many of the friends and connections from there have you met personally?" she asked pointedly.

"Lots," said Ben firmly.

"No, I mean how many as a proportion of the overall total?"

"Oh, well, err…" Ben's confidence began to desert him.

"Keep thinking about that for a second" said Sue in a surprisingly friendly voice. "I want to show you something." She pressed the key on her laptop to get a slide to appear:

The Four Levels of a successful (Networking) Relationship

- *Awareness – knows who you are. Hurrah! At last!*

- *Understanding – can describe you and your role to a colleague. Recite your elevator pitch.*

- *Supporter – speaks positively about you and seeks to be helpful, but only when asked.*

- *Advocate – actively sings your praises whenever the opportunity arises.*

"The reason I ask this is because although you may have lots relationships, you may not have many valuable relationships. Then again you may have some valuable relationships that you are perhaps neglecting. Ben, just because you are connected to someone on a social networking site does not make them someone you could ask for help, or trust with an important request."

Ben looked very hard at Sue. "I'm curious, are we talking about personal friends here?" he asked. "Or are these professional friends?"

"That's an excellent question," said Sue. "The answer is both. Even though you separate them mentally, and even use different tools for each group, there is increasing crossover between both groups. If you are going to make the most of personal and professional relationships, you need to have a consistent approach to both."

"I'm sorry," said Alan. "My personal friends and my work colleagues are two completely separate groups of people."

"Oh really?" said Sue. "What about your golfing friend?"

"My golfing friend?"

"Yes, the financier."

"Oh, well, err… Good point," said Alan. "I do regard him as a personal friend but we have worked together before."

"The reason why this is important," said Sue, "is that unless you are well organised, you will treat one group better than the other. And that's not healthy."

"Not healthy? Why exactly?" asked Barbara, who was listening eagerly.

"I believe that people need to have a good balance between their work and personal lives," replied Sue. "If you focus on developing your professional relationships at the expense of your personal ones, it may help you with your job but it does not make you a very rounded individual, as you have much less context out of work. Equally if you spend all day on Facebook chatting to personal friends, it's unlikely that you will be delivering full value to your current role."

Kate's face reddened. Although she was highly regarded by her peers and managers, she had a secret Facebook addiction. She wondered if Sue knew. She hoped nobody had noticed, and then saw that Jeff was looking at her. He smiled broadly at her and she had to look away to avoid giggling.

"Why do you need to combine them? I don't get it." asked Ben.

"I didn't say combine them. I just said you had to take a consistent approach to both," replied Sue. "When I say take a consistent approach, I mean think about them the same way."

The Four Levels of Relationship

"There are four basic levels of relationship," she continued. "Awareness, Understanding, Supporter and Advocate."

"Where do friends fit in?" said Ben blankly.

"Well those who you would regard as friends would probably fall under Supporter and Advocate," replied Sue, bracing herself for another Ben onslaught, but surprisingly he went quiet on her. "Let's start with Awareness," said Sue. "Anyone you want to have any kind of relationship with must become aware of you either by name or context."

"Context?" asked Barbara.

"Where they have met you or know you from."

"Oh. OK, thanks."

"However, just because they are aware of you, does not mean that they understand who you are, what you do or what value you bring. That's why your elevator pitch I talked about this morning is so important."

"Right," said Sue. "They should be able to describe you quickly, for example they might describe me as that 'programme manager who goes on about all that networking stuff,'" she added slightly carelessly.

"Oh I think you may be selling yourself rather short there," responded Barbara seriously. "But I get the gist of it."

"Good. The next level after Understanding is Supporter," she looked at Ben. "I think this is where your friends come in. Supporters are people who speak positively about you, and are generally willing to help," Sue reinforced the words from her slide. "However the relationship is generally passive, as they tend to respond positively rather than be proactive on your behalf."

"OK so you would count them as friends but not good friends, right?" questioned Ben.

"They may well be good friends," replied Sue. "But they are unlikely to be your closest friends. For the very close friends, your best relationships and the people who are most likely to be in the trenches with you – I call them Advocates. Generally you will have only a handful of Advocates. These are people you are close to, know you really well and are always looking out on your behalf. Your sales force if you like."

"Sales force?" enquired Alan.

"They are a small group of people who are selling you to other people in terms of your skills, abilities and personality."

"Typically how many should we have of these relationships," asked Barbara, with her pen poised over her notes.

"Good question. Usually somewhere between five and ten people in total, in some cases as many as fifteen," replied Sue. "You can think of them as the first 10 people you would have for dinner if you were celebrating a major achievement in life."

"Why so few? I mean surely you would want to have more?" asked Jeff curiously.

"Remember what I said about the importance of the quality of relationships?" said Sue. "You simply cannot spend the time needed to manage and interact with more than a very few Advocate relationships. On top of that you are generally born with at least two."

"Born with? Born with?" asked Ben incredulously.

"Your parents."

"Oh. I hadn't thought of it like that," Ben tailed off.

"You see what I mean? Their status as advocates means that the level of communication with them is generally very high and therefore time consuming," finished Sue.

"So what does this mean in a business context?" asked Barbara, imagining the next question Robin would ask her.

"It means that in order to succeed you need to find and build one or two Advocate level relationships in every role that you do," Sue answered simply. "Sometimes they are a colleague, a manager, or your mentor. It's also a very good idea to find and build an advocate on the client side, which brings me neatly on to my next slide."

Key lessons

- *Find at least one person you get on well with and can convert into an Advocate. They will help recruit people to your cause.*

- *Get your elevator pitch polished enough so that people you meet with end up with Understanding rather than just Awareness (or worse).*

Key Lessons

Jeff read the slide and laughed. "What's worse than Awareness?" he grinned.

"Meeting someone who forgets you completely," responded Sue. An appreciative chuckle ran through all the audience at this point. "I'm serious," said Sue smiling. "I don't think it's a risk for you lot, but if you don't make a first impression – remember this morning – people may forget that they ever met you and that's not good at all."

"So if I go back over my notes from today," enquired Barbara, "let me check something with you. As a rough benchmark up to 10 Advocates, 150 or so Supporters, and 500 with Understanding. How many people with Awareness should I target?"

"Well, let's go back to this morning's session. That depends entirely who needs to know who you are. Remember my project network? In your role, I would say that for you could be the whole office here and probably some key people in management internationally."

"Huh," replied Barbara, visibly considering the issue. "I sort of knew that instinctively, but I hadn't consciously thought about it," Barbara replied after a pause.

"I have a question for you," said Alan. "If you build new relationships and move people up a level in your network, how do you manage out the ones you have there already?"

"Good question," breathed Jeff.

"Good question indeed," added Sue, just overhearing Jeff. "You have to decide which people you are no longer going to actively communicate with or spend time with."

"That's pretty ruthless isn't it?" said Kate, who had recently been on the receiving end of a Facebook de-friending. Kate had been very upset about it at the time, even though the girl in question was someone she barely knew. It was the public humiliation that had bothered her rather than the absence of the annoying postings on her wall.

"OK. One, you have to do it if you are going to be effective," responded Sue crisply. "Two, it's not necessarily a question of removing them, it's just a question of not proactively communicating with them. It happens all the time, when you move role for example, you leave behind people you have seen every day for a long period of time. To continue to communicate with them at the same level is clearly unnecessary and is often likely to be unproductive. They need to get on with their lives. It doesn't mean that you cease to be friends with them, it just means that they drop back down a level or two."

"Oh, OK," said Kate. "So you are not ignoring them or anything like that, you are just not actively sending them stuff, right?"

"You can send them whatever you like," said Sue. "But I return to my original suggestion – if you wish to move people up a level, something has to give. Otherwise you will dilute yourself, and not spend time and energy on people who really matter. I don't think it's a question of moving people down a level on the list, it's more a question of moving them off the list. For example, when people move roles, many of the relationships they already have are not always relevant in their new role. It doesn't mean that their Advocates and Supporters are downgraded, just that they are no longer as relevant as before."

"Sue," said Kate, "what does that mean at a practical level?"

"It means that you no longer need to be as proactive in driving those relationships. If some of those people have become friends, then obviously that continues at a personal level."

"If I understand you correctly," said Alan, "you are saying that you archive relationships and yet maintain the ones that have become friends."

"Exactly. In fact the first of my final comments reflects on that exactly." Sue pressed a key on her laptop. "Here's my last slide you'll be glad to hear:"

And Finally

- *Do enjoy the personal friends you make through your networks, they will travel with you forever, making life richer and more rewarding.*

- *Don't allow the network to become an end to itself, otherwise you will lose sight of the reason you built it in the first place.*

- *Your network of relationships should reward you by making life simpler and more fun, however it does require discipline and effort!*

"I just wanted to make the point that I have made some great friends through my networking skills. Going back to the point I was making to Kate just now – and the point I was making to you earlier; just because I don't see these people regularly anymore doesn't mean that they are no longer friends."

"What do you mean about a network becoming an end in itself?" asked Ben.

"When you start to become accomplished at networking," replied Sue slowly, "you may find yourself trying to cram as much networking in as possible without thinking about why you are doing it. I know this because I've accidentally done it before, and it can start to annoy people."

"What happened?" asked Alan, quickly wishing he hadn't asked. "Oh never mind."

"Don't worry. In the event I got an earful from one of the senior managers for wasting his time," grinned Sue. "It's a very easy trap to fall into. You need to have a little empathy for people."

Ben frowned. There was that empathy word again. He made a mental note to look it up.

"Finally a reminder of why it's all worthwhile. It really should make your life easier and more rewarding. It does however require discipline and effort from each of you."

"Sue," asked Barbara thoughtfully, "how long do you think it takes to become really good at this?"

"I think it takes between one and two years to build a professional network," said Sue. "It's sometimes shorter if you work on a particularly intense project. If you go through a very intense experience with people, such as working round the clock or doing a long trip then you get to one of the higher relationship levels very quickly."

"Thank you," said Barbara closing her book, "that's been really great."

"Thank you Sue," chorused the others and the group started to stand up and gather their things to leave.

"Yes, many thanks indeed, that was really excellent," said Alan.

"Don't forget Monday 2pm," Barbara reminded Alan.

Alan's thoughts were already elsewhere.

"Monday 2pm?" repeated Barbara, giving Alan a very pointed look.

"Right!" said Alan. "Yes, Monday 2pm." He grabbed his things and shot out of the door; he had a phone call to make.

Back In His Office

"John, how are you?" began Alan. "Yes I'm still on for golf tomorrow, listen can I ask you a small favour? Do you have to be away straight after lunch tomorrow? No I'm not proposing another 9 holes; you remember I was working on something? I want to talk to you about it. Thank you. Looking forward to it." Alan put down the phone feeling greatly relieved. He didn't want to take the concept of the

Leopard to Robin on Monday without testing it out first, and since his last conversation with John he had been looking for an opportunity to share some of the ideas they had been creating.

He pulled out his notes from the very first day and looked at the five Principles of The Leopard: "What did we do first?" he mused, "Act opportunistically... Time... hmm." There was a knock at his office door, which startled him. It was late on a Friday and he thought most people would have gone. "Come in," he called. It was Sue.

"Was that OK?" she asked nervously.

"Oh that was really great," replied Alan, "Why?" he peered at her.

"You disappeared in such a hurry at the end. It's really not like you."

"Hah!" Alan laughed. "Your two sessions were really excellent Sue. In fact they were even better than I had imagined. The reason I had to get moving is that I had a call to make before close of business," Alan relaxed back into his chair. He decided to confide in her. "We have got some momentum now, I am seeing Robin on Monday," he said.

"Robin? You mean the Chairman?"

"Exactly. Barbara has teed me up to present our ideas."

"Wow. That's really great" said Sue, flushing with excitement, "Alan that's wonderful news!" She rushed over to Alan and gave him a spontaneous hug, which embarrassed them both.

"Oh... err, yes" said Alan awkwardly. "It is." His gaze fell on the notes he had been wrestling with. "Have you got 10 minutes?" he asked, knowing that she hadn't.

"Sure. What do you need?" replied Sue, composed and professional once again. She was keen to get going but this was great news. She was sure that Barry would understand if she was a few minutes late for dinner. "I am going to do a dry run of my presentation to Robin this weekend, and I'm struggling with all the material we have put together."

"How much detail are you going to delve into?" asked Sue.

"Not a lot to be honest," said Alan, "I just want to get the concept across, that's all. Here are the principles from the beginning. I am just trying to work out how to lay them out. So we started with Act Opportunistically, and from that came the Hierarchy of Time."

"Yes I remember it well," replied Sue, she turned to Alan. "Do you have a blank sheet of paper?"

"Yes, here you go."

"Great, thanks," Sue reached into her briefcase and pulled out her notebook and pen from it. She laid out the paper on the desk and quickly wrote out each of the five principles spaced out on the left hand side of the page. She drew a rough line down the middle and then opened her book. "OK so I agree: 'act opportunistically' is all about being prepared, which is all about time," she wrote 'Time' on the right hand side. "The next two topics we did were about the 'Hierarchy of Communications' including phone and email," Sue looked up at Alan. "Ironically I think those are all about 'Adapting to a wide variety of environments'," she commented. "We may actually be doing this in the right order."

"That can't be right," said Alan. "Surely they are about speed?"

"No. Think about it!" said Sue. "Your communications are the number one thing you need in any new environment, face to face, email, whatever."

"Maybe you are right."

"Well I think 'Networking' is also part of 'Adapting'," continued Sue. "Those are the skills you need to really get yourself moving in a new environment."

"That makes sense. What next?"

"Ironically the second half of my networking piece, 'Relationships', doesn't fit in there."

"Where does that go then?"

"I think that's all about speed," said Sue after a pause. "Think about it. If you know the right people."

"OK. So that brings us up to date. What else is there?"

"You were going to do a session on meetings."

"Yes I was, wasn't I?" Alan had quite forgotten about that session. "I have lined up Jeff to do a session on technology next week though."

"Technology? OK that definitely goes under speed."

"Really? Why not 'Act opportunistically'?"

"Technology amplifies everything we do. It's an enabler. We can do more things and do them more quickly."

"Not in my experience," grumbled Alan.

"That's probably because you are not using it right."

"Well that may be."

"Meetings, meetings," Sue said to herself, thinking. "Oh easy, that fits under 'Driving any chosen activity to a successful conclusion'."

"Why exactly?" said Alan with a furrowed brow.

"You generally cannot achieve much in this world without a meeting," responded Sue. "A meeting is a crossroads in a decision making process."

"More like a spaghetti junction!" said Alan facetiously.

"Now you are being silly. Don't forget you asked me to help you!" scolded Sue.

"Fair point. I'll behave," Alan became serious again.

"So what else are we missing?" he asked.

"I think you need something on teamwork, but apart from that I am out of ideas right now."

"I'm sorry Sue. Thanks so much, you have been a real help."

Sue gathered up her book and pen and put them back in her briefcase.

"It's a pleasure!" she said. "I am really excited about Robin."

As she got to the door Alan called out "One last thing! Where would Teamwork go?"

"Also under Drive."

"Thanks! Oh Sue?" but she was through the door and away.

Alan rushed across the room and out into the corridor to see Sue nearing the stairwell. "What about Remaining almost Undetected?" he called.

"Over to you," she called back. "Have a good weekend!" And she was gone.

Alan went back to his desk and picked up the sheet they had

worked on. He opened up PowerPoint and began copying the various topics into a slide. When he had finished he printed out the page and took it back to his desk. "Why is undetected a good thing?" he mused. "Do we really need it? If I'm undetected at home my wife may think that I'm late and will not need dinner," he giggled at himself. "What the hell am I doing here on Friday night? What is keeping me here?" he asked himself. Then he had an idea. "Bingo! Eureka! Got it!" he typed furiously on the keyboard and then picked up the phone to call Sue.

"I really wish I was undetected," she answered.

"I have it," cried Alan, "it's Discipline. Have a great weekend too!" Then he hung up.

Sue looked at her phone curiously. "Discipline?" she said to herself, "that's interesting!"

She climbed out of her parked car and went into her house. "Hi Barry, how was your day?"

Chapter Notes

The Four Levels of a successful (Networking) Relationship

- *Awareness – knows who you are. Hurrah! At last!*

- *Understanding – can describe you and your role to a colleague. Recite your elevator pitch.*

- *Supporter – speaks positively about you and seeks to be helpful, but only when asked.*

- *Advocate – actively sings your praises whenever the opportunity arises.*

Key Lessons

- *Find at least one person you get on well with and can convert into an advocate. They will help recruit people to your cause.*

- *Get your elevator pitch polished enough so that people you meet with end up with Understanding rather than just Awareness (or worse).*

And Finally:

- *Do enjoy the personal friends you make through your networks, they will travel with you forever, making life richer and more rewarding.*

- *Don't allow the network to become an end to itself, otherwise you will lose sight of the reason you built it in the first place.*

- *Your network of relationships should reward you by making life simpler and more fun, however it does require discipline and effort!*

Sue's "Principles of The Leopard" Chart

- *Act Opportunistically: Time*

- *Adapt to a wide variety of environments: Communications, Networking*

- *Operate at speed: Relationships, Technology*

- *Drive any activity to a successful conclusion: Meetings, Teamwork*

- *Remain almost undetected: Discipline*

7

TECHNOLOGY

Alan Gets Some Help

Alan was in a very positive mood when he arrived at the golf course on Saturday morning. He had always been confident that what they were doing was relevant, but had struggled to articulate it. During the short session with Sue last night he had felt that things had finally begun to fall into place. His golf game was also in good shape and he found himself striding along the centre of the fairways whilst John's wayward shots took him deeper into the woods.

By contrast John was in a foul mood. A week of difficult meetings and a couple of late nights had left him really looking forward to the golf, but right from the first tee he had been unable to take his mind off things and as a result his game had descended into chaos.

"Ooof!" he expelled as he took a particularly wild hack at his ball, which was buried deep in the rough. It hopped out, dribbled a few feet and then slithered into another tuft of long grass.

"Aaargh!" shouted John, who was by now completely exasperated. He threw down his club and took a deep breath. What did he play this game for? I mean really?

"A bad day on the course is always better than a good day in the office," said a voice behind him.

John laughed. "Too right!" he said, and turned to see who it was. There was no one to be seen apart from a black cat sitting a few feet away. John stared at the cat while he tried to compute who had made the comment. He suddenly realized he had never seen a cat on the golf course before.

"That was a pretty evil shot," said the cat. "How did you end up over here anyway?"

"Holy shit! A talking cat!" said John (who also didn't generally swear). After a moment, he gathered himself. This was very surreal. "I hooked my three iron," he said trying to look dignified and then gave up with a shake of his head. "What the hell am I doing talking to a cat?" he exclaimed aloud.

"Probably making a better job of talking than of playing golf," observed the cat. "Anyway I am a Leopard, not a cat."

"A Leopard? Now you really are being absurd!"

"Not as absurd as you look hacking at that bush," replied the cat. "Try adjusting your grip, especially your right hand."

"My right hand?" John was incredulous. "Am I reduced to taking golf lessons from a cat?" he added sarcastically.

"Try it and see," said the cat. "As I said, I am a Leopard not a cat."

"My right hand…" continued John. "What do you mean?" he looked round but the cat was gone. "Blast!" he said. "Oh well." John picked up the club, fiddled with his grip briefly and then addressed the ball. He took a slow calm swing and, with a loud thwack, made full connection with the ball. "Oh! Good!" he said as the ball arced towards the green. He looked round again to see if he could thank the cat for the tip. Then he paused to contemplate his state of mind. "I really must be imagining things," he added and set off to join up with Alan.

Post Lunch Dialogue

After lunch John and Alan took their coffees to a quiet corner of the clubhouse.

"So what was it you wanted to share?" opened John.

"You remember when we had that chat a few weeks ago? You know the one where you were thinking about packing it in?"

"Oh yes. I remember. Interesting. You were very fired up about something at the time but wouldn't share it with me," replied John mischievously. "I took your advice," he continued. "In fact right now the only thing I am actively thinking of giving up is golf!" He laughed ironically.

"A bad day on the golf course is always better than a good day in the office," said Alan.

John's brow furrowed at the familiar sound of the phrase. He started intently at Alan. "I suppose you are right," he answered. "It's about the only exercise I get. Anyway, going back to our conversation a few weeks ago…"

"Yes," said Alan. "I am ready to show you what I was on about." He pulled out a folded piece of paper and a pen from his jacket pocket. "Before I begin I think we are both agreed that the formality of the business world – and indeed the world at large – has changed since you and I cut our teeth."

"I couldn't agree with you more old boy – if I remember, that was what I was complaining about last time."

"Exactly" said Alan. "Not only has it lost its formality and structure, it is a much faster-moving world." Alan unfolded the paper on the table in landscape format; written across the very top of the page was the definition of the Leopard:

The species' success in the wild owes in part to its opportunistic hunting behaviour, its adaptability to a variety of habitats and its ability to move at up to approximately 58 kilometres (36 miles) an hour. The leopard consumes virtually any animal it can hunt down and catch.

Alan turned the piece of paper round and showed it to John who pulled out his glasses and peered at it intently.

"That's very interesting," said John slowly. "But what exactly has it got to do with what we were discussing?" John's mind was whirling – 'Leopard, Leopard – hadn't that bloody cat been muttering about Leopards? No don't be stupid, talking cats don't exist... just my imagination, he thought. He peered at Alan sharply, his eyes fixing him in an intent stare.

"Think about it John," he said. "The Leopard is the perfect metaphor for today's business world."

"Alan, you and I have been friends for a very long time," said John carefully. "And I have to tell you that I think you are starting to lose it."

Alan laughed. He had fully expected this reaction from John. He knew that if he could get John on board today then Robin would be a much easier proposition on Monday.

"Maybe," he said. "But if you could humour me for a couple of minutes before you call the men in white coats."

John shook his head ruefully. "Keep digging," he added.

Alan drew a wavy line down the middle of the paper. "Consider for a minute that this creature is a very successful predator across the globe, and yet very rarely seen."

"Well I have been on safari many times, and I still haven't seen one," commented John.

"Exactly – that's my point. They are operating successfully all around you and yet you never knew they were there."

"And your point is?" asked John evenly.

"There are five key characteristics of the Leopard that make it successful." Alan wrote them in order spaced out down the left had side of the page. "First they act opportunistically," he said softly. "They can adapt to a wide variety of environments; they operate at speed."

John watched him closely.

"They drive any chosen activity to a successful conclusion and remain almost undetected," finished Alan.

"That's very interesting," said John. "So how do you relate that to the skills and approaches that we use today?"

"I'm glad you asked that," said Alan with a grin. "To get through the gate of 'Acting opportunistically', you need to examine your use of Time."

"Oh – time management – I see," John jumped in.

Alan shook his head.

"No, not exactly," he replied. "Time management is normally about aligning tasks with priorities and strategic goals – which is fine. What we are considering here is how we each think about time. We drew up a hierarchy of time. Basically we break down time into 4 key components – the most valuable of which is Unallocated Time, followed by Creative Time which you need for thinking and brainstorming; Functional Time for doing things and finally Dead Time for tasks such as sleeping," he finished. "It's a mind-set thing – to be able to act opportunistically, you have to be much more flexible about your time and therefore how you think about it."

Alan paused for a second and John remained silent. "Am I making any sense here?" he asked hopefully, anxious that John was still missing the point.

"I think so. What about the other the skills and approaches?"

"OK. Good. Well once we are through acting opportunistically, we need to adapt to any new environment, and for that we need communications and networking."

"Oh I can certainly agree with that," enthused John.

"Good – I am making sense then," smiled Alan. "To operate at speed we need both technology and relationships," he continued.

John took out a pocket notebook and a pen and began to write.

"I am not sure I agree with you about technology," he interjected.

"You can't avoid it John. Look what your BlackBerry gives you."

"Fair enough, I'm listening," John replied.

"Then we come to 'drive any chosen activity to a successful conclusion' and for that we need meetings and teamwork," said Alan.

"Do you think meetings are really useful anymore?" said John provocatively raising a single eyebrow quizzically just like Roger Moore in a James Bond film. It was stylish gesture and Alan wished he could do it too.

"I do actually," said Alan seriously. "And it's one of the topic areas where I would like some help from you. So many meetings are badly run and attendees also have no idea how to behave."

"You are telling me!" said John emphatically. "I would be delighted to help. Let me know when."

"The final part is to remain almost undetected. This is all about discipline," finished Alan.

"I am not sure I understand either of those," responded John. "Leopards might well remain undetected but why should people?"

"Actually this is the most important," replied Alan. "All the above skills and approaches are vital, but to be effective they need to be an inbuilt part of people's day to day lives. They need to be an invisible part of people's capability. To achieve this requires discipline. Firstly to absorb and learn and then to focus on what each of us needs to do. To become one of a new breed of Professionals." He paused for a moment to watch John reflect.

John was still for a few moments then he smiled broadly. "I think you are probably certifiable, but I have always believed that there is a fine line between genius and insanity."

Alan laughed. "So do you like it then?"

"It's very interesting. So what exactly are you going to do next?"

"I'm seeing Robin Monday afternoon," said Alan.

"Robin? Really?" responded John. "Well he has always been much more progressive than me."

"I believe he is certainly receptive to new ideas," said Alan.

"I am going to wish you good luck and I mean it," said John. "Let me know what I can do to help."

"It's been very helpful talking to you about it this afternoon," said Alan. "Thank you John – it's very much appreciated."

"Not at all – an absolute pleasure."

"I will send you some dates for the session on meetings."

The Meeting with Robin

Alan was emboldened by his chat with John on Saturday. He wasn't entirely sure that John really understood everything that he had explained to him, but he knew him well enough to know that if he disagreed with him fundamentally, he would have said so there and then.

When Alan and Barbara arrived at Robin's office at 2pm, they were shown straight in to find Robin in a warm and friendly mood.

"Alan, Barbara – come in!" he enthused. "I am fascinated to hear what you have to say. Leopards and all that – sounds very exciting!"

Alan and Barbara glanced at each other. They had agreed to keep the Leopard title out of Barbara's conversation with Robin.

"Leopards?" asked Alan, curious to know how Robin had become aware of the idea.

Robin smiled.

"All right I will confess," said Robin with a twinkle in his eye. "You do know that John and I worked together many years ago, don't you? Anyway, he rang me first thing this morning. He told me that you had run the ideas past him at the weekend; he told me that while they might seem a little odd I should listen carefully and take you seriously. What do you think of that?"

Alan laughed. "I don't know what to make of that, honestly!" he said.

"Oh you mean you didn't actually put him up to it then?" replied Robin with a mischievous grin.

"Certainly not," said Alan tartly. "Although I confess I did use him as a sounding board after we played golf."

"Well he spoke very warmly of you anyway."

"We have known each other a long time. He's a good friend and also a good man."

"So, what have you got to share with me?" suddenly Robin was all serious again.

"Well, I am starting from the supposition that the business world we operate in today is a far cry from the formal and structured world in which we began our careers," Alan began. "We operate in a fast moving, informal environment with few rules, where there is a price to pay for missing opportunities as well as a much more visible one for making mistakes."

Robin nodded, "I would not disagree with you."

"I have been thinking hard about the need to bridge the divide and how we could develop a new way of working – a new level of professionalism," Alan continued. "In fact I have been working on it informally for a few weeks with a few like-minded people." He pulled out the piece of paper from his session with John. He had thought long and hard about how to present this to Robin. He had eventually decided to place his bets on the authenticity of his written prototype rather than putting together a more polished PowerPoint slide that might appear soulless. Alan opened the paper, turned it round and placed it in front of Robin. "The concept is based on the characteristics of the Leopard," he continued. "It is one of nature's most successful predators, and its opportunistic approach maps well onto what needs to be done to move the game forward."

Robin looked at the sheet carefully. "I see." He said bluntly. It was pretty clear that he didn't.

There was an uncomfortable silence. Robin's brow furrowed and then straightened. He looked hard at Alan for a moment and decided that he would make an effort to understand. "So these are the characteristics on the left of the page?" he asked. Alan breathed out gently.

"Exactly," he said. "The skills and approaches that relate to each characteristic are on the right hand side. We are working through each one slowly."

"Let me ask you a question," said Robin. "Why on earth do you think this is relevant to our organisation and what benefits do you think it can bring?" he looked hard at Alan, who met his gaze directly.

"If we change the way people think and operate as individuals – no matter what level – I believe we can make a 20% improvement in productivity." Alan kept his voice calm and level. "If we can combine this with a similar progress in teamwork and co-operation I believe we will see a really significant improvement in how this company operates."

Robin's face was expressionless for a couple of seconds, and then his face softened. "Really?" he said. "So what makes you think that we are not already at our maximum level of productivity? You do know that there are teams in this company working round the clock and weekends on a whole pile of projects."

Alan shook his head emphatically. If he got this bit wrong he might need a new job. "If regularly working weekends and nights is regarded as an example of good productivity then we have a real problem. What I am talking about here is helping individuals to be smarter, better connected and much more agile. Several members of the team we are working with are from the new graduate intake. They think about the world in a completely different way from you and me and yet they are keen to tap us for our experience and knowledge."

Robin sighed heavily and went quiet. There was a long and pregnant silence in the room. "Where exactly have you got to?" asked Robin eventually.

"Well we are up to Technology, although the material isn't pulled together yet," began Alan, missing the trapdoor that was opening in front of him.

"When is the next meeting?" asked Robin.

"Err... Friday," replied Alan, suddenly aware that he might get a reprimand for using company time on what had been up to now a pet project.

"Good – let me know what time, I would like to attend if I can. Please send me a calendar invite. Oh – one more thing – what do you think should be done with this concept and set of ideas?"

"I would like to see the company consider adopting it as a universal training programme, which is why I involved Barbara." Alan was still unsure how to read Robin's reaction.

"Alan, thank you. This is interesting – but I want to learn more.

Thank you for bringing it to my attention." He looked at Barbara. "I am going to add a very short piece to the AOB section of the board meeting next week," he added. "I think we need to flag it to Bill [the CEO] and the team as work in progress – that is if you support it Barbara?"

"Thanks Robin. Yes I do indeed," said Barbara who had, up till now, let Alan do all the talking, "I went to last week's session and I must say it was terrific."

"Oh what was it about?"

"Networking and relationships."

"Interesting – I look forward to catching up on that one. Thank you both for coming up to see me, I look forward to Friday."

Alan and Barbara took their cue and departed.

"That was short and sweet," said Barbara as soon as they were in the corridor.

"I was a little surprised, I must say," admitted Alan. "But then again, you and John had already done some pre-selling."

"Nonsense Alan, you are a senior member of the management team," chided Barbara. "Friday will be interesting though. Robin is rather clueless about technology if I remember correctly."

"Well let's see if we can educate him then," replied Alan. "Mission accomplished for today. I'd better phone Jeff and Sue."

The Big Technology Session on Friday

Ben and Jeff arrived early for their big session. They had spent several evenings preparing, and had brought an array technology and gadgets with them. They walked into a large conference room with a row of plush leather chairs on castors and large glass windows from floor to ceiling. There were several impressive framed photographs of the company's different facilities spaced out across the walls as well as a number of large screens for video conferencing. "Wow! Cool room," muttered Ben.

"You are telling me," murmured Jeff, pleased that Alan had

managed to score them such a good space.

They set everything up on a table at the front of the room, eventually covering it with a sheet just before everyone arrived.

Alan hadn't told them that Robin would be there. He had debated with himself long and hard about whether he should, eventually deciding that their preparation would be very stilted if he told them.

"Is that who I think it is?" whispered Ben as Robin walked in.

Jeff also recognised him immediately, but decided to downplay it also. "Not sure," he said absently. He stared hard at Alan until he caught his eye, and made a gesture as if to say "What's going on?"

Alan smiled back at him and made a gesture to indicate that the floor was all theirs.

"Thanks," muttered Jeff.

Just as he was about to start, the door opened and several additional people came in. It was now Alan's turn to be surprised as Barbara stood up, greeted them and organised seats without introducing them.

"Who are they?" Alan hissed at Barbara.

"The word is out," she smiled back. "These are just a few folk I know who are keen to get involved." Alan was about to reply when Jeff stood up.

"Hi everyone!" began Jeff. "Ben and I are going to do a session on technology this morning. For those of you who are technically minded some of this will be familiar; for those less so we hope it will lift the veil. Before we begin I wanted to get an idea of what technology you already have and what you use. How many of you have a smartphone?"

"It depends exactly what you mean by a smartphone," said Robin, pulling a slightly old fashioned mobile phone out of his jacket pocket. "I do have a mobile phone, but I'm not sure whether it is 'smart' or not?"

"A basic phone can do calls, contacts and texts," responded Jeff, glancing quickly at Ben. "In our book a smartphone does email, allows you to browse the web and has other applications on it such as social networking."

"Well why would I need all that on my phone?" asked Robin, giving Jeff a steely look.

Jeff paused for a second, mostly for dramatic effect. "In truth, you don't have to have all that on your phone," he replied simply. "If you have easy and regular access to a PC or laptop, you can do all those things from there. However, if you have a busy day, or you are travelling, or you don't have access to a broadband connection, you may not get a chance to use your laptop or PC. That's why having your email, broadband and applications on a smartphone can be really useful," he finished.

"OK," replied Robin. "So are you going to show me how this stuff works?"

"Absolutely!" answered Jeff. "But before we do, who else has smartphones? Or not?"

"BlackBerry," responded Barbara.

"Me too," added Alan.

"Great, what else?"

"iPhone," responded Kate. "But you know that!"

"Windows Phone," responded Sue.

"OK – great, thanks!" said Jeff. "Let's turn to computers. Do most of you have laptops?"

Most heads nodded in agreement.

"I use a desktop mostly," said Alan.

"I guess I have what you would call a desktop," said Robin reluctantly. "I have a laptop too but I never use it."

"We are going to look at both approaches. Any Macs at all?"

One of the new arrivals put his hand up. "I use a MacBook," he added cautiously. "I do a lot of photo and video work."

"Thanks – me too," grinned Jeff.

"I thought we only gave PCs to our people," grumbled Robin.

"Oh we do generally," countered Jeff without elaborating further. He walked over to the table and with Ben's help pulled the sheet off to reveal a display of laptops, technology and devices. "Ben and I gathered together all the standard issue corporate technology that we give out to everyone. We have also added some non-standard technology that people sometimes use – such as Apple MacBooks. Before we did the session, we wanted to understand what everyone was using as standard, and what people could also use with a bit of invention. We discovered that there is actually a lot of choice and flexibility, but firstly most people don't understand what they need; and secondly if they can't find what they need, they don't ask for help."

"I'll start with my MacBook," he turned to Robin. "This is my machine and not the company's," he stated. "I have used Macs since I was a kid and I would have used it at home anyway. I also do a lot of photography and video work, but most importantly I wanted to get everything I do onto one machine. If I am going to do that, it had to be an Apple, so I have loaded it so that I can run a version of Windows 7 on it as well as the Apple operating system."

Alan suddenly felt a cold chill running down his spine, what the hell had Jeff been up to?

"When I joined I went to see the IT folks," Jeff continued, "and we had a long discussion about it. They support a few Macs for number of technical applications, but we worked out a deal where they have given me a standard build of Windows and Office, but on my Apple."

"Well I never," said Robin. Alan heaved a big sigh of relief.

"The first point I am making is that you need to get everything you do onto one machine – desktop, laptop, PC or Apple."

"What if you have two machines?" asked Robin, now fully engaged.

"First you really need to decide which one you want to use as your primary machine and transfer everything onto it. If you deliberately split things between two machines, at some point you will end up getting caught out by finding the programs and data you need are on the wrong machine."

"I can personally tell you that will end up wasting a lot of time and causing unnecessary stress," chipped in Ben, "and as someone who does do a lot of work on data, I learned that lesson the hard way," he added.

"So what should I do? I have both a desktop PC and a laptop?"

asked Robin. "I don't use either very much, as I must confess that my PA does a lot of my computer work for me."

"Do you have any of the machines we have here?" asked Ben.

"Oh, err, let me see." Robin put his glasses on his nose, stood up and walked over to have a look at the tale of devices. "The desktop is not here, but this is the laptop I have," he said pointing at one of the largest machines on the table.

"Now I know why you don't use it very much," said Jeff. "It's a fabulous machine which is so powerful that it's generally used for doing things like developing applications for smartphones. It also has an extended battery." He picked it up and hefted it in his hands. "It is also probably the heaviest machine on the market. Which I guess is why you don't use it very much. Correct?"

"It weighs a bloody ton," replied Robin. "I always hesitate to take it with me because of the weight, so that's why I don't use it."

"I also suspect that you don't need all that processing power, you probably only want it for email, Internet and reading documents," added Jeff.

"That's about all I use my desktop for," said Robin.

"OK well in that case can I make a suggestion? Why don't you trade it in for a smaller machine such as this one? It's so slim that it's called an Ultrabook." He lifted a very neat looking laptop off the table and handed it to Robin.

"My word, this doesn't weigh much!" exclaimed Robin.

"It's got a solid state disk inside," explained Jeff. "That means that its data storage is all done on memory chips and there is no hard drive storage. It saves a huge amount on weight and power, but it does make the machine more expensive."

"I like this, I really do!" exclaimed Robin. He turned to Jeff with an air of boyish enthusiasm. "So if I could swan about the place with this slip of a machine," he continued, "how do I do things such as printing that I do from my desktop?"

"You can print wirelessly over the corporate network, or you could get a wireless printer for your office," replied Jeff. He gestured at the

Ultrabook.

"You may find that you can trade your existing machine into the IT department for that Ultrabook," said Jeff. "Your existing laptop is such a top spec machine that they will be only too pleased to have it back!"

"Well that's me sorted. What about everyone else?" said Robin as he turned to face the room, smiling.

"Although the lifetime of machines is pretty short these days, a lot of people are lumbered with heavy, slow and outdated machines," continued Jeff. "It's a real problem, and one that individuals struggle to solve. They have really got three choices: live with it, buy their own machine or find a halfway house like I did with my Apple Mac."

"Jeff, how do you think we should approach this as a company?" asked Barbara.

"Some firms are starting to give people a laptop 'allowance' instead of a machine," replied Jeff. "It's known as BYOD or Bring Your Own Device and it does make a lot of sense as they get the machine they want and they are responsible for it if it gets damaged, lost or stolen."

"That's interesting," added Barbara. "Do the economics work?"

"Yes," said Jeff. "It lowers insurance and warranty costs as well as removing the whole asset tracking hassle. It also means people look after their machines better as they have to fork out for a replacement."

"Well we should look at doing it," pitched in Robin. "Barbara will you make a note to speak to IT?"

"The other approach is just to buy the machine you need anyway," said Jeff. "I know it seems an odd thing to do, but I strongly believe that these tools are so important to our professional and personal lives not to allow company policy to limit your capability. It's not very expensive to get even a basic laptop, and they all have things like built in cameras for video calling on Skype."

"What about the issue of having work data on a personal machine?" asked Alan. "And for that matter what about personal data on a work machine?"

"Hah," Barbara snorted. "Both are an issue for us right now. Official policy says no to both things, however Jeff seems to have found one way round it."

"I knew I would have to get permission for work data on a personal machine," said Jeff. "And that works quite well with the separate setup for Windows on my machine. However I confess that I also carry some folders of personal data on that setup, which kind of hits on the second point."

"I can see that this is a bit of a grey area," said Robin.

"I go back to what I was saying about one machine," said Jeff. "In order to make life – both personal and professional – work efficiently, you always end up with some personal data on your work machine. My belief is that provided you follow company security guidelines, don't break the taste and decency rules or introduce a virus, I can't see that it should be an issue."

"Well you might not see that but I am pretty sure that the IT security folks are going to have a problem with that," said Sue. "I know it makes sense in principle but if you make it policy, it's a carte blanche for everyone to use their work laptops at home for all sorts of purposes."

"I hear you Sue," replied Jeff. "But the reality is that people use work laptops for personal use anyway. Why not acknowledge it?"

"I'm not sure we are going to solve this today," intervened Alan. "Can I suggest that we accept that while our company policy disapproves of this in principle, our people generally disobey in practice?"

"OK so let me finish up my bit and then I'm going to hand over to Ben to talk about Data," said Jeff. "But let me re-cap first. You need to have one machine with everything on it. It needs to be fit for purpose and almost certainly portable," he raised a hand as he could see Alan about to interrupt him. "Some machines need to be desktops, especially if security is an issue, or they have to run special applications or devices. But there are huge benefits to having a portable machine whenever possible, as it means your office really does travel with you. If you are choosing a portable machine make sure you chose the lightest and most compact machine you can get. You are going to carry it around and you don't want to strain parts of your body carrying it. Always get a spare battery for travelling and additional power supplies – one for home and one for the office." He finished.

"That's a lot of extra stuff," added Barbara. "Is that all really needed?"

"Yes, it is," replied Jeff. "The battery makes sense if you are on a plane or working somewhere there is no power. You would be surprised how hard it can be to find a power socket in some buildings. There are also some really cool external battery packs that can power both your laptops and smartphones for long periods of time. As for the power supplies, it saves you time and hassle every day when you get to the office or get home, and it also means that if you lose your travelling power supply, you have a spare at each location. If you can fit it in, it's also worth investing in a Mi-Fi device."

"A WHAT device?"

Jeff smiled.

"It's a little box about the size of a mobile phone and it converts 3G Mobile phone data into a mobile Wi-Fi hotspot so you can surf the web wherever you are."

"Well I never."

"We all need to understand and remind ourselves that the laptop and the phone are the two of the most important tools in people's lives. I don't necessarily expect people to buy their own machines like I did, but they should be prepared to invest their time and money making them work."

"What approach should we take to the smartphones you were talking about earlier?" asked Robin. "I'm curious now. Do I need one as well as my new laptop? And a Mi-Fi of course?"

"I would say that you should definitely have a smartphone," said Jeff, "because it will really help you to get more done when you are on the move."

He walked over to the table and picking up several examples. "Here are the main choices, but I think you will need to do some research yourself. Here's the iPhone, which I have."

"Is this a company device?" asked Alan.

Jeff laughed. "No, it's mine," he said. "And before you ask I did get approval and yes it does work with the company email system."

"Is this any good," asked Robin poking hopefully at the iPhone.

"I think it's great," said Jeff, "but it may not suit you." He handed Robin another phone. "This is a BlackBerry," he said, "Alan and Sue have this and I think it's really excellent for email and text messages and pretty good for browsing the Internet. The iPhone is also good at these but it does lots of other things such as music, navigation and other applications."

"I think my daughter has an iPhone," replied Robin. "What else is there to look at?"

"This is the Windows Phone," replied Jeff. "It's has these very neat tiles on it for all your applications, it's very good at email and synchronising with contacts as it works really well with Outlook, as well as social networks like Facebook and LinkedIn. This particular one is made by Nokia."

"Now I don't know where to start," said Robin.

"Yes, it can be confusing," agreed Jeff. "That's why we dug out all these phones today. It's very similar to the discussion we had about laptops just now. As an individual, you need to invest some time and money figuring out what you need and making it work. If you know someone who has each type of device, you should ask them for their input and decide if it could meet your needs. Alan's a big BlackBerry fan, Sue has the Windows Phone and your daughter sounds like she would help with the iPhone," he suggested.

"Thank you Jeff, that's very helpful," said Robin still playing with the phones absently. "I think that's exactly what I am going to do."

"How do we work out what the company should and should not support here?" asked Barbara.

"This is much easier than laptops," said Jeff. "For a start, most phones have a SIM which can be switched out, so if people want to change or upgrade their phone – let them. The only major issue is secure email integration."

"But I like my BlackBerry and I don't want to change it!" cried Alan.

"And you shouldn't have to," replied Jeff. "If you have something that works then great."

"We also don't give a mobile phone to everyone," said Barbara. "Or do you think we should?"

Jeff paused for a second. He knew that this was an emotive issue, and caused some resentment with those that were denied. "My personal opinion is that they should only be given to those who are in client facing roles, those who travel a lot and have to do international calls. Let's face it the cost of making national calls is incremental and if you are in the office you can use a desk phone."

"I would like everyone to have a mobile or better still a smartphone," said Barbara. "It would make my types of communication so much more sensible."

"Pretty much everyone has some kind of phone already," responded Jeff. "The real question is really whether everyone should be upgraded to a smartphone."

"Well – what's the benefit to the company if they do?" boomed Robin.

"That's easy – you can create smartphone applications to make all our company systems really mobile," shot back Jeff. "Think about the power that would put at people's fingertips. Imagine getting management data on a weekly or even daily basis delivered directly to your phone!"

"That could be really useful," replied Robin. "Barbara that's another one for the next Board meeting."

"Finally Robin, you might also want to take a look at this." Jeff walked over to the table, reached under the sheet and pulled out an Apple iPad and handed it to Robin.

"I must say, I have seen people using these on the train," said Robin. He looked at Jeff. "Is it any good?"

"I like it," said Jeff. "This is my own personal one."

"So could I possibly use it for doing email and Internet on the move? Couldn't I use one instead of this laptop?"

Jeff smiled. "Good question. You probably could, and increasingly we will all use tablet computers as day to day devices. On the one hand it's fantastic for reading, viewing and doing email and pretty good for Internet. On the other hand it's not secure, typing long documents is hard and it's not terribly private physically," replied Jeff. "I don't think that's such an issue for personal content but if you are reading confidential documents and email then you need to be aware."

"What do you mean?"

"People can easily read stuff over your shoulder or when it's laid flat on a table, unlike a laptop where the screen can be hidden unless you are right in front of it. Also if you lose it or it's stolen, the data on it is not encrypted means that anyone can get at it."

Robin swiped the screen several times. "Even so, this is very nice. I must say I am tempted."

"If you have Apple stuff already then it's probably a good thing to have. That said here's something else for you to consider." Jeff reached into his bag and pulled out another tablet computer.

"What's that then?"

"This is something I have borrowed from a friend. It's a one of the new Windows 8 tablet computers."

"How nice is that!"

A small group stood up and began to gather round Jeff and Robin as they played with the two tablets.

"This," said Jeff quietly gesturing towards the Windows 8 tablet, "will be the way forward in my humble opinion."

"Why do you say that?" asked Barbara.

Jeff reached over and touched the screen and flipped it back to a familiar PC view.

"Firstly you get the best of both worlds in one machine – you can use this with a wireless keyboard. Or touch."

"Oh, wow."

Jeff reached into his bag and pulled out another smartphone, unlocked it and passed it to Barbara.

"This looks exactly the same," she blurted out. Jeff smiled.

"Exactly. The new Windows Phone operating system works exactly the same way as the tablet. So it doesn't matter which machine you use, everything works in exactly the same way across devices."

"That is very cool indeed," admitted Barbara.

"You haven't seen the best bit yet," added Jeff, "both machines also have a whole new Office suite that's designed to work with touch. Here I will show you," he opened up PowerPoint application on the tablet and swiped through a few pages of a presentation to much cooing.

Sue intervened. "Jeff, what do you think tablets are best used for?"

"Tablets fit neatly into the gap between laptops and phones, the touch interface is fantastic for sharing stuff and the applications make it really easy to get at information quickly."

"Anyway I will leave those for you to play with and now I'm going to hand over to Ben to talk about data," finished Jeff. "But just before I go here's a short hand-out for you all on personal technology strategy. I hope it's useful. Thanks everyone. Ben, over to you!"

"Thank you, Jeff!" came from the audience, along with a generous round of applause. Jeff sat down smiling, much relieved to have finished his part.

Ben Steps Up

"Hi everyone," began Ben nervously. He coughed then straightened himself and launched into his subject. "As a data specialist, I have my own particular interest in data. Every day, each one of you generates a significant amount of important data without realising it. Both at home and work, you increasingly receive, process and create vast amounts of data and yet I will guarantee that very few of you have any kind of robust process for managing, backing up and pruning that data."

"Pruning?" spluttered Robin. "But that's what I do to my roses!"

There was a murmur of laughter in the room.

"Well imagine doing the same thing to all the documents you have on your computer," explained Ben patiently. "Pruning in the data sense is just deleting files you don't need and re-organising the ones that you do. Simple really!"

"Fair enough – well put," said Robin.

"So I want to ask you all," continued Ben, "if you understand how important your data is?"

"Doesn't IT back up all our computers for us?" asked Barbara innocently.

"They back up the servers and the intranet sites. But unless you have made a special arrangement, they will not back up your work desktop or laptop. That's your responsibility!"

Barbara thought for a second. "Most of our important stuff is on the servers so that's fine," she replied. "But I must admit there is quite a bit of correspondence on my laptop which doesn't make it onto the server."

"I hate to tell you this," said Ben. "But there is an IT policy that requires you to back up your machine, although it's not enforced."

"Oh," said Barbara. "Well I probably need a refresher on that one, then."

"Maybe," said Ben. "But think about what Jeff was saying earlier. This isn't just about your work machine – this is about all your data. Think about all your home photographs, emails, music and videos. I'll lay down some money that pretty much all of you don't back these up. Am I right?"

There was some muted murmuring in the audience.

Ben took this to mean that he had their general agreement. "So let me put a scenario to you. 5 maybe 10 years ago, you would have pasted all your personal photographs into an album along with some labels. And the only thing that would have threatened a completed photo album would have been a fire, a burglary or a flood of some kind." Ben paused to let this sink in. "Now you risk losing every single photograph that you have taken over the last 5 years though the simple but entirely possible failure of your PC hard disk. Before you ask, yes it does happen."

"So what are you suggesting here Ben?" asked Sue, right on cue.

Ben flashed a rare smile.

"I'm glad you asked," he said, walking over to a white-board in the corner. "It's very simple actually, there are just three rules," with which he began writing.

The Three Rules of Backup

1. *Treat both your professional and personal data with the same serious degree of respect.*

2. *Back everything up at least on a weekly basis if not daily.*

3. *Everything you have needs to be held in at least three separate places.*

Before Ben could explain in more detail he was interrupted by Robin. "Hang on a second, I am not sure that I'm following you," Robin had a puzzled expression on his face.

"It's very simple," responded Ben. "How many PCs do you have at home and at work?"

"Oh, err, two, three if you count my monster laptop," replied Robin. "I mean seriously what do I need to do?" he asked earnestly and somewhat humbly.

Alan watched Ben to see if he really understood that his Chairman was actually asking him for help and guidance. "Well firstly you need to get an external hard drive to back up your PCs onto. You can get a wired one which means that you have to connect it to each computer, which is fine if you have one or two machines. If you have more than two machines you need to do it properly and buy a network hard drive which can plug into your home network and connect to all your PCs. These are relatively inexpensive and can be set-up and connected very easily. Secondly you need to set up a backup from each PC on the network – that's become really easy if you have PCs with Windows 7, if you also have Macs it's very straightforward as they have software called 'Time Machine' that does it all for you."

"OK Ben – what if you don't have a home network, just a Wi-Fi connection?" interrupted Barbara, "I mean how simple could I make this?"

"A Wi-Fi Connection is just the same," replied Ben. "It's just wireless, that's all. When you do the backup for the first time it will take some time over a home Wi-Fi connection, but once you have done it once it will be much quicker second time around. If you then follow my Rule 2, you should do a backup for each PC once a week. If you have to plug in the wired hard drive to each PC doing this weekly, it becomes a real chore. On the other hand if you buy a network hard drive, you can set up each PC and Mac to automatically do a backup when it sees the network hard drive. Much less hassle if you ask me! Oh I almost forgot, if you just have Macs in your household, you can buy an Apple network drive called a 'Time Capsule', and if you are a PC nut there is the Windows Home Server which you can use for all sorts of other interesting things. But I digress."

Sue's brow was furrowing. "So if I follow Rules One and Two, what do I need to do for Rule Three?" Sue peered intently at the white-board. "What is it you said? Everything you have needs to be held in at least three separate places?"

"I am glad you asked," replied Ben. "The third rule is the most vital piece of the strategy. Doing a regular weekly backup is a great strategy that gets you to about 90% security level. I mean both your PCs would have to fail or be stolen plus you would have to lose your home drive as well to make this a serious risk. But it can happen. I'll give you an example of a friend of mine who lost everything in a house fire a couple of years back. He had diligently backed up everything but both his laptop and his backup got irreversibly damaged in the fire and he lost years of work and personal data. So – how many of you have heard of the Cloud?"

"The Cloud?" asked Alan mischievously.

"Yes. The Cloud. And by the Cloud, I mean cloud computing."

"Yes I have heard of it," replied Alan with a grin. There were other nods in the room. Robin looked blank.

"For the purposes of this morning you should think of cloud computing as an approach where a multitude of computers and data storage are directly connected to via the Internet and can be easily accessed from any device or location."

Ben was getting some blank looks, so Jeff decided to intervene. "Look: lots of you have used websites and smartphone applications," he began. "These all use cloud computing. You can see the website or use the application, but you don't know or care where the computer is that's delivering it or where it's stored, you just know it works!"

"Oh I get it," said Barbara, "it's like online shopping too, you don't know where the shop is but you know it will be delivered by mail."

"Exactly," said Ben, much relieved. "The third part of the strategy is to use cloud computing and data storage to provide the third place where we hold all the data that is important to us."

"That sounds complicated," observed Robin.

Ben sighed, and Alan tensed as he could see Ben's famous short temper beginning to fray. "It's not actually that hard, there are at least four very good services you can use which are very easy to set up – Apple has its iCloud service, Microsoft has SkyDrive, there is Google Drive and there is also another service called Dropbox. Again this requires a little effort to set up, and a while to sort through your data each month, but eventually you will have a complete and secure Internet backup of all the important stuff you have on your PC."

Robin was shaking his head again. "Alan, Ben – I have to say that this sounds like an awful lot of work," he began vaguely.

Alan held up his hand to prevent Ben from interjecting.

"Robin," he began. "At this stage I think it is important to make something very clear. The world we operate in is driven and operated by digital information. Like it nor not, that's how it is. This company lives and breathes data. Therefore we as individuals have to learn to take the same approach to our professional and personal data. Otherwise we will put all our hard work, success and reputation at risk." As an afterthought Alan muttered "here endeth the lesson" which he had not intended to be overheard, but was actually audible to Robin and everyone. It broke the momentary tension and Robin grinned as everyone else chuckled.

"Fair point Alan," he said.

"Well I will agree, at first glance it does not look straightforward," said Ben. "However these simple cloud services are very inexpensive to install and once you have set one up, it just runs in the background. I'll tell you what, Jeff and I will come over and set it up for you," Ben finished triumphantly.

Jeff started as he had thought his contribution was over. He and Ben exchanged glances, waiting to see if Ben's gamble would pay off.

"Thank you Ben, Jeff. That's very kind and I would very much appreciate it." Robin replied in a humble tone. They were off the hook for now but would have to up the ante at a later date!

"That's no problem. We'll make a plan," said Ben, very relieved to have got over the hurdle.

"Oh one last point on that," Jeff stirred himself into action, gesturing to the Windows tablet that was back on the table.

"The next version of Office has all this cloud stuff built in so you don't even have to think about it."

"Well that would be fantastic," said Robin eyeing the Windows 8 tablet with envy.

"OK next up – and I guess this goes back to the Data Pruning we were talking about just now," Ben gave a rare grin, he was beginning to enjoy himself. At last he was being recognised for his expertise! "File management and versioning. Doesn't that just fill you with dread when I say it?" he asked ironically. "So let's make this really simple."

"What folders and files do I need and what should I call them? It depends entirely on what you are working on, so here are some good starting points, these would include projects you are working on, clients you work with, people you work with, teams you work with and industry topics you are interested in and an admin folder for everything else including personal data. I'll be candid – it's very hard to create any kind of standard structures for how you organise things. It's very much up to each one of you as individuals, but there are two rules of thumb for organising your stuff:"

1. *Damning with Faint Use – If you create a folder and don't put very much in it, it is probably time to delete it or archive it.*

2. *Divide and Conquer – If you create a folder you put a lot of things into and then can't find them, it is probably best to create some more sub folders and divide the topic.*

"As for files that you are putting into each folder – well there are two useful rules for those too:"

1. *Versioning – For every new version of a file, add an updated version number to it so you make sure you only work on the latest copy of a document. You might think this is trivial thing to do but it avoids a lot of unnecessary hassle and wasted effort – particularly if you have a deadline to hit. It also means that if you have to go back to an idea which you earlier abandoned, that you have the original copy and have not deleted it.*

2. *Ownership – If you are sharing a document with other team members, add your initials at the end each time you make changes. It makes it really clear who was the last person to do it so you can accurately track multiple contributions.*

"So what about this pruning lark then?" Robin was waiting patiently.

"Simple really," replied Ben. "When you have finally got your files and folders organised, you need to go through them ideally once a month at least and delete document versions and archive folders that are no longer needed. It's really quite similar to your roses – you trim the ones that need trimming and uproot the ones that are dead."

Robin chuckled. "That's good," he admitted. "I can relate to that."

"Oh and as one final word," continued Ben, "if you follow Jeff, Sue and Alan's guidance on email – what is it called?"

"The Eleven Rules of Email," Jeff, Sue and Alan piped up together.

"Yeah that's it. Anyway they have a really good rule on Email Inbox management in there. It strikes me that if you set up and follow the same file structure as you have in your email, that would make really good sense."

"I'll send it to you all," added Sue as she artfully passed a notepad to the new attendees in the group. "I'll just need your email addresses."

"Well done Sue," thought Alan, "let's stay one step ahead anyway."

"OK I'm going to wrap up now," announced Ben. "I have just one last thing to say – which is the most important topic of all – and the one all the IT folks get most worked up about. Security."

He walked into the centre of the room, as much for effect as to gain their attention. The room went quiet. "I want you to think about this building for a second," he began. "If someone wanted to steal something physical from this building, they would find it pretty hard work – right?"

Everyone looked at each other momentarily and then back at Ben.

"Absolutely," said Barbara. "The front desk is very secure – all the rear doors require swipe passes and have video monitoring on them, and you need a swipe pass to get into the car park."

"Exactly," said Ben. "The point is that we have thought very hard about what we need to do to secure the premises – in a physical sense. Everyone instinctively understands this. The security rules are pretty simple and everyone knows them. Correct?"

There was a murmured collective agreement.

"So I'll bet none of you know where the fibre connection point is, what router ports are open to the Internet and which individuals run our day to day IT security policy. Correct?"

"Easy – that's Jim Langford." A voice at the back of the room named the company's IT Director.

"You are right. Jim will know but it's not Jim who does it," replied Ben. "Actually to be honest – it doesn't matter who does it as long as the company's board knows that it is being done as effectively as possible. However despite all the work they do and the significant investment the firm makes in IT security, nearly every electronic breach of security is of someone else within the firm making a really simple, schoolboy error. So Jeff and I put together something called the Thee W's – and before you say it – no it's not the World Wide Web!"

Ben picked up a marker pen and moved across to the white-board to write:

The Three W's of Electronic Security

1. *Who? Don't send stuff to or from people you don't know well. Qualify them first and make sure you are sending or receiving documents that are approved and appropriate.*

2. *What? Think about what you are sending. Does it really need to be in writing and could you communicate it verbally? Is the information sensitive? In which case should it be communicated as a printout rather than something that could be forwarded electronically?*

3. *Where? Be careful what you leave lying around on your desk – or on your screen. Think who might be able to see it when they walk past.*

"When Jeff and I began the preparation for this session, we took a walk round the office and we were amazed what printed material was left lying around and what was left up on screens. I know we agreed that this was a 'secure' environment, but we let our clients, partners and associates into this office every day."

When he finished writing, he threw the pen down on the table emphatically. "That's all folks!"

The room broke into several conversations at once. Alan looked across at Robin who was scribbling notes furiously.

"Very well done to your chaps," breathed Barbara into his ear. Robin looked up at them.

"Alan – I must say this is a bit of a revelation. I am not sure I can take it all in at once, but I really have learned something this morning. When's the next one?"

"Err... next Friday."

"Bingo," said Barbara.

Getting Executive Help

As they streamed out of the room after the Technology session, Alan allowed himself a moment to bask in the glow of what they had started. Robin had been completely converted to the cause, so much so that Alan was beginning to worry about how to control Robin's enthusiasm.

Aside from attending the next session, Robin now wanted Alan to brief him on the overall plan for the project, and the whole Leopard concept again. Alan was quite happy to do this but adding it on top of his existing workload meant he was beginning to feel overwhelmed. He agreed to email Robin some suitable times as they exited the room, and then grabbed Sue and Jeff before they could head off.

"Lunch? Over the road? I'm buying," he said quietly.

"Where are you off to now?" queried Barbara, sensing an opportunity.

"You too if you want," said Alan.

"Me too?" queried Barbara

"Lunch. Over the road. I'm buying," repeated Alan. He was actually quite happy to have Barbara attend. She had helped get Robin on board, and her support would continue to be invaluable.

"Oh good! I just love that place!" Barbara enthused.

Friday lunchtime meant that the Bistro was pretty packed, but Alan charmed the manageress and got them pretty much the last table at the back of the restaurant. They chit-chatted until the food was ordered and as the waitress walked away, Alan decided to level with all of them. "Well how did you think that went?" he opened.

"What did you think Alan?" asked Jeff directly, as the session had been at Alan's request.

"I thought you and Ben did a superb job," replied Alan honestly. "I'd like to apologise for springing Robin on you."

"I'll say," added Jeff with a wry grin. Alan smiled back.

"I had to decide whether it was better to tell you beforehand or not," he responded. "I think you both reacted remarkably well."

"Well you could have at least told me!" Jeff's indignation was beginning to wane.

"Jeff it would hardly be fair for me to tell you and not Ben."

"I suppose."

"Anyway as I was saying. I thought you both did a really superb job. I must admit I didn't expect Robin to ask so many questions, but you both dealt with him really well."

"You do realise that as a result we both have to go round to his place and set up his storage system don't you?" Jeff hadn't quite finished.

"I do and I regard it as quite a coup," Alan smiled sardonically. "So you know that Barbara and I went to see Robin last Monday morning and walked him through the whole Leopard concept; this session was the try-out for him to see if he liked it."

"I know," Sue leant forward. "So what happens next?"

"Well he's put it on the minutes for next week's board meeting," replied Barbara.

"What we have asked for is to turn the project into a company-wide development programme."

"And he has agreed?" asked Jeff.

"Well he wanted to come to a session first, and that was today," answered Barbara. "I think you both did very well and I for one learned a lot."

"Me too," said Sue. "I must say I normally find technology and data very complicated. But I thought today was simple and well structured."

Jeff blushed a little. "Thanks guys," he muttered.

"So what do you see happening at the board meeting on Wednesday?" Alan asked Barbara.

"It's an agenda item so when it comes up, Robin will explain a little of the background and what he got out of the session today. Oh and by the way he will also have briefed Bill [the CEO] beforehand."

"So what will Robin recommend?" persisted Alan.

"He will look to me as someone who has been involved and would normally provide guidance," replied Barbara slowly.

"And?"

"Well I will suggest two things. Firstly that we have some more work to do to finish the concept. Secondly, we probably need to either submit or present a paper to the board when that's done." Barbara looked directly at Alan.

"I'm not stalling here – and you know I am a big supporter – but I think you need to polish the edges somewhat before you present at board level."

"I know, I know," said Alan. "Anyway whatever you agree, we will know by next Friday's session as Robin is now due to attend."

"Oh Robin will be there, have no worries," said Barbara.

"It's supposed to be me – perhaps with some external help – doing a session on meeting etiquette," said Alan.

"Yeah that was the one you were supposed to do this week," grinned Jeff.

"I know, I know," Alan waved his hand; "we'll get there." At that moment the food arrived and the conversation fragmented. When they had finished lunch, they wandered back to the office, separating at the front entrance with good wishes for the weekend ahead.

Jeff's mobile rang. He waved goodbye to the others and picked up the call.

A Dinner Date

"Hi Jeff. What happened to you at lunchtime?" It was Kate who was a little crestfallen not to have been included in the lunchtime gathering. Jeff felt guilty.

"Sorry Kate," he replied breezily, trying not to acknowledge the awkwardness he felt. "I got tied up. My fault entirely." As he was saying the words a further wave of regret washed over Jeff. While he had enjoyed the lunch, he was beginning to really like Kate, and yet he hadn't done anything about it. "So why not?" he asked himself. Before Kate had a chance to respond to his guilt-driven protestations, Jeff instinctively decided to do something.

"Actually Kate, forget lunchtime. What are you doing for dinner tonight?"

"Oh, I, err." Kate already had some informal plans for the evening, but Jeff's sudden change of tack had caught her completely off guard.

"Good. That's settled then. My treat to make up for lunch," finished Jeff, who was now on a roll. "7pm?"

"I...err... yes that would be lovely," Kate felt herself flush with excitement and emotion as all the feelings she'd had for Jeff since they had met at business school came flooding back. Why had he taken so long? Why was he always so aloof, and so maddeningly busy! Never mind, finally she was going to dinner with him.

"Let me work on a good restaurant this afternoon and I'll let you know," replied Jeff. "See you later!" He was also invigorated with his direct approach, which had surprised him almost as much as it had Kate. He hung up the call and then reflected back on his actions. Had he been a little hasty? I mean he really liked Kate but they worked together. Was this a smart move? I mean they had known each other since business school so it wasn't as if they had just met. But dating someone in the office? Were there company rules about this sort of thing? To hell with it! He liked Kate and it would be fun, he told himself. He scanned though his iPhone for Alfonso's, which was his favourite haunt. I'll never get in there, Jeff thought to himself, especially at this late hour – but hey let's give it a go!

Alfonso's was, as expected, full, but a little banter with the Maître D' got Jeff a table at 6.30pm prompt. He texted Kate: "Meet me 6.30pm at Alfonso's," and then had another moment of self-doubt. I have never been put with her on a date and yet I'm taking her to Alfonso's. Am I nuts? He wondered to himself. "Oh well, it's done now," he said out loud, to no one in particular.

Chapter Notes

Jeff's Personal Technology Strategy

- *Invest the time and do your research — make the most of understanding and using your technology.*

- *Smartphone — Search out the device that suits you best and if possible get one device for both home and office use.*

- *Laptop & PCs — unless you need the power, security or storage capacity of a desktop, find a laptop that is as small and light as possible as you have to carry it. If possible aim to have one laptop for both home and office use.*

- *Tablets — Do look at tablets and see if they will help but remember for most of them their strengths are email, reading documents and Internet browsing.*

- *Reduce the friction — add what you need to make it easier and as fast as possible. Pay for it yourself if you have to as it's your time saved.*

- *Do ask for help — find someone you know to help you with problems and training. Do pay for a specialist to help you if you need it— it will save you time in the long run.*

- *Renew your own technology together — try to refresh everything you have onto the same technology cycle.*

- *Get the best — when you do refresh, get the best technology you can afford. Technology cycles are short and buying the best helps extend the lifecycle and gives you better value.*

The Three Rules of Backup

1. *Treat both your professional and personal data with the same serious degree of respect.*

2. *Back everything up at least on a weekly basis if not daily.*

3. *Everything you have needs to be stored in at least three separate places.*

File Management & Versioning

1. *Damning with Faint Use — If you create a folder and don't put very much in it, it's probably time to delete it or archive it.*

2. *Divide and Conquer — If you create a folder you put a lot of things into and then can't find them, it's probably best to create some more sub folders and divide the topic.*

3. *Versioning — For every new version of a file, add an updated version number to it so you make sure you only work on the latest copy of a document. This avoids a lot of unnecessary hassle and wasted effort — particularly if you have a deadline to hit. It also means that if you have to go back to an idea which you earlier abandoned, that you have the original copy and have not deleted it.*

4. *Ownership – If you are sharing a document with other team members, add your initials at the end of the filename each time you make changes. It makes it really clear who was the last person to edit the document so you can accurately track multiple contributions.*

Example high level folders include:

- *Projects you are working on*
- *Clients you work with*
- *People you work with*
- *Teams you work with*
- *Industry topics you are interested in*
- *An admin folder for everything else including personal data*

The Three W's of Electronic Security

1. *Who? Don't send stuff to or from people you don't know well. Qualify them first and make sure you are sending or receiving documents that are approved and appropriate.*

2. *What? Think about what you are sending. Does it really need to be in writing and could you communicate it verbally? Is the information sensitive? In which case should it be communicated as a printout rather than something that could be forwarded electronically?*

3. *Where? Be careful what you leave lying around on your desk – or on your screen. Think who might be able to see it when they walk past.*

8

THE CELL-LIKE TEAM

Coffee Bar

Alan headed off to pick up a coffee in the Coffee Bar after lunch – a newly acquired habit. He was just getting his thought process around a macchiato he had ordered when he saw a colleague and friend he had not seen for a while striding though the lobby.

"Sam! Sam! Over here."

Sam was a senior sales director and Alan's peer. He was a suave and well-dressed man of indeterminate age. Alan reckoned he must be in his late forties, but his exceptional levels of personal fitness and immaculately fitting suits made it hard to tell. Alan was very fond of Sam but Sam was always on the move and rarely available for any lasting conversation.

"Hi Alan! How are you doing?"

"Got time for a coffee?" asked Alan.

Sam looked at his watch. "Yes, I do actually. That would be great."

They ordered Sam's coffee and settled back in a couple of chairs on the periphery of the Coffee Bar which was doing a roaring trade.

"I don't normally see you in here," stated Sam.

"Indeed you didn't. But you will now!"

"Ringing the changes are we?"

"I am indeed ringing the changes," replied Alan confidently. "In fact in some very radical ways. But never mind me; I haven't seen you for ages. What have you been up to?"

"Oh boy. There have been some radical things happening at my end. You are aware that there have been some departures in my area, aren't you?"

Alan nodded, "I heard. Hard to fathom out why but I am sure you had your reasons."

"Reasons? I wasn't given a lot of choice if truth be told. But that's life in sales I guess. We had to deal with some deep-rooted problems that frankly are not unique to this firm, but are very typical of sales departments pretty much everywhere. I feel a little naïve not to have seen it coming." Sam leaned forward and lowered his voice. "Typically in sales you get paid just enough to live on as a basic salary and you make up the rest through bonuses and commissions. It's a common way of doing things. Most companies try to put in a compensation system that drives the sales guys to leave no stone unturned in their drive to win new business," he paused for a second. "If however you have some smart and self-interested sales execs with a bit of an insular streak, they spend their time 'gaming' the bonus system to pay them the maximum without doing what's best for the client. Or for the company either. It's not that we were doing badly – in fact we were ahead of budget. But the behaviour was a ticking time bomb. We had to do something."

"Ah," said Alan. "I see. I never quite understood that was what it was all about," he peered closely at Sam. "But didn't you set-up the bonus system and hire most of those guys in the first place?" he added neutrally, aware that this must be a very sore point for Sam.

"Oh yeah, that was me," smiled Sam ruefully. "I actually offered Bill my resignation when all this blew up, but given that he also signed off on the original approach, we both agreed that I should stay and fix it."

"Wow. That must have been pretty stressful," said Alan.

Sam shook his head. "Not really. It goes with the territory," he said.

"So what are you doing now?" asked Alan.

"Well I spent a lot of time talking to clients and the sales people about what we were actually doing and I found a whole range of problems beneath the surface. There was no coordination. People were all doing their own thing. And that meant lots of duplication internally with different people visiting the same client on the same day without knowing about it. We had no training programme, no succession planning. We found that out when we let go several of the key offenders. So I have had to be pretty radical in my solution. And it seems to be really working."

"The first rule I imposed was to tell everyone that while they have individual responsibility, no one works as an individual any more. I decided that the whole department had to work as a series of small teams. Everyone had to be part of a team and contribute to that team rather than acting alone."

"That's very interesting," said Alan quietly. "Why?"

"Individual skills and contributions are vital but if we don't act collectively we neither act on our client's behalf or ultimately the company's. Individual behaviour is too unpredictable and large teams are too unwieldy to act quickly. So I chose what I have called the 'cell-like' team as the ideal model. Three is the minimum number of people and mostly the rule, although I do have some five man teams for larger accounts."

"Why three?" asked Alan.

"It's an incredibly efficient way of working. It provides an excellent level of client responsiveness and enables the team to operate at a higher level of detail. If on the other hand you make the team any smaller, for example a two man team, if one person leaves then the whole thing struggles as you no longer have a team."

Alan chuckled. "That's so true!" he exclaimed.

"So we still have a bonus scheme that rewards individual contribution, however now are balancing this with a similar one that rewards each team for their collective performance."

"And how would you say it is going so far?" asked Alan.

"Very positively indeed. Despite the departures, morale has returned and is much better than before. The numbers are up but much more importantly the clients are happier and are telling me so. Of course some of the initial team selections haven't worked that well so we have had to reshuffle, but that's to be expected."

"Has Barbara been involved in this process?" asked Alan curiously.

"Oh sure. She's been terrific!"

"Good," replied Alan leaned forward slightly conspiratorially. "Sam I have a big favour to ask. I am working with Barbara and a few others on a new project internally. We are looking at radical new ways of working. I am fascinated by what you have just described and I would love to have you come and tell us about it properly."

"Delighted Alan. The problem is when! I'm rolling the structure out to Europe next month and I have to finish all the preparation work and do the meetings for that next week."

"So you will be in the office then?" Alan skilfully interjected.

Sam sighed. "Yes I will be in the office."

"Friday 10am?"

"I'll check and let you know."

"Great. By the way Robin will be there."

"Will he now?" asked Sam, somewhat surprised.

"Yes indeed. He came to our technology session this morning."

"Technology? Do tell?" Sam had got up to leave but his curiosity was now heightened.

Alan reached into his jacket pocket and pulled out the handwritten note, which he had shown to Robin on Monday. "OK, so before I explain, would you agree that we operate in a fast moving, informal environment with few rules, where there is a price to pay for missing opportunities as well as a much more visible one for making mistakes?"

Sam laughed out loud. Several heads nearby tuned to see what the noise was about.

"Isn't that what we have just been chatting about for the last 15 minutes?"

"So the project that Barbara, myself and a few others have been working on is all about developing a new way of working. A new era of individual professionalism."

Sam peered at the piece of paper. "So what's all this about a Leopard?" he asked evenly.

"Well we reckon that the most desirable characteristics are very close to those of a leopard." Alan continued – "The leopard is one of nature's most successful predators, and its opportunistic approach maps well onto what we think needs to be done to move our game forward."

"And these are the related skills and knowledge areas on the right – correct?"

"Absolutely. So, as I said, we just did the first session on Technology this morning; I'll get Ben and Jeff to send you the notes."

"Hmm," said Sam. "And right below Technology is Teamwork. OK I see. How much material do you have? What's going to be happening with all this?"

"Quite a lot. Except it's not terribly well structured right now," replied Alan.

"Looks pretty organised to me," interrupted Sam.

"Thanks. As for next steps it's going to the board next Wednesday. The aim is to get approval to develop it into a formal training programme."

"Well that should be easy if you have Barbara's backing."

"Not necessarily so. Robin thought I was going nuts when we first showed it to him."

"Well I think it's really interesting. If possible I would like to see what I can incorporate into the new sales training programme."

"Deal," said Alan. "Trade you for the teamwork section!"

"Done," said Sam. They stood and shook hands.

Distraction

As they rose to walk out the rays of the afternoon sun shone through the glass of the entrance foyer, a tall cavernous space now packed with people arriving and leaving but mainly frequenting the Coffee Bar.

Suddenly there was a commotion by the security gate. The crowd parted as a tall, elegant woman walked through the assembled crowd. She was wearing a mid-length but relatively low cut black dress displaying her ample cleavage, as well as a pair of outrageous high heels which clicked rhythmically across the floor. The crowd in the Coffee Bar fell silent. The men gaped and the women studiously ignored her. She brushed past Alan and Sam without a word and continued to stride purposefully down the hallway in a piece of short but very memorable theatre.

"Who exactly is that?" murmured Alan.

"She," replied Sam, "is Rafaella."

"Oh? You know her?"

"I do. She's a senior executive at one of our best clients."

"But she just walked past without a word," Alan looked at Sam quizzically.

"That's Rafaella for you." Sam shrugged, giving nothing away.

"Oh," said Alan.

"A word of warning: she's trouble."

"Really?" asked Alan who, despite himself, was looking after her departing figure.

"Trust me."

"OK fine," said Alan. His curiosity was heightened but his sense of tact kicked in. Subject closed for now. But he did wonder.

Dinner With Kate

Jeff arrived early at Alfonso's. He checked in with the Maître'D and made sure that the table he had booked was up to scratch. He decided to wait at the bar. Jeff was feeling nervous which was unusual for him – as an eligible bachelor, he was used to dinner dates, but he was simply too busy to take dating very seriously. In truth he had never seriously thought about having a proper girlfriend, it just got in the way of work and his outdoor pursuits. Although he had known Kate for several years, having made the decision to ask her out for dinner, he was desperately keen to make sure that the evening was a success.

Kate was about 10 minutes late, by which time Jeff was actively fidgeting with anything he could find on the bar. She was wore a stunning long dress which floated around her. Jeff slid off the barstool and greeted her warmly with an uncharacteristically clumsy embrace. Kate managed to contain her surprise, but at the same time all her uncertainly about the evening faded away.

"Shall we?" gestured Jeff and they moved through the restaurant towards the table. As they walked, they passed a full length mirror and Jeff caught a quick glimpse of them both. He paused to admire the view for a second. Kate was suddenly aware that he was no longer with her, turned and also saw the mirror. She looked back at Jeff.

"What are you doing?" she said with a smile at the corners of her mouth.

Jeff grinned sheepishly. "I was just thinking what a great looking couple we are," he said. There, it was out.

As Kate walked back towards him, she reached out and squeezed his hand. "Thank you," she said simply. "I'm so pleased that you invited me, we never get the chance to spend time together alone."

Jeff gazed back directly into her eyes and smiled. "I am only sorry that we didn't do this ages ago," he replied.

Monday Morning

Alan had a restless weekend. Even though he wasn't playing golf, a series of prolonged downpours kept him cooped up in the house. He'd been thinking about Sam's ideas and although excited, he was now quite concerned that they might not transfer across fully to what they'd been working on. First thing Monday morning, he picked up the phone and called Sam.

"Sam? Hi, Alan here. Hope you had a good weekend… Yes, apart from the wretched rain… Listen could you and I spend 30 minutes having a chat before Friday's session? I know you are very tied up this week but I do think it's vital. 5.30pm today? Thanks so much." Alan was concerned on two fronts. Firstly that everyone would dismiss Sam's thinking as a 'sales' issue rather than something that had a wider purpose. His second interest was to clearly identify the areas that linked Sam's teamwork ideas to the overall Leopard concept.

Alan had just got off the phone with Sam when Robin called, full of enthusiasm. "Good morning Alan, hope you had a good weekend."

Alan implied he'd had a good weekend but before he could go further Robin got straight to the point.

"What's on the agenda for Friday?"

"Ah – glad you asked. Friday's session will be about teamwork. I think you will enjoy this one."

"Any particular reason why?"

Alan smiled. "It complements work we are already doing."

"Good stuff," said Robin before ringing off.

"I hope so," thought Alan.

Monday Morning Behind the Bike Sheds

The weather was simply glorious. So much so that Jeff decided to cycle in early.

He was locking his bike in the yard behind the office, when he suddenly felt the presence of someone else. Sure enough he looked round and there was the black cat.

"And how are we this morning?" asked the cat.

"Pretty damn good actually," replied Jeff.

"Anything to do with dinner with a certain young lady on Friday evening?" asked the cat.

"How the hell did you know about that?" asked Jeff who was

incredulous as he had been very discrete in organising the meal. Then he remembered he was talking to the cat. "Of course you would know about that," he muttered, being facetious. Then he paused for a second.

"You are always full of advice, especially about cycling gear," he said. "Any wisdom you care to share?"

"I refer you to the characteristics of a Leopard," replied the cat evenly.

"What has that got to do with it?" asked Jeff.

"Last time we spoke you told me you had just looked them up."

"I had," Jeff started to say, looking up. But the cat had gone. He shook his head and went inside to change out of his cycling clothes.

He had 5 minutes to kill before he was due to meet the gang for a coffee, so he pulled up the Leopard characteristics on his laptop. "Well it's not adapting to any environment or acting opportunistically. It's certainly not operating at speed" he grinned to himself. "So I guess it must be driving any activity to a chosen conclusion or remaining almost undetected. Or maybe both." He snapped the laptop shut. "Well I am certainly going to remain undetected on this one."

Coffee Bar

Kate was already at the Coffee Bar when Jeff arrived. They greeted each other casually and as Jeff went to get the coffees, she wandered over. "I had such a great time on Friday," she said with a secret smile playing around her mouth.

"Me too," grinned Jeff.

"I do think we need to keep it from the office vultures," she added, all serious all of a sudden.

"I agree with you totally," said Jeff. "I'll text you later and we'll make a plan." He handed Kate her coffee and suddenly they were both all business again.

Rendez Vous

Alan knocked at Sam's door at 5.30pm promptly. He was conscious of the limited time that Sam had this week and the need to prepare properly for Friday's session.

"Hello? Come in. Hi Alan. Please grab a seat."

Despite Sam's very neat personal appearance his office was in a state of disarray – and indeed Sam was not at his eloquent best in his shirtsleeves. "Sorry I've been in since 7am this morning. It's been chaos."

"No problem. Sorry for stealing more of your precious time. Two things I wanted to talk about. The first is to focus Friday on the purely teamwork aspects of what you are doing and avoid the compensation issues. I do understand that the compensation issues are a massive component of your brief, but I want to see how we can use your thinking on a wider basis."

Sam nodded. "That's fine. So, what do you suggest?"

"Can you go through the structure in a little more detail so I can understand it better?" asked Alan.

"Sure. There are five key principles in what I have implemented so far. As you know, the First Principle is that while everyone has individual responsibility, no one works alone."

"Got that," said Alan. "It makes sense and is very transferrable."

"The Second Principle is that the three person team is the standard for three good reasons: client responsiveness, efficiency, and operating detail."

"Interesting," said Alan. "That actually still applies except I suspect I might change the word client and replace it with relationship."

"Sorry I don't understand?" queried Sam.

"If you look across the company aside from your division, some people have external relationships, some have internal ones and some have a mixture of both."

"OK I get it."

"One further question though. What do you think would happen if you increased the team from three to four people?"

Sam chuckled. "That's an easy one. Sure you can do more with an extra person, but you double the number of internal relationships within the team. With three people you have three relationships that have to work. Adding one more person doubles that to six. It's unwieldy and increases the chances of tension and disagreement – in my humble opinion!"

"I hadn't thought about it like that," confessed Alan.

"The Third Principle is about team roles. There are three team roles, Senior, Associate and Administrator."

The Roles in a Cell-Like Team

- *The Senior's role is to guide and manage the team, provide the thinking, drive the planning and take responsibility for progress against the plan.*

- *The Associate's role is to contribute to the thinking, execute most of the plan and to do the actual reporting against the plan.*

- *The Administrator's role is simply to reduce the day-to-day friction of the team – to organise travel, meetings, preparation, communications and administration.*

"The thinking for this principle is to support the Senior guys in doing what they do best, challenge the next level of people to support them and take the lead whenever possible and finally to have the whole thing very professionally organised and very well run."

"You have an Administrator for every team? I am amazed that you had got the sign off for the head-count!" exclaimed Alan.

"Not yet but we will do. A number of teams share the

Administrator role right now but that will change. We are recruiting several new positions right now."

"How in hell's name did you get sign off for that?"

"Ah glad you asked. It's very simple, I cheated!" Sam grinned mischievously.

"It's all in the career progression. If I was just asked to hire executive assistants with no further role progression then I would have been shot down, no argument. What I'm doing is hiring Administrators from the junior graduate programme and other recruitment sources where people have not had sales training or experience but do have good customer facing skills. The objective from day one is that if we take them on as an Administrator, we aim to promote them to an Associate programme within two years, and if they do well to a Senior within five years. Sales roles always have a high degree of turnover, and this approach provides a pipeline of new talent along with the continuity within a team."

"What a good idea," said Alan. He thought for a moment. "How can you expect to progress people from such humble beginnings to such a senior role within such short timescales? I mean normally you would need ten years to reach such a senior level."

Sam smiled. "The team structure accelerates their learning and assimilation of knowledge," he replied. "If these people want to get their promotion, they have to pass a series of interviews and assessments that are set by Barbara, myself and several other folks including their team members."

"So what if they have someone within their team that they don't get on with?"

"That's one of the risks we face. But I must say so far it's been pretty obvious," replied Sam. "If you work together in an open plan office, it's pretty clear which teams work well and which teams don't. And that brings me neatly to the Fourth Principle. It's what I call 'Drive Progress through Challenge, not by Objective'."

Sam continued: "As a department, we are normally given a set of objectives for the year. Some of these objectives are client related, some of these are individual and others are team based. I know you didn't want to talk about compensation packages, but this is how we used to do it. I spend time with the Senior from each team who will negotiate the objective with me after I give it to them. When we are agreed, he or she will also divide the objectives amongst each team member and then return the final document to me and it goes into the formal HR Appraisal process."

"Part of the objectives is all the usual reporting – weekly monthly and quarterly – quarterly being the point at which we might change or add something if we need to do so. This is all pretty vanilla stuff, its complicated, time consuming and although it all goes into our 'Balanced Scorecard', I think pretty much everyone hated the process, including me. So I'm replacing it with something much simpler. I have asked the board to give the department no more than six high level challenges for the year. I am then going to take the challenges to the teams and ask them each to write a detailed plan of how they as a team are going to rise to the challenges."

Alan was scribbling away on a pad. "Thanks Sam. That makes sense and actually fits quite neatly. Take a look at this." Alan slid the diagram of Creative versus Functional across the table. "This is the work we did to illustrate how people approach time and how their personality types divide accordingly. In short Creative Time is about lateral thinking and ideas; Functional Time is about getting things done. People naturally fall into one or the other approach, hence the diagram to illustrate the benefits and shortcomings."

Sam started at the diagram for a long time. Eventually he spoke, "I have done quite a lot of exercises on this area over the years. But what you are suggesting looks really simple. Maybe too simple?" he countered.

"Maybe," replied Alan. "But to get everyone – and I mean everyone – engaged, it has to be really simple."

"So what's the ideal scenario here?" asked Sam, leaning back in his chair and putting his arms behind his head.

"I'm not entirely sure yet," responded Alan. "I mean I think we have figured out some of the basic issues. My instincts tell me that the first step is to make people aware of which type they are and to recognise the instinctive behaviour of that type."

"I suspect that the second step is to train them in the opposite behaviour – to take them out of the comfort zone; and the third and final step is to help them find a way to balance both behaviours so that they can use them whenever appropriate."

"So if I'm looking at your team structure," continued Alan. "I would assume that the Senior is definitely a Creative, the Associate can be either and the Administrator is probably Functional."

"Then again those characteristics could be reversed at each stage," countered Sam. "And actually it wouldn't matter as long as the team was balanced!"

"Exactly!" exclaimed Alan. He paused for a moment to think.

"In fact your team structure could drive the entire Creative/Functional learning process. And if you add your Fourth Principle, Driving Progress through Challenge not by Objective, then you have a great motivation that drives the learning process from the outset."

Alan sat back in the chair. "This is really great stuff," he enthused. "In fact I think this is the missing link."

"Steady on," said Sam.

"Sam, I'm serious. I've got to thank you. By the way, what is the Fifth Principle?"

"Ah, I thought that you would never ask. I actually pinched it from the Boy Scouts: Fun, Action and Adventure."

"You are kidding?"

"I am not. It has got to be fun otherwise no one is going to do it. Action because it's all about getting things done, and adventure because it should also be about the new and the unexplored. Oh and I think these are great principles for life in general."

Alan nodded, "I like your ambition Sam."

"Me too!"

Wednesday Afternoon

Alan had spent all day Wednesday visiting a major customer. It had been an intense day of presentations and planning and he was so preoccupied that the board meeting had slipped his mind. He picked up a voicemail from Barbara on the way home and suddenly he was agog to know what had happened. He called her right away.

"How did it go?" he asked before even issuing a greeting to Barbara.

"Good afternoon to you too!"

"Sorry, been wrapped up all day."

"Haven't we all?" retorted Barbara with just a hint of irony. "Robin was very enthusiastic and I didn't have to say much. I am not sure he understands exactly what we are trying to do but he does understand the opportunity to improve. The changes in Sales have helped to pave the way. The long and short of is that you have the green light to continue with the Friday sessions and an invite to the next board meeting – probably next month."

"That's brilliant news! Thank you Barbara."

"One word of caution, Bill is still neutral on this and could easily go the other way. We should brief him personally."

"Thanks again – good point."

Friday

After the positive output from the board meeting, Alan had organised a bigger meeting room for the Friday session, which had turned out to be a fortuitous move as the room was half full when he and Sam arrived. It was a modern theatre-style space, well lit but without the glass outlook of the smaller rooms.

Barbara was already there and was busy working the room. He couldn't see Robin.

Sam stood up and the room went quiet in anticipation. "Unlike most sales folk I only have one slide for this session." There were a few good-natured chuckles. "However true to form I am going to talk a lot. For reasons that I will not go into in detail, we have recently completely changed the nature of how we work together as a team. The main driving force behind this change was to radically improve our collective relationship with our clients."

"Having spoken with Alan and others at length, the principles used would seem to have value throughout the business. There are five principles to our approach and the core idea is to create what we call cell-like teams which are a number of autonomous small groups that are far more effective than the sum of their parts."

Sam tapped his laptop and pulled up a slide onto the screen.

The Five Principles of the Cell-Like Team

1. *Everyone has individual responsibility, no one works alone.*

2. *The three person team is the standard for three good reasons: client responsiveness, efficiency and operating detail.*

3. *There are three team roles, Senior, Associate and Administrator:*

   a. *The Senior's role is to guide and manage the team, provide the thinking, drive the planning and take responsibility for the progress against the plan.*
   b. *The Associate's role is to contribute to the thinking, execute most of the plan and report progress against the plan.*

   c. *The Administrator's role is simply to reduce the day to day friction of the team — to organise*

201

travel, meetings, preparation, communications and administration.

4. *Drive Progress through Challenge, not by Objective.*

5. *Fun, Action and Adventure.*

He continued: "The First Principle is that everyone has individual responsibility: no one works alone. This doesn't change the individual's responsibilities in terms of actions and commitments. But it does mean that they get shared within the team so if someone is struggling or unable to deliver, the team can cover it."

"The Second Principle is around the three-person team which is the standard for three good reasons: client responsiveness, efficiency and operating detail."

"Why three people?" asked Sue. "Why not two?"

"Two people can easily form a good team, but what happens if one of them leaves or is away on holiday? Then there is no team any more. Three people solve this problem with the minimal number of internal relationships."

"So why not four?"

"Think about it: if you add one more person to a three person team you double the number of internal team relationships. It can work with four or even five man teams, but three is the magic number. I should also add that client responsiveness applies to internal clients as well as external clients."

"How do you mean?" asked Ben.

"I mean that a cell-like team should aim to manage internal relationships in the same way as client relationships."

"Interesting," said Ben. "Having never worked in sales, I am not sure I know what a client relationship looks like."

"It's mainly about making sure you deliver to people's needs and manage their expectations accordingly," interjected Alan, who didn't want Sam to get side-tracked by Ben.

Ben nodded, "OK thanks," he said. Alan was surprised at this response, he wondered if Ben was perhaps becoming a little more subdued?

"The Third Principle is that there are three team roles, Senior, Associate and Administrator. Let's start with the Senior. The Senior's main role is to lead the team rather than manage it. The Senior should set the direction, drive the planning and take responsibility for progress against the plan."

"Why not manage the team? I mean in that case who manages the team?" asked Jeff.

"This is the radical part. The team should really manage itself."

"So how does that work exactly?"

"The team works that out independently. Basically we are treating them like grown-ups and letting them figure it out for themselves."

"Huh! That is pretty radical," replied Jeff.

"OK next is the Associate role which contributes to the thinking, executes most of the plan and reports progress against the plan. The best way to think of this role is as understudy or deputy for the Senior or team leader. Finally the Administrator's role is simply to reduce the day-to-day friction of the team – to organise travel, meetings, preparation, communications and administration. This could sound quite mundane but actually it's vital to drive the efficiency of the team."

"A really good Administrator can make the team incredibly slick and productive. There are a number of personal benefits such as clear career progression and career development and learning in each team. From the company perspective, there is also good succession planning structure in place which means we don't lose critical client relationships when an individual leaves."

"So how do you get promoted from being a Senior?" asked Jeff.

"You get to set up a team to run a group of teams."

"I thought you said there really wasn't any management?"

"There isn't. It's really about leadership and aligning with the company objectives."

"But surely that means management?" persisted Jeff.

"This leads me neatly onto the Fourth Principle, which is to drive progress through challenge, not by objective. By challenging the leader of each team to respond to an issue, rather than issuing objectives, it gives them the space and responsibility to lead."

"The Fifth Principle, I happen to think, is the most important: Fun, Action and Adventure. It also happens to be the motto of the Boy Scouts." There was some animated amusement in the room. "It means that working in the team should be fun, the action part is about getting things done and adventure is all about trying new things, stretching yourself and innovating."

"That's pretty much it folks – over to Alan."

There was a ripple of applause from the audience and Alan stood and moved to the front of the room. "Thanks Sam, that was really useful. I want to take us off on a separate path for a few minutes, but I shall return," he said looking directly at Robin who had slipped in late and was sitting at the back of the room.

"I would like to put it to you that people generally divide into two distinct types: those who are great at getting things done and those who are great at ideas and solving problems. Occasionally there are people who are great at doing both, but most people excel at one or the other."

"However everyone who is naturally one type or the other faces a challenge when they need to exhibit the opposite behaviour. For example even those with the best ideas have to wash the dishes!" Some humorous appreciation followed. "So the challenge for the naturally Functional person is what I call 'The Search for Lateral Thinking' which is the ability to take an alternative approach to problem solving. For the Creative type person, it is 'The Struggle for Discipline' which is all about focusing on what needs to be done and not being distracted by other new ideas."

Alan put up a summary slide:

Creative Versus Functional

- *Functional people are brilliant at bringing structure and order to things, executing tasks and making plans.*

- *Functional people struggle with making the leap and approaching something from an alternative perspective.*

- *Creative people are able to look at things differently and solve problems that seem simple with hindsight but need inspiration.*

- *Creative people struggle to prioritise their creativity and often don't have the patience to work through tasks thoroughly.*

Robin stirred himself. His patience was running low. "Alan, this is fascinating, but how does it relate back to the team structure Sam was talking about?"

"I am coming to that right now," replied Alan. "Is everyone OK with this?"

"Isn't this just the same as 'left-brain / right brain'?" asked Ben.

"Similar. Except that most people wouldn't be able to tell you which side of the brain does what! The idea is to make these dominant characteristics recognisable to everyone, which I think they are. The reason this is really important becomes clear when I take you back to the three roles in the cell-like team that we discussed earlier. To make the team work you have to get a good balance of Creative and Functional personalities."

"Aha indeed!" interrupted Robin, who then became aware that everyone was looking at him. "Sorry Alan."

"Once you as an individual have recognised your dominant

personality type, your one challenge is to balance both your behaviours so that you can switch when you need to. The cell-like team really helps that challenge because it naturally balances your dominant behaviour as well as providing the opportunity to learn the naturally opposite behaviour from people who are dominant in the opposite type. Does that make sense?" Several heads nodded.

"So given we haven't yet been reorganised like Sam's team, how do we go about organising ourselves in cell-like teams?" asked Jeff thoughtfully.

"I thought you might ask," replied Alan. "Here's how it works:"

Creating your own Cell-Like Team

1. Understand whether your behaviour is predominantly Creative or Functional.

2. Look for a project to apply it to – this may be one of your own projects or it may be someone else's project that needs help.

3. Work out which one of the three roles you would naturally play in that project.

4. Identify who could play the other roles and see if you can co-opt them in to help. As a rule, Administrators can generally help or work on several teams.

5. Always remember the Fifth Principle – Fun, Action and Adventure.

Jeff read the slide and laughed. "That's not far off how we have been working on the Leopard project anyway," he exclaimed. "You, Sue and I have ended up trading roles."

"I know! Fascinating isn't it?" replied Alan.

"Ah yes the Leopard," boomed Robin. "Very keen to see how that fits in."

"Well Teamwork is all about driving a chosen activity to a given conclusion – or in Leopard terms hunting down and killing your chosen prey…"

"Oh now I see…"

"Anyway, that's it everyone," concluded Alan, "I would like to thank Sam for putting this session together on top of everything else that is going on."

There was a brief round of applause and the meeting began to break up.

"Thanks Alan, I hope that was useful," began Sam.

"That was spot on," responded Alan enthusiastically. "This organisation badly needs to follow the lead you have taken," he stopped, aware that he was being rather dogmatic and that Robin was watching him with some amusement.

"Why do you say that?" Robin asked with good humour.

Alan sighed. "Honestly Robin," he replied candidly, "the time when we dictate to our people to do what we tell them as an organisation is finished. It's time we asked our people to band together and help us work out what we need to do instead."

"You really believe that don't you?" smiled Robin.

"Actually I do," replied Alan earnestly.

"I think you may well be right."

Chapter Notes

The Five Principles of the Cell-Like Team

1. *Everyone has individual responsibility, no one works alone.*

2. *The three person team is the standard for three good reasons — client responsiveness, efficiency, and operating detail.*

3. *There are three team roles: Senior, Associate and Administrator.*

   a. *The Senior's role is to guide and manage the team, provide the thinking, drive the planning and take responsibility for the progress against the plan.*

   b. *The Associate's role is to contribute to the thinking, execute most of the plan and report progress against the plan.*

   c. *The Administrator's role is simply to reduce the day to day friction of the team — to organise travel, meetings, preparation, communications and administration.*

4. *Drive Progress through Challenge, not by Objective.*

5. *Fun, Action and Adventure.*

Creative versus Functional

- *Functional people are brilliant at bringing structure and order to things, executing tasks and making plans.*

- *Functional people struggle with making the leap and approaching something from an alternative perspective.*

- *Creative people are able to look at things differently and solve problems that seem simple with hindsight but need inspiration.*

- *Creative people struggle to prioritise their creativity and often don't have the patience to work through tasks thoroughly.*

Creating your own Cell-Like Team

1. *Work out whether you are predominantly Creative or Functional.*

2. *Look for a project to apply it to – this may be one of your own projects or it may be someone else's project that needs help.*

3. *Work out which one of the three roles you would naturally play in that project.*

4. *Identify who could play the other roles and see if you can co-opt them in to help. As a rule, Administrators can generally help or work on several teams.*

5. *Always remember the Fifth Principle – Fun, Action and Adventure.*

9

THE MEETING

Call to Action

At the end of the Team session, Alan decided to call a council of war the following Monday afternoon. After they had agreed a time, he avoided the now customary Friday lunch at the Bistro and returned to his office. While he was exhilarated about Sam's session on the Cell-Like Team, he knew he had to keep the momentum going. He picked up the telephone and called John. John was in a meeting, but his assistant promised Alan that he would call back, and sure enough about 20 minutes later the phone rang.

"Hi John. Hope things are good with you?" and when John indicated that they were, Alan plunged right in. "Do you remember the session we had talked about you doing on meetings? I think we had pencilled in next Friday as a possible date. Will that still work?" asked Alan hopefully.

"Well to be frank it had quite slipped my mind," replied John, there was the sound of a keyboard clacking on the other end of the line as John pulled his calendar up on the screen. "Funnily enough, though, I still have it in the diary. There are a couple of other things in there too. Do you need me to do it next Friday?" John paused and there were a few moments of silence.

"It would be great if you could still do it," replied Alan.

"Delighted to, old boy, but I will need to move the other things around," replied John. "How exactly do you want me to deliver this?"

"I'll tell you over golf tomorrow," replied Alan.

Golf on Saturday

As Alan and John stood on the first tee, the mist which was shrouding the course began to clear and the sun began to peer through. They both hit straight drives onto the fairway and after collecting their clubs strode off purposefully. Alan certainly felt very relaxed and for once they were both playing consistently. On the fourth hole John eventually decided to address the subject at hand. "So I'm intrigued by the session next Friday, but I really have no idea how you want me to approach it," he began.

"Well, you chair at least three major boards that I know about," replied Alan. "That says to me that you know as much about driving successful meetings as anyone. The Friday sessions we have been running so far last for at least an hour, sometimes more," he continued. "We have a subject matter expert who walks through the topic under discussion and then we follow up with a pretty wide-ranging question and answer session."

"So how do you think I should approach it?" enquired John.

"If it were me I would approach it as though it were a normal board or committee type meeting," suggested Alan. "I know it's an educational session but you could treat it like a normal meeting and then explain each step of the process."

"Let me think about that," mused John. He was silent and thoughtful for most of the next hole, and then as he sunk his putt, he walked over to Alan.

"Got it!" he exclaimed, "Here's what I want you to do."

Monday Morning

As soon as he got to the office on Monday, Alan checked his email and sure enough there was the note from John, who was brief and succinct:

> *Alan,*
> *Please find below an agenda for Friday's meeting. Please can you:*
>
> *1. Add the room details.*
> *2. Distribute to the relevant people inside your firm.*
> *3. Ask them to confirm their attendance.*
>
> *I will arrive just before 9.30 am and look forward to seeing you all then.*
> *John*

Alan looked at the agenda and smiled, this was going to be fun. He made the change that John had asked for, added a line with John's background, and then attached the agenda to an electronic invitation. Alan quickly phoned Barbara, who was in a meeting so he left a voice message. "Barbara, hi it's Alan here. You should have Friday's meeting invite and agenda. Please can you forward to all those who attended the last session plus anyone else you think should come and ask them to respond. Thanks."

He looked at the agenda again. It was intriguing:

> *The Enduring Value of A Properly Run Meeting*
> *Friday 25th October, 10am to 11am*
>
> *Chair: John Abercrombie*
> *Venue: Room 101*
> *Attendees: To be confirmed*

1. *Types of meetings (5 mins)*
2. *Stimulating Progress (5 mins)*
3. *The Purpose of an Agenda (5 mins)*
4. *The Role of the Chair (5 mins)*
5. *Gaining agreement / driving progress (5 mins)*
6. *7 Deadly Sins that Blight the Meeting Landscape (20 mins)*

   i. *Lateness*
   ii. *Not Paying Attention*
   iii. *Lack of Preparation*
   iv. *Disruption*
   v. *Disagreements*
   vi. *Following up & actions*
   vii. *Tracking Progress*

7. *Side Benefits (5 mins)*
8. *The Two Meeting Rule (5 mins)*
9. *Questions & Answers (5 mins)*

The First Moment of Regret

Jeff was in some distress on Monday morning. Following his every successful date with Kate the previous weekend, they had both managed to keep everything under wraps at work the following week. They had planned to spend the second weekend together, and everything had been going brilliantly, indeed Kate had stayed over Friday night. They had a wonderful day on Saturday and another great evening.

On Sunday morning, as usual, Jeff had got out of bed and into his cycling gear without really thinking about it. It was what he did every weekend without fail.

"Where are you going darling?" he could hear Kate's sleepy voice enquiring.

"Bike training. I've got a triathlon in 3 weeks," he grunted.

"Oh. What time will you be back?"

"Sometime this afternoon."

"Oh."

He had thought no more about it, but when he got back Kate was gone. No note, no phone message. Nothing. Jeff was filled with self-recrimination, "I really could have missed a week's training," he thought to himself miserably. Now he had to face Kate at work on Monday morning. Sure enough as he strode through the lobby towards the Coffee Bar, Kate was sitting there with the usual group.

"Calm and polite," he reminded himself. "But seriously where do I stand?"

Kate returned his greeting neutrally. She was furious with Jeff and also herself. She had known Jeff for a long time and had built up a very specific image of him in her mind. She wasn't quite sure whether she was angry because she felt let down and abandoned when he had disappeared, or because she had opened herself up to him and ended up feeling very hurt. Either way she was adamant that she was not going to speak to him until he apologised, although she hadn't yet worked out how she was going to deal with it when they had to work together. Jeff got his coffee and with the minimum of greetings headed off upstairs. Round one was over.

Friday Morning

John was as good as his word and at 9.25am on Friday morning he walked through the front door into Reception. Stylishly dressed in an impeccable Savile Row suit with Church's shoes, he strode purposefully across the floor, filled with energy.

"I say – nice suit John," commented Alan as they shook hands warmly. "Mind you I would have expected nothing less!"

John smiled. "Important to look the part on any day – but particularly today," he replied.

Alan introduced Barbara and they moved across the lobby to the Coffee Bar.

"Good coffee, thank you" noted John as he sipped his cappuccino. "Does anybody actually get any work done with this place here?" he gestured to the Coffee Bar.

"You would be surprised," responded Alan. "It's fantastic for bumping into people and also as a place to have a 'one-to-one.'"

"I am not sure I am familiar with a 'one-to-one,'" replied John amicably.

"Oh sorry that's just our own internal expression for a face to face meeting," added Barbara. "It's not part of the formal HR manual but meeting someone down here for a short chat has become an integral part of the culture here. I agree it's very informal, but it has worked very well."

"I suppose I am a little old fashioned," commented John. "So this must be your equivalent of my 'having a quiet word' with someone."

"Exactly," responded Alan, "the difference here is that there is a natural place to do it inside the building."

"Hmm – that's an interesting idea."

The Enduring Value of A Properly Run Meeting

When they arrived in the room, the furniture had been reconfigured into a 'U' shape so that everyone could sit at the table.

"Thank you Alan, that's perfect," added John as he moved to the Chairman's seat in the middle of the 'U'. Alan watched him intently as he went through his preparation routine: pulling out his notebook and MontBlanc pen, removing his watch and arranging them in front of him. John pulled out a pair of rimless spectacles, put them on and then turned to Alan.

"Do you have the copies of the agenda?" he asked. "Also the attendee list?"

Alan dug them out and handed them over. "I still don't understand why you needed the attendee list?" he commented.

John smiled. "I don't really, it's just to make a point," he responded. "How many seats do we have?" he peered over his spectacles at the room.

"We have eighteen attendees on the list and the room holds twenty five," replied Alan.

"I'll distribute the agendas," said Barbara helpfully.

"Thank you both," replied John crisply.

The room had begun to fill up. Alan heaved a big sigh of relief when Robin arrived in good time. Robin came straight over to welcome John who greeted him warmly.

Getting Started

At 10.00am precisely, John looked over at Barbara. "Please would you be kind enough to close the door?"

"OK. But should we not wait a few minutes for latecomers?" replied Barbara without thinking.

"No. Thank you. A 10.00am start is a 10.00am start," said John precisely.

Barbara blushed and mentally kicked herself. John was after all a very senior and very experienced professional. She wondered what would happen to the inevitable latecomers and she didn't have long to wait. Before she had even sat down, the door opened and two heads popped round. It was Ben and Kate. Jeff winced in anticipation.

"Good morning!" said John. "Can I help you?"

"Err, we're here for the meeting session," began Ben, a little confused.

"Well this is the right place," replied John. "And your name is?"

"Ben."

"I'm Kate."

"Well Ben and Kate, the meeting began at 10.00am," replied John mildly. He peered at the list in front of him, "are you both on the invitation?"

"Oh yes," replied Kate, relieved that she had done something right.

Ben hesitated, "well I normally come to these sessions," he said lamely.

John looked at the list. "Well I don't see a Ben down here," he added mildly. "Never mind, do please take a seat."

Ben and Kate had just got settled when the door opened again.

"Good morning!" said John again. "Can I help you?" The rest of the room couldn't help themselves and a murmur of amusement ran round as a couple more people slipped in. John smiled. He was making his point very effectively.

When the next two interrupters had sat down, he began. "Good morning all, my name is John Abercrombie. While some of you will know me, I believe Alan put a little background on the meeting invitation. You should all have a copy of the agenda I prepared," he scanned the room. "Yes? Good!"

Types of Meeting

"You will note from the agenda that I have nominated myself as the chair of this meeting. This is a role I am very familiar with as I chair the board of several major corporations. However whether it's a board meeting, a routine department meeting or a gathering of a social club, unless a meeting is chaired effectively it is nearly often a waste of everyone's time."

"I will come back to my role in a moment but before we begin, I wanted to ask you all what sort of meetings you have today and why you have them?"

There was moments silence and then Jeff spoke up. "Weekly review meetings," he began, "for tracking progress on the projects I'm working on."

"Good, thank you," said John scribbling on his notepad.

"One-to-one's," added a voice at the back. John lifted one eyebrow in his theatrical fashion.

"For managing my direct reports," added the voice.

"Management team meeting."

"Marketing meetings, customer meetings, sales briefings" the suggestions flowed in.

After a minute or so John brought the flow of suggestions to a halt. "Thank you all." He looked down at his notes. "If I look at this list I believe I can divide your suggestions into two distinct groups – meetings where there are open discussions and those that are designed to drive and monitor progress. Is that fair?" He looked round and several heads nodded in agreement. "If you look up the definition of a meeting in the Oxford English Dictionary, it describes a meeting as an 'assembly of people for a particular purpose.' While I think we can agree about the 'assembly of people' part," there were several chuckles at this point, "the 'purpose' of meetings has, in my humble opinion, rarely been considered properly before many meetings are held. Is that a fair comment?"

There was a murmur in the room, then Ben of all people spoke out.

"I would definitely agree with you, but sometimes we don't have a lot of choice. We have to attend anyway."

"Oh indeed. But that doesn't excuse the meeting from lacking purpose, does it?" smiled John.

"A poorly planned meeting is a travesty on any organisation, public or private. Aside from the direct consequences in people's wasted time, there is the opportunity cost of something more productive that could have been done with the time instead, and finally there is the risk of disengagement and negative sentiment arising from a poorly run event. In short it is an expensive disaster."

"What do you mean by disengagement and negative sentiment?" asked Barbara leaning forward.

"Well after a poorly run internal meeting, in my experience people often begin to question why they work for an organisation that wastes their time and talent, to be blunt. My personal rule number one is that a formal meeting should only be convened if there is no other way to stimulate progress."

Stimulating Progress

"So how else can you stimulate progress?" asked Alan earnestly.

"Well that depends on the people and issues, but I find that speaking to the right people individually, whether by phone or in 'one-to-one's' as you describe them can often resolve things without having to gather everyone together."

"But returning to your list for a moment, and assuming that your meetings are all good purposeful events," there was a good deal of laughter in the room at that point, "we are dividing meetings into two basic camps: open discussions, which are what you might call Creative meetings," John looked at Alan. "And meetings which I suppose are best described as Functional meetings, designed to monitor and drive progress. The dynamics of both of these meeting types are very different, and to be effective they will both need an agenda and Chairman."

"Let's take the easy one first: the Functional meeting which is like your weekly review meeting," John gestured at Jeff. "For example a project review meeting. For this meeting type you need a detailed agenda that leaves no stone unturned," Jeff nodded in agreement. "And timings associated to each item on the agenda."

Jeff shrugged. "Well we do sort of," he began.

"I see. Who chairs the meeting?" John asked.

"I do actually," confessed Alan.

John smiled. "Well for those meetings, provided you have a good agenda, the Chairman's job is very simple. There are three basic tasks."

1. *To keep the meeting on track and on time.*

2. *To make sure that each point is covered in sufficient detail.*

3. *Make sure that missing items, actions and follow ups are noted.*

Alan sighed. "Sometimes it works, sometimes I struggle with the timing," he confessed candidly.

"Me too," Robin had stirred.

"It's quite a common problem," responded John. "And it brings me neatly onto why a Chairman or indeed Chairwoman is needed!" A little humour buzzed around the room again.

The Role of the Chair

"As the Chair, you effectively own the meeting. Much like the captain of an airliner, you are in charge until you land at the next airport. Heaven forbid you are perhaps late, pre-occupied or someone else has prepared the agenda. This should not matter. As you begin each session, you need to take a minute to pause and set the tone for the meeting. That can include welcoming people you don't know, reminding people of the schedule and quickly checking whether the owner of each section intends to stick to the allotted schedule. You might like to think of this as the captain's pre-flight introduction," he looked at Robin.

"I must say that's very interesting. I had never thought of it like that before," confessed Robin.

"Well it's vital to winkle out any disruptions before they take you by surprise."

"The next point – which is vital – is to be absolutely objective in your approach when you are chairing the meeting. It's no good setting the tone, and then indulging one contributor at the expense of someone else. I raise this as it's one of the hardest challenges for the Chair."

"Often there are people who never speak up on an issue and there are those that talk all the time. It is very natural for the chair to get viewpoints from those that offer them rather than making sure that all the right people have contributed."

The Purpose of an Agenda?

"So if you can do all this as a chair, is an agenda really necessary?" Kate had found the courage to speak up. She knew what the answer was likely to be, but wanted to get John's insight.

"I always like to write or 'own' the agenda," replied John, "because it allows me to set the expectations for the meeting. Any agenda must cover the meeting objective, content including subsections, timings of each section and people. For more Creative meetings the agenda should be very simple and section timings should be removed. I will talk more about agendas when I talk about preparation later on."

Gaining Agreement and Driving Progress

"So that brings me to the final trick of the Chair, which is gaining agreement and driving progress. So if we are chairing a Functional meeting with a proper agenda, it should be possible to drive progress quite easily. In theory! How often do we get tripped up by something that we have missed or something that someone has just raised? It's very easy to get side-tracked, especially if it's important, and it is vital to recognise when this happens and take action. There are two choices:"

"The default approach is to agree with one of the meeting attendees for them to take it as an action item to follow up later. You can move it to the end of the meeting, but that may minimise its importance."

"If it is a Priority "A" issue that supersedes everything else in the agenda then you may need to re-organise the agenda timing on the spot. But this is the exception and should be avoided at nearly all costs."

"Do the same approaches apply if you are just meeting one person?" asked Sue brightly.

"Good question. Yes if that person is of significant importance, such as a client, but I suspect you need to judge whether it needs the formal structure. I'd say it's optional. Does that make sense?"

"Yes it does – thanks."

"I have a question," Ben had recovered his confidence from his late arrival at the meeting. "I really haven't chaired very many meetings so far, but I do go to a lot." He paused, looking a little sheepish. "So, what exactly should I do with the insight you are giving us here?"

There was a sudden hush in the room. Alan sighed inwardly. Trust Ben to be awkward again. But he didn't need to worry.

John put his pen down, looked at Ben and smiled. "That's a perfectly reasonable question. Tell me, how many of the meetings that you attend do you find frustrating?"

"Oh man. Loads! I mean there aren't exactly many people who know how to run them."

"Precisely," responded John. "I am willing to bet you only a few of these people 'who don't know how to run them' are here in this room. Correct?"

"Yeah, that's pretty much true," Ben had the good grace to look guilty at this point.

"So I am hoping that by the end of this session, you will be able to educate them about what they need to do."

Ben's brow furrowed. "I'm sorry I don't understand."

"If you know how it can be done better, you can perhaps ask them the right questions that will help them improve."

Ben looked puzzled.

"For example, the three things you can do as an attendee when you arrive is ask who is chairing the meeting, where the agenda is or – heaven forbid there is no agenda – what the meeting objective is and if the meeting is likely to finish on time."

The penny dropped. "Oh I see."

"In a minute we are also going to cover the bad meeting habits that everyone at the meeting can improve on," finished John with a mischievous grin; he was beginning to adopt a much more informal and jocular tone.

The Seven Deadly Sins that Blight the Meeting Landscape

"Right. Now we are going to talk about some of the other issues that blight meetings. Even if the chair is fully organised and in control, he or she will still need the co-operation of all the other meeting participants to conduct a successful meeting. I have called this section the Seven Deadly Sins, and to follow up that young man's comments, addressing these sins is something to which everyone needs to pay attention." As he glanced up from his notes, John happened to see someone at the back of the room still tapping furiously at their smartphone.

Not Paying Attention

"I was going to start by talking about lateness but I see that I am given the opportunity to go straight to the second Deadly Sin of Not Paying Attention."

A murmur rippled around the room, and slowly everyone turned to follow John's gaze. Their gaze fell on a somewhat stressed looking and dishevelled woman executive who took a few seconds to realise that everyone was staring right at her. She blushed deeply and dropped the offending phone into her bag. "Sorry, so sorry," she began.

"My dear lady, I am sorry too," responded John with a wistful smile.

"There are two very simple rules here: one for participants, one for the Chair. If you are participating in a meeting, and something comes up that is more important than the meeting, then by all means slip out quietly and go and do it. It's a judgement call for each person. By staying in the meeting and trying to do something else, you are neither doing justice to the meeting, nor the issue you are trying to deal with."

"So what you are saying is?" interrupted Ben.

"What I am saying is: either pay attention or leave the meeting. What's really dangerous is that other people will assume that because you are present at a discussion, you are fully aware of the subject matter and decisions made. If you don't bother to pay attention then you risk major mistakes and misunderstandings. In short don't do it!"

There was a muted silence in the room. The guilty lady executive had turned a deep shade of red and was avoiding eye contact with everyone.

"The second part of this issue lies very firmly with the Chair," said John in a softer voice. "If the meeting is not engaging people properly, then the Chair must either get the meeting back on track or close the meeting and re-schedule it."

"Really?" it was Robin's turn to interrupt.

"Absolutely. If a meeting is so dull and tedious that everyone is struggling to pay attention and follow the discussion, then it's better to give people their time back and re-convene at a later date. It also suggests that perhaps the agenda, attendees and reason for the meeting may need re-visiting."

"I hate to say this, but sometimes we have no choice," intervened Ben. "I mean sometimes we have to attend meetings that are excruciatingly dull and unavoidable."

"Well if you have not managed to train your Chair fully or influence the agenda, there are a couple of other things you can do to make these meetings worthwhile which I will cover at the end."

Lateness

"I am now going to come back to the first 'Deadly Sin' which is Lateness. Some of you found the door closed at the start of this meeting. None of you were very late but I was trying to make a particular point. I apologise if you were offended, but as a Chair I have to be firm."

"What do people say to you if you're late to a meeting?" Ben felt he had nothing to lose by asking a cheeky question, "I mean you're very senior so a meeting chair is hardly going to say anything, are they?"

John smiled. "If I am late to a meeting, which is very rare, the meeting chair usually lets me know of their displeasure using a little irony or sarcasm. If I am actually chairing and cannot make it on time, I will ring ahead and ask someone else there to chair in my place. Lateness is a fact of life. Sometimes it's unavoidable; but all too often it is merely a bad habit. Lateness around meetings is a particularly bad sin, as it wastes not only your time, but the collective time of everybody at the meeting. There are nineteen people of us here this morning, so every 3 minutes wasted is a very expensive hour of people's time that will never be recovered. So my point is simple: if you accept an invitation to a meeting, then you must make every effort to arrive at least 5 minutes early, and allow enough time in your diary for the allotted meeting time."

"Whoa," said Jeff. "So what happens when a meeting overruns?"

John smiled. "That issue lies firmly with the Chair," he said. "If a meeting looks like it will overrun, all you need to do is indicate 10 minutes before the stated end time that you have to leave on time. Make it the chair's problem, not yours. Alternatively, you can indicate that you have some time to overrun if needed, but at least you have raised the issue."

"OK. Thanks."

Lack of Preparation

"Now I will move onto Deadly Sin Number Three… Preparation! Far too many meetings are held without proper preparation," continued John. "Firstly all meetings should have an agenda – even if it only a few points on the meeting invitation. As I said earlier, an agenda must cover: meeting objective, content including subsections, timings of each section and people. Frankly, no matter how junior, meeting attendees are perfectly within their rights to veto an agenda item if they haven't seen the agenda in advance."

"Really?" asked Barbara. "You are joking I take it?"

"I really do believe in this," replied John. "If the meeting owner isn't serious about the agenda, then why should the attendees be?"

"OK," Barbara was still digesting her surprise.

"So as well as preparing a proper agenda, meeting owners should also prepare relevant background reading such as articles, whitepapers and previous presentations that should be included. Assuming that everyone at the meeting has the same level of knowledge is a regular but serious mistake and will undoubtedly waste precious meeting time if some of the participants have to be brought up to speed."

"How do you decide if a meeting requires detailed briefing notes?" asked Sue.

"Good question. Three rules of thumb. The first says that briefing notes are less important for meetings under an hour. The second says it's more important if it is a complex or detailed subject, and the third says it is a must-do if the topic to be covered is mostly new to the participants."

Sue scribbled the notes.

"If you do send out a proper meeting pack, it's the duty of every participant to read it before the meeting. No excuses."

"How far in advance should you send it out?"

"At a minimum two days and preferably a week."

"Why two days and not twenty four hours?" Ben was curious.

"Twenty four hours gives far too little time for most people to accommodate it in their schedules, forty eight allows the possibility that they can create some time to read it." He held up a small book-shaped electronic device. "I'm a pretty old fashioned chap, but I do believe in moving with the times. I have my assistant send every meeting pack to my Amazon Kindle by email, that way my reading list is always with me and I can catch up on it between other events in my day."

"What a marvellous idea," exclaimed Robin.

Disruption and Disagreements

"Next up are Deadly Sins Four and Five – Disruption and Disagreements – which I will deal with together to contrast them. Whatever you do there will always be people in a meeting who are disruptive, want to hog the conversation and argue unnecessary points.

I am going to return to my earlier comments about driving progress. As Chair you need to decide either a) this is a debate for another time and to get the meeting back on the agenda or b) to push the agenda back to have the debate in more detail."

Alan thought back to the first meeting where Ben had disrupted his entire agenda and smiled quietly. He looked over at Ben who was expressionless.

"While you may find that disruptions can be a pain, you have to be very careful not to dismiss alternative viewpoints as they may well be right in the longer run – objectivity is crucial. Disagreements however are slightly different to disruptions in that you have two sides that may have equally valid points; again it's important to be as objective as possible. The real question is whether there is enough available information to support either viewpoint at the meeting. If not then it's easy to move the disagreement to a follow up meeting. If a decision is needed, then the best approach is to get each side to summarise their viewpoint in three key points, record these in the notes and take the decision accordingly."

"Isn't that really risky?" asked Barbara.

"Actually it's much safer than many decision processes," replied John. "If you have recorded both sides of the argument in the notes and then follow up with the decision and the rationale for making it, you have an excellent record of what took place."

"Don't you find that people find it safer to defer a decision until they have more information?" asked Robin.

"Yes I do, but they should know that under my watch that they only get to do that once!" There was some laughter at this point.

Follow Ups and Actions

"Now I shall be moving on to Deadly Sin Number Six. Follow Ups and Actions."

"Sorry to be dim," said Jeff, "but how can Follow Ups and Actions be considered a sin?"

"You are quite correct," said John. "They are not sins in themselves but they are the source of two of the greatest Deadly sins: Not Following Up and Not Completing Actions. I keep them in the positive sense to encourage people. When I attend meetings that I am not running, I often find the notes, actions and follow ups are not always consistent and leave a lot to be desired."

"Should the Chair always make notes?" asked Barbara earnestly.

"I believe the Chair should make their own notes to ensure they have not missed something, although it's always preferable to have someone else take detailed notes."

"If the agenda is properly prepared, then it's easy just to make short notes against each section. These should be short and concise. If you are doing your chairing duty properly anything more is impossible unless you have someone with you to take detailed notes. Action items should be highlighted and numbered, with a date attached. Assigning them to an individual to own is also critical, otherwise nobody will action them. If you nominate someone who is not at the meeting, then someone at the meeting must own the action to send them a copy of the notes and get agreement on the action point."

Tracking Progress

"Finally we come to the seventh Deadly Sin, which is Tracking Progress or rather, Not Tracking Progress," John paused for a second and looked up. "Why would we need to track progress?" he asked to see who was paying attention.

"To drive the activity to a given conclusion," murmured Alan, but not many people could hear him.

"Very good Alan but you know this all too well."

"To make sure that the meeting was a worthwhile use of our time." The answer came from the female executive who had previously been caught using her phone and was now paying close attention.

"That is absolutely right, you must remember this sin otherwise there is no point having the meeting in the first place." John gave her a warm smile and despite her positive contribution, she went bright red again. "As Chair you must ensure that the follow ups and actions rest with the designated people and communicate these to the person who will track progress against these."

"Can you give an example of who this person might be?" asked the lady executive.

"Well when it is the main board, this is usually the company secretary, but typically I would expect this to be the head of the business unit or the project that the meeting is covering."

"Thank you."

"Now that I have dealt with the Seven Deadly sins, let us come onto some brighter points – the unseen side benefits of meetings."

Side Benefits

"Ben, you were asking me earlier about what to do at meetings that were unavoidable and dull. I am going to suggest to you some unseen benefits of attending dull and tedious meetings! I have a fairly full agenda these days but I do look out for meetings that are 'useful' for me to attend. When I say useful, I am not critical to the discussion but it's useful for me to see what's going on. In other words I volunteer for what you might regard as dull and tedious meetings!"

"Why would you ever do that?" said Ben incredulously.

"I do this for two reasons, the first is to make contact or what you might call 'network' with people I do not normally see or speak to. It's very useful to see them in action and understand what they are thinking. The second reason is opportunistic. In these meetings topics occasionally come up to which I can contribute my expertise. I generally try not to intervene, but if I can be helpful I will do so when it's obvious that there's an issue. I call this approach 'Occupying No-Man's Land'."

"Occupying No-Man's land?" Alan was curious.

"Finding a subject of which I have some knowledge and of which other people are unsure," replied John. "I then become the intellectual owner of the topic until such time as I delegate it to someone else."

"Sorry," asked Ben. "But what exactly is the point of doing that?" He was still astonished that John would willingly attend a meeting he didn't have to.

"My dear boy," smiled John. "Considering you have to attend so many dull meetings, I would have thought you might want to try and gather some of the more interesting topics when you get an opportunity?"

"How do you mean?" said Ben.

"You have to wait opportunistically for a discussion to drift onto a topic which you know, and then you can volunteer to take a follow up or action on that topic. You have to learn to pick carefully if you can, but for those of you who harbour any kind of career aspirations it's one of the best ways of getting noticed."

"Oh" the frown slowly eased from Ben's face and he smiled. "What a good idea," he said firmly.

The Two Meeting Rule

"Finally to finish," John continued, "I am going to share with you a masterstroke that I learned from a friend of mine who runs a large law firm. As you know law firms usually operate as partnerships and that as partners are all individual owners of the firm, there are often heated debates about strategy. The two meeting approach is used when there is an unavoidable and contentious issue that has to be resolved."

"In the first meeting, the meeting has an open agenda with plenty of time with the single proviso that no decision will be made at that meeting, although everyone who has a view is strongly encouraged to share it at that meeting. It is vital to make sure that every key person attends and it is critical that there is enough time allotted. If people cannot attend they need to understand that their viewpoint may not contribute to the outcome. You could consider this a Creative meeting like we discussed earlier."

"Anyway the input from the first meeting is gathered and although the decision will not be 'made' until the second meeting, the first meeting should lay out all the issues in the open so that those that need to drive the decision process can have the appropriate conversations before the second meeting. The second meeting's sole purpose is to make the decision, it has a short agenda, and a relatively short amount of time allotted. Again, from our discussion earlier, you could call this a Functional meeting. The agenda for this second meeting lays out the options very simply and provides all the necessary supporting information so that a decision can be made quickly."

"Because everyone who is involved has had a full opportunity to contribute in the first meeting, it is much, much easier to reach a decision in the second meeting." John paused. There was a stunned silence in the room. "Well that's pretty much it, ladies and gentlemen," finished John. At which point a rash of chatter broke out.

Alan stood up and held up his hand to silence them all. "I would just like to thank John for kindly giving his very precious time to come here this morning and enlighten us," he began before a ripple of enthusiastic applause ran through the group, with several calls of 'thank you' ringing out.

"You are most welcome," replied John standing up.

Robin wandered over. "Can we persuade you to stay for a spot of lunch?" he asked John.

John looked at his watch. "Sadly I have to go on to another appointment, but that's a very kind thought," he replied.

"We'll make another plan," added Alan.

"That would be great."

"I'll walk out with you," added Robin, visibly enthused with the morning's session.

Alan was a little relieved, as he needed to speak to Sue and Jeff.

Next on the List

A few minutes later it was just the three of them left in the room. "First the good news – that was another very good session."

"You are telling me!" exclaimed Jeff.

"I must say John was very good," added Sue.

"I thought he would go down well," admitted Alan, "However that almost certainly means that Robin is going to ask us to pull this together pretty quickly. We need to be ready. Jeff, can I ask you a favour?"

"Sure."

"Please could you gather the material we have collected so far and run the principles past your group of friends that you meet with?"

"Well I don't know about that," Jeff was hesitant.

"Come on Jeff, they have already been really helpful already," Sue weighed in.

"Oh well, I suppose…"

"Thank you, that's brilliant," Alan's enthusiasm was overwhelming.

"I'll need a week though," said Jeff thoughtfully. "It takes a few days to get space in the diaries."

"Well as soon as you can organise it," said Alan hopefully.

"Come on you two, let's go and get some lunch. I'm starving," said Sue.

Chapter Notes

The Agenda

The Enduring Value of A Properly Run Meeting
Friday 25th October, 10am to 11am

Chair: John Abercrombie
Venue: Room 101
Attendees: To be confirmed

1. *Types of meetings (5 mins)*
2. *Stimulating Progress (5 mins)*
3. *The Purpose of an Agenda (5 mins)*
4. *The Role of the Chair (5 mins)*
5. *Gaining agreement / driving progress (5 mins)*
6. *7 Deadly Sins That Blight the Meeting Landscape (20 mins)*

   i. *Lateness*
   ii. *Not Paying Attention*
   iii. *Lack of Preparation*
   iv. *Disruption*
   v. *Disagreements*
   vi. *Following up & actions*
   vii. *Tracking Progress*

7. *Side Benefits (5 mins)*
8. *The Two Meeting Rule (5 mins)*
9. *Questions & Answers (5 mins)*

Other Notes

- *A formal meeting should only be called if there is no other way of stimulating progress, such as speaking to people individually.*

- *Meeting types divide into Creative meetings for brainstorming and Functional meetings to monitor and drive progress.*

The Role of the Chair

1. *To keep the meeting on track and on time.*

2. *To make sure that each point is covered in sufficient detail.*

3. *To make sure that missing items, actions and follow ups are noted.*

The Purpose of the Agenda

The agenda sets the expectations of the meeting. Its content should include:

- *Meeting objective*
- *Content*
- *Timings*
- *People attending*

The Seven Deadly Sins

1. *Lateness*

    -   *Make every effort to arrive at least 5 minutes early.*

    -   *If you are chairing the meeting and are unavoidably late, call ahead and have someone else take the chair until you arrive.*

    -   *If the meeting looks like it will overrun, let the chair know at least 10 minutes before the end that you have to leave on time.*

2. *Not Paying Attention*

    -   *Participants should either pay attention or leave the meeting (slipping out quietly) if something urgent arises.*

    -   *It is the chair's responsibility to keep the meeting focussed or reschedule if needed.*

    -   *Others will assume you are fully aware of discussions and decisions during the meeting. Pay attention to avoid mistakes!*

3. *Lack of Preparation*

    -   *Every meeting with more than two people should normally have an agenda.*

    -   *Attendees should be able to veto an agenda item if an agenda has not been provided in advance.*

- Relevant background reading should be provided along with the agenda to form a meeting pack.

- Agendas or Meeting Packs should be sent out two days to a week in advance.

4. Disruptions

- The Chair must remain objective and be careful not to dismiss alternative viewpoints.

- The Chair must decide if this is a debate for another time or push the agenda back to have a more detailed debate during the meeting.

5. Disagreements

- It is important for the Chair to be objective.

- Decide if there is enough information to support a decision.

- Get each side to summarise their viewpoint, record these in the notes along with the decision taken and the rationale for the decision.

6. Following Up & Actions

- The Chair should make notes, although ideally someone else should make detailed notes.

- Number action items and assign a date by which they should be completed.

- *Actions should be assigned to people at the meeting, if someone is nominated for an action and is not present, then someone at the meeting must take the action to follow up with them.*

7. *Tracking Progress*

- *Track progress from every meeting to make sure that it was a valuable use of people's time. If this is not done by the Chair, the Chair must give this responsibility to a regular meeting attendee to whom the meeting topic is most relevant.*

10

GUIDANCE FOR
PROSPECTIVE LEOPARDS

Get Together

Jeff knew exactly what he had to do, so he did the easy bit first, a note to Rufus.

> *Rufus,*
> *Been a while – like to get together with you and Peter as soon as possible. Thursday 7pm?*
> *Jeff*

Rufus couldn't do Thursday but could make Friday, so Jeff confirmed and then thought for a few seconds. Should he invite Peter and Kate? The coward in him said no. After all he tended to regard Peter as a makeweight, and as for Kate? Well, that was just awkward. He sighed deeply and his conscience weighed heavily on him. Easy one first: he sent the same note to Peter, changing the date to Friday. Back came the predictable response.

> *Sorry Jeff – madly busy here, might just be able to squeeze in, but so much important stuff to do. Peter*

Jeff smiled, shook his head and replied:

Too bad – Rufus has already confirmed.

And sure enough back came:

Just checking again. Think I can make it. Peter.

Jeff smiled. Peter was so predictable.

And now for the tricky one. "Just do another email," his cowardly-self suggested.

"No! You have to call her!" replied his conscience.

He sighed and picked up his iPhone. "Here I go," he muttered. Much to his surprise, Kate answered. "Hi Kate, Jeff here." He hadn't really thought through what he was going to say.

"Yes Jeff," Kate was curt to the point of rudeness. Jeff paused for a second and told himself to keep calm.

"Listen – Rufus, Peter and I are getting together Friday night," he tailed off.

"And?"

"Well I, err… we would love you to come also," he finished lamely.

There was a fairly long silence. Jeff caved in first. "Aside from catching up, I am going to share some of our latest stuff with them."

"I see," was the icy response. Jeff had had enough of the cold shoulder.

"Well if you want to come, we are meeting at the Trattoria at 7pm on Friday."

"I am busy tomorrow but I will think about it."

"Fine. See you around." Jeff hung up. He was annoyed but glad he had got it over with.

Kate on the other hand was filled with remorse. "Was that really necessary?" her conscience asked her.

"Yes it was!" she snapped back at her conscience, but somehow she couldn't shake off the nagging guilt that she was behaving like a child. The feeling of guilt stuck with her for the rest of the day, and even when she finally got home she still couldn't shake it off. She sighed, pulled out her iPhone and tapped in the appointment to meet with them at 7pm on Friday. As she put her phone away, she was surprised to find that the feeling of guilt suddenly lifted.

Friday

Jeff was first to arrive at the Trattoria on Friday and managed to secure a booth so they could have some privacy. He checked his phone messages and then made sure his phone was switched off. He got out his papers and made sure they were into the right order. He ordered a coke from the waiter. No sense in starting on the beer just yet, and suddenly Kate arrived. This was awkward. After their conversation Jeff hadn't thought for one minute that Kate was coming.

Kate, for her part, hadn't imagined for one minute having to speak with Jeff on his own.

Jeff stared at her for a few seconds. She looked fantastic. All the more so as he could see she was becoming flustered. He decided to break the ice first and smiled warmly. "Hi Kate, I am really pleased, if but a little surprised, that you decided to come."

The relief flooded across Kate's face. She took off her coat and slide onto the opposite side of the booth. "I must admit I wasn't intending to come," she replied. "But it seemed the right thing to do."

"I'm glad," replied Jeff and was surprised to find that he actually meant it.

"It doesn't mean you are forgiven," Kate bitterly regretted the words the second she had said them. Jeff began to bristle for a moment then he swallowed hard.

"For what it's worth, I am so very sorry about Sunday," he said. "If I could go back and change things I would."

Kate looked directly into his eyes. "I was very angry with you," she admitted. "But it is hard to keep it up." She smiled.

"I would like to make it up to you," said Jeff earnestly.

"I would like that," she said. "Perhaps over a coffee tomorrow morning?"

"That would be lovely. I'll text you."

"So aside from all the usual chit chat, what are we covering this evening?" said Kate.

The waiter brought Jeff's drink and Kate ordered herself a glass of wine.

"What's up with you? This is Friday!" Kate enquired gesturing at his coke.

"Going to hold off for a while," Jeff replied. "I have to concentrate. Alan wants me to walk you through some of the project content to date – to check that we are not going wildly off base."

"Oh good," replied Kate. "I must say I have really liked what I have seen and heard so far."

Jeff was trying to calculate if he had enough time to give Kate a preview when Rufus arrived.

"Hi all!" he greeted them enthusiastically. He was just settling himself down when Pete turned up.

"Hi Peter, how's things?" asked Jeff.

"Oh simply amazing," began Peter. Rufus and Jeff winced, anticipating that Peter was about to go 'off on one'. Much to their surprise he didn't. Instead he sat down, tuned his phone off and glanced up. "More importantly, how are all of you?" he continued.

"Great thanks," replied Rufus. "It seems ages since we have seen each other, although I am sure it has only been a few weeks."

"It has been a while," admitted Jeff. "My fault mostly."

"We were helping you out with that very interesting project," observed Rufus, "in between rescuing Peter's career of course. How did it go Peter?"

Peter had reddened slightly but quickly recovered. "I really owe you guys," he said quietly. "You really saved my bacon."

"So it's back on track now?"

"Absolutely. Very much so."

"Good. So Jeff what's happening at your end?"

"So glad you asked. That was one of the reasons I wanted to get you all together."

"Oh yes?"

"We've made a lot of progress on the project and I wanted to share it with you and if possible get your feedback."

"Great. What have you got?"

"OK here goes. To start with I have three key questions for you:"

1. *Do you find your work or home life at all stressful?*

2. *Do you consider that your world is unpredictable?*

3. *Do you want to make the very most of your opportunities when they come past?*

"I have them here on a piece of paper." Jeff passed them across the table. "I want you to think about them but don't give me an answer yet."

Jeff gave them a few seconds. "Now tell me out of three how many you would answer yes?"

Rufus went first. "Two I think, although that last question is a bit loaded."

"It's meant to be," replied Jeff.

"Well maybe three then," replied Rufus.

"Two definitely" replied Peter.

"Three," added Kate.

"OK great thanks," responded Jeff.

So my next question is pretty obvious.

"If you could have less stress, make your life more predictable and be able to nail all your opportunities, you'd want to do that, correct?"

"We're with you," said Rufus.

"Do you know what a leopard is?"

There was a curious silence around the tale.

"Err Jeff – what's this got to do with things?" asked Peter. "I mean we all know what a leopard is."

"Well in case you forgot here's an outline description."

Jeff slid a second piece of paper across the table with the description on it.

> *The species' success in the wild owes in part to its opportunistic hunting behaviour, its adaptability to a variety of habitats and its ability to move at up to approximately 58 kilometres (36 miles) an hour. The leopard consumes virtually any animal it can hunt down and catch.*

"I'm sorry I still don't get it," complained Peter.

"Think about it for a second," replied Jeff. "The leopard is one of nature's most successful predators. Read that description again, and see if you can identify the principles to its success."

"Because it's fast and furry?" ventured Peter, who was starting to become a little facetious.

"Very funny Peter," responded Jeff, trying to keep a straight face. "OK I'll lay it out for you. The Leopard can act opportunistically, adapt to a wide variety of environments, operate at speed, drive any chosen activity to a successful conclusion and remain almost undetected."

"That's really interesting," Rufus was deep in thought but completely engaged. "So if I understand you correctly, your goal is to translate these successful principles of the Leopard into the human arena."

"Rufus, you were always the clever one," interjected Kate with a grin.

"Exactly! You got it in one," affirmed Jeff.

"OK so what do these principles mean in the human world?" prompted Kate.

Act Opportunistically

"So glad you asked," countered Jeff. "If you lay out the five principles, you can then work out what you need to do to fulfil each one. So the first one is the ability to act opportunistically – which is all about how you use your time – remember the Hierarchy of Time?"

The penny finally dropped for Peter.

"Oh wow! I get it. So if you can work out how to divide your time between Creative and Functional, you can free up time to do other things?"

"I think you need to add Creative versus Functional. It's not just time, its personality too," added Kate.

"That's a good point."

"So how do you work out that whole Creative versus Functional thing anyway?" asked Peter. "I mean we got it fairly quickly but there must be a way to work it out?"

"Good point. I'll take that back with me," Jeff scribbled another note.

Adapt to Any Environment

"So, moving on to 'Adapting to a wide variety of environments.' The view we came to is that communications and networking are vital for this. So from the discussions we had have come the Hierarchy of Communications, the Rules of Responsiveness and – ta da – the Eleven Rules of Email. I'll share these with you in a second."

"OK so I understand why it's important. I mean we get dropped into all sorts of environments in life. But explain to me why you think communications and networking are vital for this?" asked Rufus.

"Simple. Two reasons. Firstly, to find out what's going on in a short timescale, you will need to quickly communicate with a lot of people to make sure you understand fully. Secondly you will need to make the right people connections quickly, which is why networking is so important."

"But what about relationships?" Peter again.

"I'm coming to that next."

"But aren't they important for adapting?" Peter was off the mark again. Jeff sighed.

"Once you have the right relationships, you have already adapted," explained Jeff. "The first part of the process is networking to build enough relationships to survive. The second part is managing those relationships, which is what you need to do to succeed, and indeed operate at speed."

Operate at Speed

"So I understand that Leopards do things quickly, but why is this important to us humans?" asked Rufus wryly. Jeff sensed that Rufus was testing him.

"I will refer to the First Principle. If you are operating slowly, you are hardly going to have time to act opportunistically."

They all laughed. "Well put," responded Rufus.

"So why relationships and technology then?"

"Well to achieve most things in life you are going to need help," clarified Jeff. "And if you have the right relationships you will be able to do more and do it more quickly. Simple really. As for the technology, it simply serves to amplify what you are doing. Email is a great example; you can get a written message out to a huge audience, very quickly and with very little cost. Imagine doing that even 20 years ago? Rufus, a few weeks ago you were telling us how you have automated parts of your business modelling process. That's another good example of operating at speed."

Rufus chuckled. "Touché," he said. "But why do you think speed is so important?"

"The quicker you do something, the sooner you can find out if it is working or not. If it's not working, you can try something else, and if it is working you can move on and do something else much earlier."

"Well that makes sense."

Drive Any Chosen Activity to a Successful Conclusion

"So the next one is about driving a chosen activity to a successful conclusion."

"I can relate to this one," said Peter. "This is what I do best."

"Almost, Peter. But there are a couple of points I would like to make here. This principle is about prioritising what you execute. The word 'chosen' is critical. You need to choose which activity you are going to conclude. By the way success should not always mean concluding everything you do. A successful outcome may also mean handing over things to other people so you can focus on your own 'chosen' activities."

"Oh," said Peter, rather crestfallen. "So this about saying no?"

"I am not sure you always need to say 'no'," interjected Kate.

"I think it is more about re-directing things to where they belong. Getting you off the hook so to speak."

"Oh OK," said Peter. "I can relate to that. There are times I would definitely like to be off the hook."

Remain Almost Undetected

"So moving to the last one," began Jeff.

Rufus snorted. "This one is ridiculous, I am sorry. I don't want to be undetected thank you very much."

"OK let me explain. This one is not about being invisible. It's about having the discipline to get on and do things without making a big deal about it. There's a great saying: 'there are those who make things happen, those who watch things happen and those who wonder what happened'. The idea of this principle is to occupy the first category, not give away too much to the second category and keeping the third category bemused. For you Rufus, I would think this is the most vital principle. I mean if your competitors knew what you were up to you wouldn't have a business."

"Good point," admitted Rufus.

"The other side of this point is that too many people are far too busy tweeting their business on the Internet and sharing it on blogs and social networks without thinking."

"Oh boy you are not kidding," said Kate.

"Of course, these things all have a use," added Jeff. "But they need to be used effectively. In other words with discretion."

"Hey Jeff, you know what would be useful?"

"Try me."

"If you could just do a short description of each of the principles. Otherwise they will need an explanation like you just gave us."

"I have to say Jeff, this is illuminating and I am fascinated," concluded Rufus. "A leopard indeed!" He shook his head, "Who would have thought it? What happens next?"

"Well we have done a whole pile of sessions internally on things like networking, relationships and technology, and we are turning it into a company-wide training programme."

"That's an interesting move. So what's the big driver for the company?"

"Well the traditional dogma says that we could spend a lot of money on organisational change programmes," explained Jeff. "But the exciting thing is that if we can get this adopted, it will help people as individuals to become more successful. That will be a much bigger win in my humble opinion." Jeff paused and leaned back in his chair. "Look, what I would really like to do is to share the project and all the materials as we progress." Jeff turned to Kate. "I know you will see it all anyway but I would really like to get Peter and Rufus' input on it as well."

"Oh I think that would be great," enthused Kate.

"Are you two up for it?" Jeff asked Peter and Rufus.

"Absolutely," Rufus beat Peter to the punch line for once.

"Me too," Peter wasn't going to be left out.

"OK great – how are you guys fixed for Monday evening?" asked Jeff.

"Oh, err, let me see," Rufus' brow furrowed.

"I'll buy dinner," volunteered Jeff.

"I'm there," replied Peter, adding. "I know, I know I am such a tart," with a degree of self-depreciation they had rarely seen before.

"I don't know if I can make it," replied Rufus glumly. "Look, leave it with me – I might be a little late."

"Kate?" asked Jeff absent-mindedly, forgetting any sensitivities.

"Oh I'm sure I will be able to make it," replied Kate blankly. Rufus looked her quizzically wondering if there was an undercurrent there. Kate caught his gaze and managed to keep a neutral expression until Rufus looked away.

"Great! Enough of all that for now, I need a beer!"

Later that Same Night

Jeff got home quite late that evening. Normally he would have gone straight to bed but his brain was still wired and now he had to get something ready for the session on Monday. He walked into the kitchen, opened a bottle of Rioja and poured himself a glass. A wistful pang of regret washed over him. If he hadn't trashed his relationship with Kate they would be chatting and laughing together now. At least I'm seeing her tomorrow he thought. He smiled; that was tomorrow and this is now.

He sat down, pulled out the papers from earlier and spread them out over his kitchen table. Immediately his brain kicked out of melancholy and back into gear. He pulled out a blank piece of paper and re-wrote his notes from earlier. As he finished, he reached for his MacBook and began typing the notes into an email. "Let's get this out tonight and see what they think," he said out loud to the empty kitchen.

Rufus, Peter, Kate,
Try this as a starting point!
Jeff

The Principles of the Leopard: Summary

1. *Acting opportunistically* – create time in your day to balance both Creative and Functional activities.

2. *Adapt to a wide variety of environments* – equip yourself with the skills and habits to tackle new projects.

3. *Operate at speed* – organise both your relationships and your technology so you can be effective and responsive more quickly.

4. *Drive any chosen activity to a successful conclusion* – find the right collaboration to succeed with your chosen priorities.

5. *Remain almost undetected* – build your priorities into your daily routine so that they happen automatically, leaving you free to focus on new opportunities.

He was just about to shut the laptop when an email came back from Rufus:

Shouldn't you be in bed?

Jeff laughed and typed back:

Bit lost. Only got as far as the wine rack so far!

He quickly snapped the MacBook shut before he could get distracted by Facebook or any other emails for that matter.

Monday

Jeff strode through the lobby on his way to the Coffee Bar; as he arrived he immediately saw Kate sitting with a small group. She was sitting next to Ben who was telling some sort of story and as Jeff arrived she threw back her head and laughed. He stopped for a moment to watch her. Saturday had been great but they were both a little bruised and had parted with a firm agreement to meet up again.

"She's so fabulous," Jeff thought. "How did I miss her for all these years?" He shook his head. Today was work. "Morning Kate. Morning Ben", he called our cheerfully. They both waved their acknowledgement and carried on chatting, so he bought himself an espresso and headed for the hills. He had a busy day ahead of him.

The Leopard Meeting

Alan wore a worried expression as Jeff walked through the door to Alan's office at 10am. "How are you getting on?" he asked Jeff impatiently.

"Pretty good I think," replied Jeff dropping into the chair. He reached into his bag and pulled out a printout with his email he had written on Friday night. "What do you think about this as a starting point?"

Alan studied it intently as Sue walked in.

"Hi Jeff, hi Alan," she greeted them warmly. "How's things?"

"I'll tell you when Alan's finished reading my note," replied Jeff with a grin.

Alan looked up. "What you have written makes reasonably good sense to me," he began. "It's a good starting point as any. Where do you go from here?"

"I have a plan for each section, and I think I can get you a draft this week. But I'm a bit stuck on the first section," replied Jeff.

"We have an instinctive idea about the difference between Creative and Functional behaviour. And by the way Alan you covered the principles really well in the session on teamwork, but we really need to be able to help people understand the difference between the two. What I need is a very short set of questions that people can ask themselves to determine the difference. Is that something we could discuss in this morning's meeting?"

Alan's worried expression vanished and a smile began to play around his mouth.

"For once in my life," he thought to himself, "I have actually bet on the right people."

"If that's what's needed, then let's do just that," he replied breezily. He reached into a file on his desk and pulled out the slide with the description. "Here's the summary slide if that helps:"

Creative Versus Functional

- *Functional people are brilliant at bringing structure and order to things, executing tasks and making plans.*

- *Functional people struggle with making the leap and approaching something from an alternative perspective.*

- *Creative people are able to look at things differently and solve problems that seem simple with hindsight but need inspiration.*

- *Creative people struggle to prioritise their creativity and often don't have the patience to work through tasks thoroughly.*

They gathered around the table to look at the slide. "So I'm a Creative and Sue's Functional," murmured Jeff. "But we still don't know what Alan is yet."

Alan smiled but said nothing.

"Well shall I start off then?" said Sue. "If it was me, I would ask three questions."

"Do you leave any Unallocated Time in your daily schedule? A no answer is a Functional response. A yes answer is Creative."

Jeff laughed. "That's me, I always have gaps," he looked at Alan who was giving nothing away.

Sue continued "Next question. If you had to take on a really interesting project right now, could your clear your schedule immediately to do work on it? Functional people hate doing that. I know I do, but for a Creative person an interesting project is music to their ears. Again, no for Functional, yes for Creative."

"OK, that makes sense," commented Alan neutrally. "Go on."

"Final question. When you go to find something at your desk, do you find it by memory or by system? If the answer is system then, you are definitely Functional." Sue paused and looked around at Alan's office which as ever was immaculate as ever.

"So where is all the Leopard filing then Alan?" she tried a sneak attack.

"In the cabinet under L," Alan murmured without thinking.

"Hah – got him! A Functional!" exclaimed Jeff.

Alan went very red with embarrassment.

Sue suddenly felt very mean. "I'm sorry Alan, but I just don't understand why you won't tell us," she exclaimed, trying to be sympathetic. "It's not as if we are going to broadcast it from the rooftops!"

Alan sighed. "I'm sorry," he said. "I think I am actually a Creative but by necessity, I have managed to acquire so many Functional habits it's probably hard to tell. The reason I didn't want to tell you wasn't that I wanted to be secretive, I just wasn't sure until right now."

"But we tripped you up with the third question," added Jeff. "So maybe that question doesn't work?"

"We should add a couple more," agreed Alan. "That way we can be sure with people who are marginal."

"OK, here's another," said Jeff. "Do you regularly back up your laptop? Yes is mostly Functional, no is probably Creative."

"Fair enough," replied Sue. "I think it's a little marginal though. We need one more."

"How about: 'Do you know exactly what is in your laptop bag?'"

Jeff and Sue both laughed. "Why's that so funny?" said Alan, slightly crestfallen. "I can tell you I absolutely have no idea what's in mine."

"Me neither," said Jeff.

"Um, I know exactly what is in mine," smiled Sue self-consciously.

"OK thank you for those questions, they will make good starting points. I will let you know if we can come up with anything better tonight," said Jeff casually.

"Tonight?" asked Alan.

"The team is meeting up tonight to go through it all, I am buying them dinner."

"Are you indeed?"

"Can we catch up on Thursday afternoon? Also by the way do we have a session on Friday?"

"We do," said Alan. "It's a short one on presenting. Thursday is OK with me."

Monday Dinner for the Team

Jeff was first to the Trattoria, and as they arrived he handed them each a folded piece of paper. "First things first," he said. "This is a short questionnaire with points attached. It's to see whether you are Creative or Functional."

There was a short silence while they each read the questionnaire. Rufus was the first to look up. "Creative. Definitely. That's me," he stated.

"Oh Functional definitely. But you all knew that!" said Peter. "Is that a bad thing?" he added worriedly.

"I don't think so at all," said Jeff candidly, "after all you are really very good at executing what you do."

"Thank you Jeff," said Peter with a sudden sense of pride.

Kate was very quiet. Although he already had a good idea of what she would say, Jeff hoped she wasn't going to suddenly get all sensitive about this topic.

"I'm Functional," she said quietly.

Peter opened his mouth to exclaim surprise, and then catching Jeff's expression closed it suddenly with a loud "clop." Everybody looked at him, and he blushed. "Sorry," he began, "forgot to engage brain before mouth." They all laughed and relaxed.

Jeff opened out a copy of the email from the previous Friday. "Did you get the email I sent to you all last Friday? Good. Thoughts?"

"It helps to explain each principle of the Leopard but it doesn't help us understand what we have to do in practical terms," came a rather succinct reply from Kate.

"I'll second that," replied Rufus. Peter nodded agreement.

"Good because that is the purpose of this evening," grinned Jeff. At that point the waiter arrived and they all scrambled for the menus.

After they'd ordered, Jeff brought the conversation back. "So let's start with the First Principle." He pulled out a large sheet of paper and wrote clearly across the top in marker pen.

Acting opportunistically – create time in your day to balance both Creative and Functional activities.

"So for what it's worth I think the first thing to do is the Creative versus Functional questions I just gave you. The second thing to do is to take the hierarchy of time – remember that? – and apply it to your schedule."

He pulled out a copy of the Hierarchy of Time and passed it across the table. "You need to mark out Dead Time, Creative Time, Functional Time and Unallocated Time. So the challenge is for Functional people to free up some Creative space and for Creative people to set aside some Functional space for getting things done."

"Interesting," replied Kate. "How much time as a percentage do you think that should be?"

"I would think a minimum is 20% or one day a week for both types."

"That seems a hell of a lot," complained Peter, "I mean for me to free up a whole day."

"No silly," said Kate. "It's one day's worth of time over an entire week."

"I still dunno if I could do that," chuntered Peter.

"My suggestion would be that it could include Unallocated Time as well," said Jeff helpfully. "But Peter seriously, just think if you had done this sooner you would have had a whole day's worth of time to think through your project in the first place," contributed Rufus.

"I suppose you have a point." conceded Peter, still looking concerned. "I will give it a go, that's what I'll do!" He beamed at them.

"Question for you," asked Rufus looking at Jeff. "For a Creative type, should this Functional Time that I need to add include time for doing email?"

"Good question," Jeff thought for a moment and shook his head emphatically. "No, I don't think so," he replied. "Your Functional Time should be for gathering and completing discrete tasks. Even with the 11 Rules of Email, no-one could describe doing email as a discrete task."

"Fair enough," admitted Rufus as the others laughed.

Jeff was busy writing on the large sheet of paper, the conversation lulled for a few minutes until he finished and held up to show them what he had done.

"Here it is!" he exclaimed.

Guidance for Prospective Leopards (1)

- *Acting opportunistically – create time in your day for both Creative and Functional activities.*

Creative vs. Functional

- *Using the Creative vs. Functional questions to first determine whether you are naturally Creative or Functional in approach.*

Time

- *Use the Hierarchy of Time to analyse how you are spending your time during a given day; get rid of activities that are neither meaningful nor compulsory.*

- *If you are Functional you will need to prioritise your diary to add sufficient Creative space to consider new possibilities. This should be 20% of your working week and can include Unallocated Time.*

- *If you are Creative, you need to gather all your Functional tasks and organise them within regular blocks of time so that they don't interfere with your Creative Time. This should be 20% of your working week and excludes time spend doing email.*

- *The goal is to balance both behaviours so that you reap the benefits of both Creative and Functional activity.*

"I must say," said Kate, "that is actually quite easy to understand."

"Well when you do try it, please let me know how you get on," said Jeff. "Now for the next one."

Adapt to a wide variety of environments – equip yourself with the skills and habits to tackle new territories.

As he held up the second piece of paper, their dinner arrived so the dialogue was interrupted for a while as they ate.

Adapt Before Dessert

"I suspect that the first two points on this one may be easier," declared Jeff. "There are three things we have already talked about: the Rules of Responsiveness, the Hierarchy of Communications and the 11 Rules of Email."

"I must say the 11 Rules of Email are magic. You sent me a copy a couple of weeks back and my email is so much better than it was," added Rufus.

"I agree with that, actually I like all of these," added Kate with a sparkle. "Of course particularly the Rules of Responsiveness which I participated in personally."

"Indeed you did," acknowledged Jeff sincerely. "So why don't we start with that. What should people do with it?"

"Try it for at least a week in my opinion," said Peter.

"OK thanks. So what about the Hierarchy of Communications?"

"I think you probably need to apply it first to yourself and work out what you actually use and how much impact it is having. Then I suppose you should apply it to the handful of people you deal with most, say five?" contributed Peter thoughtfully.

"If those five turn out to all be on Facebook you may have a problem," observed Rufus ironically. "There's not much hierarchy to understand if you all use the same communications tool, is there?" Kate laughed.

"Oh thank you so much," responded Jeff drily. He was also a major user of Facebook and Kate knew it.

"How do we measure success with the 11 Rules of Email?"

"Easy, 20 emails or less at the end of every day for a week. Although I'm a long way from getting there right now," smiled Rufus.

"Thanks guys," said Jeff who was writing furiously.

"And now for networking."

"I hate networking," stated Peter dully.

"It's fundamental, especially if you want to further your career," countered Rufus.

"But it's just so complicated," exclaimed Peter. "And I hate it when people ignore me or don't return my emails!"

"You don't need to take it so personally," suggested Rufus.

"I'll do a follow up session on networking with you Peter," suggested Jeff. "My colleague Sue has done a super piece on it. For now I am going to make a suggestion here about starting a networking project," he scribbled a couple of lines and passed the sheet around.

Guidance for Prospective Leopards (2)

- *Adapt to a wide variety of environments — equip yourself with the skills and habits to tackle new territories.*

Communications

- *Try the Rules of Responsiveness for a week and see what impact it has on your work and social life.*

- *Think about what tools you use to communicate — where are they on the Hierarchy of Communications? What tools do you use to communicate with the 5 people you communicate most regularly? If the answer is just Facebook, then you may have a problem...*

- *Make sure you have implemented the 11 Rules of Email, measure your results by how many emails you have in your inbox at the end of each day. If you succeed in having less than 20 every day, try and create another email rule of your own design!*

Networking

- *Chose an objective, project, or new area of business that you are interested in and where you don't know people very well.*

- *Make a list of all the people you can think of in that area, making a preliminary guess of People Types and their preferred Hierarchy of Communications.*

- *Begin networking with people in that area, updating and expanding your list as you progress.*

Finishing Off

When Jeff got home at the end of the evening, he found that he was exhausted. He contemplated an early night but his conscience pricked him and he sat down and started tapping away, entering all the notes from the evening. On reflection it had been pretty successful. They had completed four of the five sheets that he had set out to do, however they didn't have the time or collective energy to tackle the Fifth Principle. He had sensed the mood and had deliberately closed out the evening with what they had already covered. He had said a warm goodbye to Kate and although he was pleased to be back on speaking terms, he reflected that he was not missing her as much as he had done the previous Friday.

Jeff finished typing and pulled up a new email to Alan and Sue headed, "Four down, one to go!" On reflection he was pretty happy with the evening's work. The Fifth Principle deserved more discussion anyway.

He hit send, snapped his MacBook shut and went to bed.

Chapter Notes

Guidance for Prospective Leopards (1)

- *Acting opportunistically – create time in your day for both Creative and Functional activities.*

Creative vs. Functional

- *Using the Creative vs. Functional questions, first determine whether you are naturally Creative or Functional in approach.*

Time

- *Use the Hierarchy of Time to analyse how you are spending your time during a given day; get rid of activities that are neither meaningful nor compulsory.*

- *If you are Functional you will need to prioritise your diary to add sufficient Creative space to consider new possibilities. This should be 20% of your working week and can include Unallocated Time.*

- *If you are Creative, you need to gather all your Functional tasks and organise them within regular blocks of time so that they don't interfere with your Creative Time. This should be 20% of your working week and excludes time spend doing email.*

- *The goal is to balance both behaviours so that you reap the benefits of both Creative and Functional activity.*

Guidance for Prospective Leopards (2)

- *Adapt to a wide variety of environments – equip yourself with the skills and habits to tackle new territories.*

Communications

- *Try the Rules of Responsiveness for a week and see what impact it has on your work and social life.*

- *Think about what tools you use to communicate – where are they on the Hierarchy of Communications? What tools do you use to communicate with the 5 people you communicate with most regularly? If the answer is just Facebook, then you may have a problem...*

- *Make sure you have implemented the 11 Rules of Email, measure your results by how many emails you have in your inbox at the end of each day. If you succeed in having less than 20 every day, try and create another email rule of your own design!*

Networking

- *Chose an objective, project or new business area that you are interested in where you don't know people very well.*

- *Make a list of all the people you can think of in that area, making a preliminary guess of People Types and their preferred Hierarchy of Communications.*

- *Begin networking with people in that area, updating and expanding your list as you progress.*

Guidance for Prospective Leopards (3)

- *Operate at speed – organise relationships and technology so you can be effective and respond more quickly.*

Relationships

- *Make a list of everyone you know using your contact list from your smartphone or Outlook as a starting point. Identify the level of each relationship with it.*

Technology

- *Review and organise all your personal and work technology – is it doing everything you want it to? Do you have all your data and contacts in one place? Can you easily find documents and emails you need?*

Guidance for Prospective Leopards (4)

- *Drive any chosen activity to a successful conclusion. Find the right collaboration to succeed with your chosen priorities.*

Teamwork

- *Work out how you can create your own cell-like team using the five principles.*

Meetings

- *Make sure all your own meetings are properly chaired and meaningful. At other meetings ask questions and make suggestions to help participants improve.*

11

REMAINING UNDETECTED

Nailing the Fifth Principle

Jeff did not have a further meeting with Alan and Sue planned until Friday but he was conscious of the momentum he had built up the previous evening. As he waited in the queue at the Coffee Bar on Tuesday morning, he tapped out a short email to both of them asking if they could free up some time later that day or on Wednesday. No sooner had he sent it than he turned round to find them both standing behind him.

"Oh hi. I was just emailing you both," he exclaimed.

"We know," smiled Sue.

"Really good work last night," added Alan.

"But we still need to nail the Fifth Principle," finished Jeff.

"Exactly."

"Well I can free up an hour now if you want? Sue?"

"Yes, I can join you."

"Let's take our coffee upstairs then."

As they walked towards Alan's office, Jeff threw out the challenge. "Thing is," he said, "I'm not sure we fully understand what it means in practice."

"Well, let's start with what we have already," replied Alan as they reached the door of his office. As they walked in he picked up a marker pen and walked over to the flipchart.

"Let's begin with what you defined the other day and understand whether we still agree with it." He began writing on the chart. "Remind me of your description again?"

Jeff reached into his bag and passed over a printout:

Remain almost undetected – build your priorities into your daily routine so that they happen automatically, leaving you free to focus on new opportunities.

"Just because leopards remain undetected doesn't mean that humans should," added Sue mischievously.

Alan shook his head. "I disagree. I think this is really important. It might be the most important principle. In the beginning I thought it was all about being discreet. After all in today's world, very few people are discreet any more, and for that matter privacy is much harder to achieve."

"I do think that is part of it," began Jeff.

"But probably not all of it, right?" said Alan.

Jeff nodded.

"Why do you think that?"

"I went back to the Leopard characteristics as a matter of fact," replied Jeff. "If you think about it, their ability to remain undetected actually means that they completely organise their own lives in private."

"That's certainly true" added Sue. "And?"

"I translated that to mean that they have organised their goals and objectives in advance, and although they are very opportunistic, they have a basic plan. Albeit simple – food, water, safety, a mate and so on. The lesson for us is that we need to have a basic plan before we venture out," he finished.

"So why do you think that lesson is part of the Fifth Principle?" questioned Sue.

"The lesson is about you setting your own objectives privately and then building them into your daily routine so that you are doing them automatically. Although you may share them, I think it's about embedding them in your life. I suspect that you cannot apply this lesson until you have worked through the other principles."

There was a silence in the room. "Wow," said Sue.

"Let me ask you something further," said Alan. "How does this make you more opportunistic?"

"I thought you would ask me that," responded Jeff with a grin. "Although you are adding structure, you also have to add discipline to the lesson also. It's not about what you plan to do it's about what you are not doing."

"You've lost me there."

"If you plan 4 to 5 objectives or priorities, in order to stick with them you will need to discard other things that get in the way."

"Whoa! Stop! That's even less opportunistic."

Jeff smiled. "You may think so, but actually it's pretty fundamental. Think back to the Leopard. Simple priorities – food, water etc. – but the Leopard can re-organise these at any time depending on what opportunity arises."

"So what you are saying is that you need to discard opportunities that are not aligned with your priorities or objectives?"

"Exactly! You also need the discipline to do this on an on-going basis."

"So I'm beginning to understand that," Sue spoke slowly. "But if you have already set your priorities then surely that limits you in terms of new opportunities?"

Jeff shook his head emphatically. "That's the whole point. You should set these objectives but you should also be prepared to review them and even discard one or more at any point in time."

"Then what's the point in setting them in the first place?" Sue was getting frustrated now.

"If you don't set them then you won't achieve anything at all," Alan added neutrally. "Am I right?"

"Yes! And that's where I got to," replied Jeff. "You need to set them, test them, review them regularly against a plan, but if you don't set them you will really struggle for direction."

Sue's expression had become more thoughtful. "So in today's world I would expect these objectives just to line up against a job description?"

"Not exactly," responded Jeff. "I mean sure there are boxes you need to tick to cover your day to day routine but these objectives have to be much more wide-ranging. They need to cover career development and personal life also. Otherwise you will never manage work/life balance and stress."

"OK! I think I'm beginning to understand," replied Sue more positively.

"I'm not saying I'm right," added Jeff. "But these are the thoughts I've been having."

"I think you may well be very right," said Alan. "So let's go back over it." He walked over to the flipchart. "How many priorities do you think is ideal?"

"No more than five," said Sue firmly. "Three is ideal but more than five is unmanageable. In my humble opinion anyway."

"I'd second that," said Alan. "It's also the number of fingers on one hand."

They all laughed for a moment.

"So what areas should these priorities cover?" wondered Sue.

"I have been thinking about that," responded Jeff thoughtfully. "I think there are three broad areas: career, personal (which includes friends and family) and health."

"Health?"

"Health!"

"Why exactly?"

"Very simple, if you have or develop any kind of serious health issue it has a massive impact on everything else. So my view is that one of these needs to be about actively improving or maintaining good health."

"OK I get that, but what does that mean in practice?" asked Alan.

"Well I will give you my example. I love competitive cycling and triathlon, so I use that hobby to drive on-going health improvement. I have a sports watch which measures heart rate, distance and stuff and I set myself goals every year in terms of training, racing and my personal stats. But my main effort as you both know is cycling to and from work every day."

"Well that's all very well for you. What about the rest of us?" asked Sue.

"It can be very simple, perhaps diet related or just walking a certain distance or even taking the stairs instead of the elevator." Jeff eyed Alan's slightly bulging midriff.

"OK so let me summarise that," responded Alan, unaware of Jeff's glance. Sue smiled and winked at Jeff.

Decide on you core priorities which should number no more than five in total divided between three areas — career, personal and health.

"Does this work?" he finished writing with a flourish.

"That's good."

"What's next?"

"I suspect," contemplated Sue, "that first you would need to break each priority down into smaller individual steps. Then probably map them into your diary?"

Alan nodded, "OK. Over what sort of timescale?"

Jeff stirred again. "Three months," he added. "That's about as far as anyone can reasonably plan in the short term. Any longer and they will not be relevant, any shorter and it will be hard to get very much achieved."

"So let me understand. You're not saying that each one needs to be completed within the quarter?"

"No. What matters is that you are making progress."

"Let me try and capture this," Alan began writing again.

Break out the individual steps in achieving each one of your priorities and then work out how you can put each step into your diary over the next 3 months.

He put down the pen and looked at Sue. "I guess we are then saying that these should be reviewed quarterly?"

"Oh yes. And also at any point in time you discard one," interjected Jeff.

"Yes quarterly makes sense. As does your point Jeff," responded Sue.

"Let me make a suggestion here," said Alan with a gleam in his eye. He picked up the pen and began writing again:

Review your objectives quarterly – or at the point in time you decide to discard one. Ensure you are making constant progress – either rework them or discard them if not.

"The last part is my interpretation," he added proudly.

"I can't disagree with you," said Jeff smartly.

Sue glanced at her watch. "Crikey! Time is nearly up," she said.

"I am going to add one more," cried Alan, who was on a roll. As Sue and Jeff began gathering their bags he wrote furiously on the flipchart once again.

Work with a mentor, close friend or colleague whom you trust so that you can be objective about what is truly important.

Jeff stopped what he was doing and gazed carefully at the flip chart. "Very good Alan," he spoke softly. "You can help me with mine next week."

Alan beamed.

"Thought you would like that last one," he said. He pulled at the flipchart sheet, tearing it off and handing it to Jeff. "As you are the keeper of the knowledge, so be it!" he said in a dramatic fashion.

"I'll write it up," responded Jeff drily.

Guidance for Prospective Leopards (5)

Remain almost undetected – build your priorities into your daily routine so that they happen automatically, leaving you free to focus on new opportunities.

- *Decide on you core priorities which should number no more than five in total divided between three areas – career, personal and health.*

- *Break out the individual steps in achieving each one of your priorities and then work out how you can put each step into your diary over the next 3 months.*

- *Review your objectives quarterly – or at the point in time you decide to discard one. Ensure you are making constant progress – either rework them or discard them if not.*

- *Work with a mentor, close friend or colleague whom you trust so that you can be objective about what is truly important.*

The Train Trip

Sue had to make a trip to visit one of the key suppliers for her project. It was quite a long trip involving several hours each way on a train, so she had put it off until she simply could not leave it any longer. It wasn't so much the travelling she disliked as the uncertainly of how much work she could actually get done during the journey, whether the journey would be tolerable and whether she would be delayed coming back as the distance was not quite long enough to do an overnight trip.

She had organised herself the night before to try and take some work papers with her so she could be productive as possible. She made a good start in the morning, sharply dressed in a well-fitting grey wool suit, managing to slip out of the house before the children worked out where she was going, or involving her in the usual breakfast chaos. Barry had been a star as ever. Today was now under control. Or so she thought.

Travel policy didn't normally permit her to travel in First Class on the train but she had asked Alan if he might make an exception so she would have space and peace to work, and he had kindly signed it off. She made the station in plenty of time, found a good seat on the train and was settling in with a coffee when she heard a loud "click-clack" of a pair of high heels along the platform and a vaguely familiar vision in red passed her window, climbed on board and slid gracefully into the seat opposite. It was Rafaella in her full glory.

Although Sue had not met Rafaella in person, she recognised her instantly and was aware of who she was. She found herself feeling rather intimidated, but worse still she was in a quandary as to what to do. Should she introduce herself and risk being snubbed or should she just keep to herself? What to do? Sue decided that she would keep to herself for now, but would say hello if the opportunity presented itself. She buried herself in her work.

Rafaella was very pre-occupied firstly by refreshing her appearance with the aid of a mirror and then moving seamlessly over to a BlackBerry which she stared at intently, flicking through her messages with zealous enthusiasm. As her perfume wafted across the table, Sue found herself glancing up again and taking a moment to admire her counterpart's appearance. Rafaella was beautifully dressed, that was for sure. Never mind Sue's grey suit, Rafaella wore an exquisite designer number which fitted her perfectly. The hair, the nails were all immaculate. "Just how does she manage to look like that on a workday?" wondered Sue.

At that moment the train started to move gently out of the station; Sue was relieved as that just left the two of them in that section of the carriage. But she was wrong. An overweight, slightly scruffy balding man in his fifties was wondering down the carriage. He was puffing from running for the train, sweating heavily and carrying a cup of coffee in a large cardboard cup which was clearly the reason why he had been late. He spotted Rafaella and an unmistakeable leer crossed his face. Spying the seat next to her was free apart from Rafaella's bag, he dropped his bulk alongside her with a distinctive thud. Rafaella had been concentrating so hard on her BlackBerry that she had not spotted her impending doom and was forced, much against her will to lift her bag up onto the table. She glared at the man. He grinned back sardonically.

Sue felt mortified for Rafaella, but at the same time she felt a little bit of schadenfreude too because Rafaella had, after all attracted his attention. No, that was mean and unfair; she pushed the thought to the back of her mind.

The man was settling into his seat, still staring at Rafaella who was now pointedly ignoring him. She pulled out a sleek ultrabook from her bag and powered it up. The man leaned forward slightly so that he could get a better view of Rafaella's more than generous cleavage. He lifted his hand and touched her on the arm to get her attention.

"Do you mind?" she said firmly. The man was delighted.

"Not at all!" he said, gazing lustfully at her. He picked up his coffee and slurped noisily through the plastic lid.

Rafaella grimaced. Sue wondered what she could possibly do to help. The train rocked slightly as it went round a corner, the man used this opportunity to lean himself against Rafaella. She turned and glared at him again. He grinned at her and then pulled a huge handkerchief out of his top pocket and began to mop his brow. Rafaella was now seriously pissed off. It wasn't a new experience for her, and while she was used to dealing with it, he was seriously disgusting, and she had another three more hours of him!

As the man slurped noisily out of his coffee again, an evil thought began to wonder through her mind. She smiled briefly before returning to ignoring the man and staring at her laptop screen.

Sue saw the smile and wandered what it was about. Surely Rafaella couldn't be enjoying this could she? The train lurched again, but this time Rafaella was ready for him. In one smooth movement she lifted her bag as if to search for something and allowed it to swing sideways across the table. The bag caught the top of the man's coffee and sent the whole thing flying straight into his lap, removing the plastic lid in the process. The man let out a piercing yell as the hot liquid covered his shirt, trousers and groin and showing a surprising turn of speed, he leapt to his feet, clutching at his scalded loins.

"Oh I am so, so sorry," purred Rafaella with a silkily sweet voice, tinged with just a little bit of evil.

"You bitch!" the man cried.

"How dare you! It was an accident!" retorted Rafaella standing up.

The train manager had been standing nearby and came rushing over. "Can I help?" he asked helpfully.

"That bitch threw my coffee all over me," exclaimed the man rudely.

Rafaella smiled sweetly at the conductor, who melted. "That man is so rude," she said with small voice. "It was an accident, and I did say sorry!"

The train manager picked up the situation instantly. "Do come with me sir, I have some towels at the bar and we can get you dried off." The man was led away still clutching at himself and dribbling coffee all the way up the carriage.

Rafaella and Sue watched him all the way out of the carriage and into the bar, and as soon as he had left they sat down again, looked each other in the eye and spontaneously burst out laughing, and soon tears were rolling down their faces.

"I can't... believe... you... did... that," sobbed Sue.

"Did... what?" Rafaella bawled back, which only set Sue off again.

Sue pulled out a bag of tissues and began to dry her eyes,

unthinking she passed them to Rafaella who also used one to dab at her eyes and then anther to try and mop up the remnants of the coffee which had got on the table. The train manager came back to dry the seat, but there was no further sign of the sweaty man. As the train manager finished wiping up, he winked at them which set them off again.

Sue caught Rafaella's gaze. "I'm Sue," she introduced herself. Rafaella and Sue shook hands.

"I haven't laughed so much in years," said Sue. "But I am sorry, he was such a pig."

Rafaella shrugged and rolled her eyes. "I am very sad to say it goes with the territory," she said. "It has happened before and it will happen again."

"I'm really sad to hear that," responded Sue earnestly. "I really don't see why you should have to put up with it."

"I don't either but then again some men would say that I was just asking for it," replied Rafaella frankly.

"Now you are being silly," said Sue.

Rafaella sighed. It was a sigh of a woman who was resigned to her lot but was nevertheless determined not to give in. "The way I dress, the length of my skirt, the make-up, blah, blah" her eyes blazed. "Shit! It really, really pisses me off! I'm a woman for heaven's sake. What the hell is wrong with looking and feeling like a woman when I go to work?" Suddenly the icy cool front dropped and a look of intense pain crossed Rafaella's face. Sue instinctively reached out and grabbed her hand and the two of them sat in silence for a few minutes.

Eventually Rafaella recovered. "Thank you for understanding," she said.

"Well I must say, I have put up with my fair share of male banter at work, but this morning was something else," observed Sue.

"Well it may have been something else for you but that for me was business as usual."

"It's a great shame to hear that," comforted Sue. "Listen I think I should confess something. I think I recognise you. I believe your firm is one of our larger clients."

Rafaella looked blankly at her for a moment, and then her eyes narrowed. "Got it," she said. "You work with Sam's crowd."

"Err… yes, exactly." Sue's mind had to race a little for the context as she didn't know Sam that well.

Rafaella eyed Sue closely. "So what did you make of me up before today?" she asked coolly.

"I haven't seen that much of you to be honest, but you always stand out. I guess that's the point."

Rafaella laughed at this. "Oh come on. What was your opinion of me before today? I'm sure you all chat together about me."

Sue sighed. It was true, there was always gossip. Particularly about Rafaella. "Alright, I thought you aloof, unemotional, and perhaps even cold. Although always immaculately dressed," responded Sue candidly.

Rafaella raised her eyebrows.

"Was I accurate?" asked Sue.

"That's pretty much how I set out to manage things, yes," replied Rafaella slowly. "Look I like to dress well and look great. It's who I am and I am not changing that for anyone. I will be honest with you, when I first started I used to be a lot friendlier but I found people took advantage and it got me precisely nowhere."

"I have never found being friendly a problem," remarked Sue.

"Well that's because you are determined to fit in," replied Rafaella. "Don't get me wrong, I am not criticising, but," she gestured at Sue. "You are dressed to fit into a man's world. I'm sorry but I have just never been prepared to do that."

Sue was taken aback for a second but her curiosity was heightened. "So tell me. What sort of response do you get when you were friendly to people?"

"Hah! They men treated me like some kind of decoration and the women ignored me completely," confessed Rafaella. "I mean – shit! – I have a first class honours degree and an MBA from a top business school."

"Oh really?" Sue was surprised. "Then why…" she caught herself just in time.

"'…do I dress like a tart?' Isn't that what you were going to say?" asked Rafaella brutally.

"Well not exactly," replied Sue, who had guiltily been thinking exactly that, "God! This is so frustrating," exclaimed Rafaella hotly. She reached over the table and grabbed Sue's hand again. "You must understand that what I am doing is so important," she said fiercely. "If I give in then they win!"

"They?"

"Pigs like him," she gestured in the vague direction the fat man had taken. "And all those who would and do behave like him. All those who belittle our contributions and want us to be slaves or just for decoration."

"I hardly think of myself as a slave," exclaimed Sue, then she smiled. "I'm not sure if I fit the decoration mould either!"

"Oh I don't know about that," Rafaella looked Sue up and down and then tactfully changed the conversation. "So what's your angle then?" she asked.

"My angle?"

"Yes. Where you are at in your life. Where you are going? That sort of thing?"

"Well," she said. "I have three children, a selfless husband who works for an NGO and I have just returned to work from maternity leave. I love working for my new boss. We have some really exciting new projects, but I spend my days very stressed trying to balance the demands of the office, life at home and the endless guilt that I am not spending enough time with my children who are all very young." The last sentence made Sue become rather emotional and she now went very quiet.

"Wow," said Rafaella softly. "That's amazing. I take my hat off to you."

"Hardly," Sue recovered, and then she blurted out. "But there is no way I can look as good as you do in the morning."

Rafaella shook her head slowly. "What I have," she said carefully, "requires a lot of effort in the morning and often a good deal of bravado, like today. As time wears on it will be harder and harder for me to keep up. And I will, mark my words! But, truthfully, I envy you because what you have will be with you forever."

"There is no reason you can't do what I have done," said Sue earnestly, but Rafaella shook her head slowly.

"I am not sure it's me. Even if I could find the right man in the first place," she added lamely.

"Nonsense," it was Sue's turn to be forthright. "I agree, you have to have the right person to share it with, but you shouldn't ever give up!"

"I don't know Sue. I'm not sure the gods are with me."

"Well you might surprise yourself yet."

"I do that on a daily basis." They both laughed again and were silent for a few minutes. "I want to ask you something," began Rafaella. "I'm curious. What sort of stuff do you get to deal with at work? As a woman I mean?"

Sue sighed. "I get two sorts. General office banter which I am OK at dealing with, and the second part is the intellectual arrogance. Sometimes the men make me feel like I cannot be right simply because I'm a woman."

"Go on."

"While some of the banter can be quite rude, I don't take it personally and have learned to deal with it. Not everyone can do that but I have found that it's better to be a participant than an objector. It's always going to go on in an office and in life generally and I would rather be a part of it."

"How do you prevent it from spilling over into the sort of thing that happened today? If that isn't a naïve question?" asked Rafaella.

Sue was surprised by this. "I presume I would just ignore it completely?" she ventured.

"I tend to stay well out of it," said Rafaella with a reflective voice, "and I am pretty abrupt if people persist. But I do wonder if it's the right approach?"

"Well it fits with your 'detached' persona that's for sure," observed Sue.

"I know. But I really do have a sense of humour and at the moment I pretty much keep it under wraps," observed Rafaella. "It's just that inevitably when I do join in the conversation always ends up getting crass and out of hand. And I hate that."

"May I make a suggestion?" enquired Sue. "That may happen because people don't know you very well. I have a couple of young engineers working with me on this project. They graduated a year or so ago and are pretty immature. They forget very quickly how to behave when I am in the room and say things that are really completely inappropriate."

"So what do you do about it?"

"Well they do work for me, which helps. So mostly I just have to nudge them when they overstep. For example I will say 'Michael I really don't think you meant to say that did you?' at which point he becomes rather embarrassed and apologises. They know I have a sense of humour, and we do joke about things but slowly I am training them to at least have some sensitivity."

"Well that's good a start. But it's dealing with the older lot, along with a couple of simpering women who coo along and encourage them," said Rafaella. "I mean really!"

"I know," sighed Sue. "But I genuinely think it will be easier if people know you better. I mean if companies do become more draconian than they are already, all it will do is divide the office into separate groups and all you and I will end up doing is wondering what they are all giggling about."

"Equally the real idiots usually end up incriminating themselves anyway."

"What do you mean?" asked Rafaella.

"People who can't control or manage their thought process usually end up putting something inappropriate in email or text, or even Facebook. It doesn't happen often but it's a good reminder," offered Sue.

"I hate getting formal about these things though, it makes the issue worse," observed Rafaella candidly.

"You don't need to – on the rare occasion it happens to me, I just quietly share it with a few key people and the problem is shared and other people help me manage it," replied Sue.

"Oh really?" said Rafaella. "That's interesting." She continued. "There is one further thing I do, which sometimes works. And that is I can be incredibly rude,"

"I know. Like just now," said Sue ironically.

"But he so deserved it," cried Rafaella indignantly, then she saw Sue's smile. They both laughed again.

"Maybe that's it!" exclaimed Sue. "That's exactly what we should do!"

"What? What?"

"When we are properly offended, be very rude indeed and then laugh like we didn't mean it."

"Never apologise, never explain. Winston Churchill I think."

Sue pulled out her black notebook and started writing in it. "That's a great one for the Leopard," she said absent-mindedly.

"The Leopard?"

"It's a really fun project I'm working on internally. I can tell you all about it."

Jeff's Expenses

Alan had a question he needed Jeff to answer; he was about to reach for the phone then he thought better of it and decided to walk down to Jeff's cubicle. He reasoned that if Jeff wasn't there he would go onto the Coffee Bar anyway but sure enough Jeff was at his desk, deep in concentration. A myriad of printed spreadsheets and piles of receipts covered his entire desk. He was so deep in concentration that he didn't see Alan at first, then he started in surprise because Alan never came to see him, he always went to Alan.

"Hi," Jeff began, a little startled.

"Quick question for you. I wondered whether you have 10 minutes for a coffee?" Alan suddenly felt very self-conscious, "shouldn't you have just sent an email and not interrupted Jeff?" his conscience told him.

"Great, thanks Alan. I've had enough of this stuff, that's for sure," Jeff got up.

"What are you doing?" asked Alan evenly.

"I am little embarrassed to say: my expenses," replied Jeff. "I got a little behind and now finance is pressuring me otherwise they say they won't pay."

"How far behind?" Alan eyed Jeff carefully who was now embarrassed.

"3 months if you must know," he muttered.

"Oh well there you are then," replied Alan not surprised.

"But it's so hard!" exclaimed Jeff. "There are so many petty rules. I cannot work out what I should and should not be claiming for."

"I know that but actually the principles are pretty simple," observed Alan.

"Yeah – if I don't do it I'm out of pocket," replied Jeff sarcastically.

"That's not what I meant actually. Let's get the coffees and I will explain – it may help you."

"Anything that helps would be great," Jeff brightened up.

As they got their coffees and sat down, Alan began. "Every organisation has problems with their expense systems. They need to strike the balance between avoiding unnecessary cost on the bottom line and enabling people at all levels to recover legitimate costs for doing business."

"I get that," replied Jeff, "I do."

"So the problem is that because expenses are so easily abused, they mostly remain on a 'low trust' system which has a lot of bureaucracy and makes it very hard for people to claim. Because the same rules have to be applied in theory to all levels of the organisation, the rules are written for the most junior level."

"OK, I understand. So what do I need to do differently?"

"Well there are three principles that I apply to all my expense claims. As a result I rarely have to think hard when I do them, which makes them much easier to do funnily enough! I think these principles are true no matter what organisation you work in."

"I'm all ears," Jeff was fully engaged.

"The first principle is that the expense should put you in a position to do your job. In other words if you were not there would you have run up that expense anyway? If the answer is yes then you shouldn't expense it."

"OK, give me an example?"

"So if I am setting off on an early morning train trip to see someone, then I always buy a coffee and a muffin at the station. Even though I'm on business I rarely, if ever, expense that."

"Why?"

"Because I could have had a coffee at home," replied Alan. "I would have had the coffee anyway, if I had come to the office for example."

"That's true," observed Jeff.

"But if I am travelling on business and I stop in a hotel for a coffee to do some email, that's perfectly alright as I would not have had to visit the hotel if I hadn't been on business."

"Oh, OK, I get it," enthused Jeff. "Thanks, that helps!"

"So the second principle is that your expenses should be reasonably consistent with your lifestyle, so even if you are taking out clients, you should not be booking places and doing things that you would never visit with your own money."

"But I like taking clients out," countered Jeff.

"I know. And I have observed that you are very good at it too," replied Alan. "But it's a good principle to follow otherwise you may end up running up a big bill which then gets questioned."

"That's a fair point."

"And the third principle is that when you submit an expense report, you should be able to look back over it justify every single line to your manager."

"Well sure," began Jeff.

"I am not sure you understand me," replied Alan. "Say for example it was me. If your expense report had been escalated to me it would mean only one thing – that you had put something in there that the system regarded as seriously out of policy."

"That would be bad."

"Yes that would be very bad."

"So you would need an explanation from me?"

"Rather more than that. I would need to know that even if it was within policy, it had been done for a good reason as I know you have good judgement. Which I think you do by the way."

The light bulb went on for Jeff. "Right," he breathed. "You would want to be sure that I had not done something that would seriously embarrass you. In other words I shouldn't let you down."

"Thank you," said Alan simply.

"Actually, thank you Alan," said Jeff. "That's been really helpful."

"There is one more," added Alan. "More of a pragmatic point really. Do you know what your expenses budget is?"

"No."

"I would find out if I were you."

"Good point. I will. Anyway what was it you wanted to ask me?"

Alan looked at him and shook his head. "You know I am embarrassed to say, I have now completely forgotten."

Jeff laughed.

"No worries," he said. "Thank you for the coffee and also for getting me out of the rut with my expenses."

"A pleasure. One more thing:"

"Yes?"

"Don't get behind again. Put time in the diary and do them every fortnight. It's your money you are losing out on."

"I know. Thanks Alan."

Chapter Notes

Guidance for Prospective Leopards (5)

Remain almost undetected – build your priorities into your daily routine so that they happen automatically, leaving you free to focus on new opportunities.

- *Decide on you core priorities which should number no more than five in total divided between three areas – career, personal and health.*

- *Break out the individual steps in achieving each one of your priorities and then work out how you can put each step into your diary over the next 3 months.*

- *Review your objectives quarterly – or at the point in time you decide to discard one. Ensure you are making constant progress – either rework them or discard them if not.*

- *Work with a mentor, close friend or colleague whom you trust so that you can be objective about what is truly important.*

The Four Principles of Expenses

1. *Any expense should put you in a position to do your job. If you were there for personal reasons rather than on business would you have run up that expense anyway? If the answer is yes then you should not expense it.*

2. *Your expenses should be consistent with your lifestyle, so even if you are entertaining clients, you should not be booking places and doing things that you would never pay for with your own money.*

3. *When you submit an expense report, you should be able to look back over it and justify every single line to your manager. If there is an escalation, your good judgement will be questioned.*

4. *Always ask what your expenses budget is — if there is not one assigned, agree one with your manager.*

12

THE RUN HOME

Setting Up for Friday

Barbara was on the phone. "Alan, change of plan, Bill wants to come and sit in on your next session," she declared.

Alan started. They hadn't got a plan for this Friday. "OK," he said for lack of anything better to say.

"Make it another good one," sparked Barbara, and then she hung up.

Alan was rather flummoxed. What to do? They had covered most of the main sessions, and yet they hadn't completely reworked all the material. He sighed and looked out the window. The summer had given way to autumn and although it was still warm outside, the trees were displaying a blaze of golden colour. He thought back over the past months to the afternoon it had all began. "Right," he declared to no-one in particular as the room was decidedly empty. He stood up, pulled on his suit jacket and walked out of his office. He marched through the building purposefully, past the Coffee Bar and out of the front door. The park beckoned – after all that's where it had all begun. He wandered through until he found the same bench, sat down and relaxed for a minute. He breathed in the fresh air and felt much better.

"Are we a little stuck in a rut?" said a familiar voice.

"Ah that must be the local Leopard," replied Alan looking round for the cat. It was sitting beside him on the bench. How had it got there?

"Well you look cheerful enough, but face it you wouldn't be out here if everything was hunky dory," said the cat knowingly.

"Too true," agreed Alan. "We are almost all becoming Leopards now, apart from the head honcho. And that's my problem."

"Why doesn't he want to be a Leopard?"

"Oh I am sure he does. He just doesn't know it yet," explained Alan. "Thing is I have to run a session to present to him on Friday and I don't know what to present on."

"That will be fine," said the cat.

"I am sure it will be fine. I just don't know what to present to him," countered Alan.

"That's what I am saying," said the cat. "You should present to him on presenting. Won't that be fun?"

"Eh what?" said Alan, but the cat had vanished just as suddenly as it had arrived. "Presenting on presenting," he repeated. "Oh I get it presenting on presenting!" He shook his head. "But that's what I was going to do anyway!" he exclaimed.

With that Alan stood up and set off back to the office. As the sun's rays shone dreamily through the trees, the breeze blew some leaves playfully across Alan's path. He smiled; he would never have come out here at all until recently. "Clears the fog," he thought to himself and smiled. "And that cat too!"

Back in the Office

As soon as he was back at his desk, Alan called Sue. She wasn't there so he left a voicemail. He wasn't worried, he had a plan. She eventually called back after 5pm.

"Hi Alan, what's up?"

"Change of plan," and he told her Barbara's news.

"Wow. Well I don't know what else we have to cover right now," responded Sue.

"Well I have had an idea," replied Alan. It wasn't his idea but what the hell. "I think we should do a short session on presenting," he ventured.

"Presenting? You know what we have been doing at the previous meetings. Well I can see how that would add value, but we haven't any collective ideas on it," she replied.

"Do you?"

"Some. I can work them up if you like?"

"Let's give examples of three different styles and summarise what's good and bad about them," mused Alan. "I have some decks I can use as examples."

"Do you really want to do that?" Sue was alarmed. Alan's presentation style was long on detail but short on audience engagement.

Alan laughed. "You don't have to say it, I know I have the reputation as a dull presenter," he confessed. "Look my approach works for some people. I will try and critique it if you like."

The relief in Sue's voice was palpable. "OK," she said. "So if I do the same and Jeff follows suit, that should work?"

"Yes but we will have to do our homework beforehand." That meant an early evening session. Sue sighed inwardly. She was seriously owed some time at home at the moment.

Alan sensed her disquiet. "Last one," he proposed. "We are really close, one last push and then Bill either buys it or we all go back to our day job."

"I hope so Alan. I love working for you, but it has been hard."

"I know," he sympathised. "And thank you. I couldn't do this without you." They fixed a time the following evening to do the preparation. Sue decided to get away early that day. At least that would brighten Barry up before she told him.

Rafaella Returns

Sue was in early the following day. She stopped at the Coffee Bar and was about to take her drink upstairs when she bumped into Barbara. "Hi Sue. I'm betting that you and Alan have a good plan for Friday," began Barbara supportively.

"I think so," said Sue. "I guess it's make or break time."

"Bill has been pretty open-minded so far. And Robin has bent his ear as you know," Barbara observed.

As they were in conversation, Sue heard the familiar "clack-clack" of high heels across the lobby. "I know who that is," she said, and turned around to see Rafaella walking towards them. "Hi Rafaella, how's things?" ventured Sue.

Rafaella scowled and then suddenly, on recognising Sue, was all smiles. "Oh hi Sue!" she said warmly, suddenly she was the friendly approachable Rafaella from the train again.

"This is Barbara our HR director"

"Lovely to meet you! Wow. Great role to have here, how long have you been doing that for?"

Sue was astonished. She stood and watched for several minutes as Barbara and Rafaella just – there was no other word for it – clicked and chatted away. She eventually excused herself and left shaking her head. One minute Rafaella was the ice maiden, the next she was ready to be friends with anybody. Well not anybody, I mean Barbara was good fun, but it was most uncharacteristic. She shook her head and thought no more about it.

The Friday Session

Chastised by the prior session on meetings with John Abercrombie, everyone was on time or early for the Friday session. In anticipation Barbara had booked one of the larger meeting rooms but between board members, management and graduates the word had spread and there was a good turnout. Bill was surprisingly discreet. He had come over to Alan to say hello and had then quietly slipped into the back row. Most of the people in the room still hadn't realised he was there. Even Ben had made it on time, and was sitting on the front row. He looked almost ready to pounce like a leopard, or so Alan thought for a minute. He suppressed a giggle.

Just as Alan was about to start, the door swung open fully, Alan looked up and there was Bennett glowering. Bennett was a large heavyset man, with jowls. His head was very bald on the top but he had thick hair round the side and back which made him look rather like a bear wearing a bandana. He also dressed in ill-fitting clothes which no-one commented on as they were mostly frightened of him. Alan suddenly had a tiny instinctive thought about why Bennett was there, but decided to be cheerful and neutral. "Hello Bennett, you joining us?"

"I don't think so," glowered Bennett. "I am looking for Ben actually."

"I'm over here," said Ben, pretty much oblivious to the political situation that was about to play out. Alan suddenly realised that Bennett had absolutely no idea that Robin or Bill were in the room.

"What the fuck are you doing here?" snarled Bennett. "You are supposed to be with me this morning working on the data architecture."

"I go to these every week," replied Ben breezily. "They are in my diary. It's no biggie. Can we do the data piece later on?"

"It IS a biggie and NO we cannot," roared Bennett. "I never approved this." Bennett's eyes were bulging as he rounded on Alan. The room had gone quiet.

"This is all your doing Alan, you deliberately lured him over here." Bennett had taken a pace into the room and suddenly became aware of all the people in it. He looked fit to burst with anger when suddenly a cough came from the back of the room.

"Hello Bennett," said Bill, who had been the one who had coughed, and, like everyone in the company, only knew Bennett by his surname, "Is there a problem?"

"Too right there is a problem," blustered Bennett, still unaware of who had asked the question. He peered hopefully at the audience and then saw Bill. Bennett suddenly turned bright red and became very crestfallen. "Oh!" he said.

There was an uncomfortable silence.

Jeff leaned over and whispered in Kate's ear: "I think I am going to wet myself…"

Kate nearly exploded with laughter but just managed to contain herself.

"I am so sorry for interrupting," said Bennett eventually, shuffling out of the room. As the door closed several people sniggered at Bennett's comeuppance. Jeff leaned over to speak to Ben.

"Oh man, I would hate to be in your shoes later."

Ben grinned. "I think we are done with him for today."

"I hope so. For your sake."

The Three Pointers for Presenting Properly

After Bennett's cameo performance Alan returned to earth very quickly. "We have a short session this morning on presenting," he began. "Short because most presentations we attend are far too long so we are going to set an example."

"In fact," began Sue, striding up to the front of the room, "we are going to use PowerPoint but we are going to start with just one slide."

Proper Presentation

Audience – understand who your audience is, the context of the presentation and their expectations. This will fully drive both your preparation and timing.

Proper Presentation (Continued)

Timing – unless you are making a depth presentation with detailed information, shortness and punctuality are paramount.

- *7 minutes and 20 minutes are good starting points.*

- *More than 40 minutes requires a break to maintain attention.*

- *Allow for questions either at the end or as you go along.*

Preparation – balance your knowledge of the topic, preparation of the content and rehearsal of the performance.

There was a moments silence and then Sue continued. "So, the first thing you are going to ask me is how long this presentation is going to last for?"

"7 minutes?" ventured Jeff playfully. Everyone laughed.

"Very good Jeff. I am going for 20 minutes including questions."

"Why? I mean how do you work out what time you actually need?"

"Often you don't get a choice. You get given a time slot on an agenda. The shortest is normally around 10 minutes, which is 7 minutes plus a couple of questions. 20 minutes is about right for the more in depth presentation that we are having today. It's a good balance between having enough time to explain and make your key points versus losing people's attention. After 40 minutes you will lose people's attention, so it's best to plan a break at that point." She paused to take a sip of water from a glass.

"But I'm getting ahead of myself. The main thing about presentations is the audience. So many things that people present on are on the topics they want to talk about rather than what the audience wants to hear. People often try and justify themselves or try and sell something in a presentation without understanding that it's not what the audience wants to hear. Audiences like to be engaged, educated and occasionally entertained. They do not want to be bored, talked at and taken for granted."

"So how do you research an audience for one of our meetings? Or even a meeting like this?" asked a tall dark haired girl in the back row.

"Typically I rely on whoever owns or is chairing the meeting to brief me on the audience," replied Sue. "Very occasionally I get tripped up but you do have to rely on the meeting owner to help. As far as this meeting goes," she grinned, "that's Alan's call so if I am missing the point, I will blame him!"

Everyone laughed again. "So beyond audience and timing, the last key point – and one I cannot emphasise enough – is preparation, preparation, preparation. If you are going to use slides – and they are not mandatory by the way – make sure you have written them consistently and that they have all the information you need. I try and get someone to look over them beforehand to make sure I have not missed anything. You need to know the topic thoroughly and be confident in your own mind that you can fully tell the story of what you are presenting about. Lastly you should rehearse as many times as you need depending on the size and importance of the audience. If you are clear in your own mind how it all hangs together you will be fine."

"How do you know when to use PowerPoint?" asked a bespectacled youth from the front row.

"Good question. I'll give you a short answer and then revisit on the next slide if I may," replied Sue.

"It depends on both the content of the presentation but also the presenter. If you are a polished public speaker and can talk off the cuff, you may choose to limit your use of PowerPoint and just talk to the audience. In this scenario, you could also use PowerPoint for one or two headline slides. If you want to be very precise you could choose to write out the text as a speech, in which case you should allow about

150 words a minute."

"For most of us – and I include myself in this – public speaking and presenting is quite hard work and PowerPoint is a great tool for structuring and organising our thoughts. It also means you have a summary to send round afterwards. Pretty much everyone has to present in today's world so I think PowerPoint is also a great help for those who lack confidence."

"What about text versus graphics?" It was the long haired lady from the back row again.

"Good audience participation" thought Sue, before she answered the question. "Text is simple and good for hand-outs afterwards," replied Sue. "Although some people do object to allowing everyone to read their slide as it arrives on the screen. Personally if you can spend time creating graphics that make sense rather than look pretty then by all means do it. Graphics, video, photos and music all enhance a presentation but they take more time to prepare and add to the complexity. They also create huge files that are sometimes impossible to email or download quickly."

"So at the risk of allowing you all to read my slides, here's the next one."

Three Typical Types of Presentation – Show, Know & Go

Show Presentation – to bring an audience up to speed on a topic with which they are not that familiar. Think of these as an advertising agency pitch. They should tell a story, be engaging and compelling to the audience if possible.

Know Presentation – to provide detailed and in depth knowledge on a topic to an audience that has some context but needs to understand the detail. This would cover financial briefings, operational updates and board reports. These presentations are all about detail and order; it is vital to make sure that the presenter knows the topic intimately.

Go Presentation – a presentation to motivate the troops and stir people into action. There are great military and political leadership examples, but above all this is about firing up the people in the room.

Sue waited for a second and looked at Jeff expectantly. He was grinning in anticipation. "Oh go on then," she said. "Spit it out!"

"So which type does this presentation represent?" asked Jeff with mock politeness.

"I will seriously kill him later," thought Sue. "At 20 minutes, this is a Show Presentation," replied Sue evenly. "Although many of you are familiar with this topic we don't normally discuss it so I have started from first principles, hence Show. I could do a Know presentation on this topic, but it would be substantially longer. More of a training session really. And that wouldn't necessarily engage all of you here today."

"I think you should actually," commented Bill suddenly. "This is very helpful."

Sue reddened at Bill's compliment, but just managed to control herself. "The point about a Show presentation is that it should serve as an introduction. Or in meal terms 'A Starter'. In order to be successful it should be engaging enough and memorable enough – tell a story – so that the audience wants more. The Know presentation is the main course. It's for people who have had the introduction and are looking for an in depth understanding of a topic. I have put reporting as a good example of this and it is – typically management teams what to drill down into the nitty-gritty of a topic and it is up to the presenter to communicate that detail on screen and through their own knowledge. These can be long and sometimes painful presentations and one of the great skills of the presenter here is to work out if everyone is interested in a particular discussion point or whether they should take a point offline with the relevant audience members."

"How do you tell?" again from the long-haired lady.

"Check for signs of boredom around the table. Also it depends on whether it's the chairman or CEO asking in which case you probably should continue."

"I would like to suggest that you don't actually," offered Robin this time. "At least at this company. Far too many senior executives use their ego to waste others time in my opinion."

"OK well there you have it," gestured Sue to the long-haired lady.

Go

"Finally the Go presentation. I won't call it the dessert but it is the presentation to finish on."

"Coffee perhaps?" Jeff was enjoying himself.

"I'll give you coffee," Sue replied tartly. More laughter. "A Go presentation is the hardest and yet the simplest presentation. Hardest in that it is for motivating what can be a disparate group of people and yet simplest in that it's essentially around the messages rather than the detail. Returning to PowerPoint for a second. Show and Know presentations generally need PowerPoint most of the time. Show to impress the audience, Know to convey the quantity of detail on the screen. Go presentations can often just be a speech or a conversation. They depend heavily on the presenter and have to answer the question 'why?' 'Why is it important?' 'Why should I do this for you?' These types of addresses are the bread and butter of military history, leadership books and business magazines, but they don't have to be all poetry and drama."

Another laugh from the audience.

"Go presentations are all about spelling out what is important and re-emphasising the message. We have to reach this number, win this client and this is what we are focusing on. And repeat the message again. Typically the audience has already received a number of important messages but what they really need to understand is what the few most important things are they need to do."

"When do you give a Go presentation?" asked the bespectacled youth again.

"Typically they are given by management at the end of a conference or offsite meeting; equally they may be more regular if you run a meeting on a project."

"Well I'm quite new and not very senior," said the youth humbly, "so I guess they are not something people at my level would normally do?"

"On the contrary, if you want to galvanise help from a team or to get an initiative launched, they are exactly the sort of presentation you will need." Sue paused. "However whichever presentation type you use will need to follow three basic steps to get the message across."

Getting the Message Across

1. *First you must tell the audience what you are going to tell them.*

2. *Then tell them.*

3. *And finally — tell them what you have told them.*

"If you follow these steps, there is a vague chance that the audience might actually remember what you said." At which point there was further amusement in the room.

"And to try and keep to my time schedule, here is my final slide:"

The Golden Rules

- *Make sure you understand your audience and the context.*

The Golden Rules (Continued)

- *Do your preparation thoroughly and above all make sure you are mentally ready.*

- *Aim to get over no more than 3 key points that the audience will take away.*

"If I was doing this as a Go presentation, this is the kind of slide I might use. I am just re-emphasising thee key points and, I hope, leaving them in your minds to take away as you go. Does that all make sense?"

Several more questions followed about PowerPoint, which Sue dealt with and then she wrapped up. "Thank you all," she looked at her watch. "22 minutes so I have run over just a little."

There was applause throughout the room and everyone began to drift out.

Bill and Robin came over to Sue who was disconnecting her laptop; Alan hovered alongside, slightly nervously. "I really enjoyed that," began Bill. "Thank you very much."

"Very well done indeed," echoed Robin.

Bill looked at Alan. "You have both done a super job," Bill continued. "I really want to see this progress. Alan, please follow up with me next week?"

"Yes, absolutely," replied Alan.

And with that Bill and Robin moved off and left the room which was now emptying rapidly.

Several more people came up to thank Sue and ask about copies of the presentation. When they had gone, Alan put his hand on Sue's arm.

"That was really very good you know," he said sincerely.

Sue was completely overcome with emotion and went very quiet for a moment. "I'm sorry," she said.

"What is there to be sorry for? You worked very hard and delivered a fantastic session."

"I don't normally get emotional at these things."

"I know but I think we have finally got there."

Barbara had been chatting to some of the others, walked over and threw her arms around Sue. "Well done," she said, Sue clung to her desperately fighting off waves of emotion. She saw Jeff standing behind Alan. "And I am going to kill you when I get a chance!"

"Who me?" asked Jeff in mock indignation, and suddenly they were all laughing. When they had calmed down, Alan spoke. "What are you all doing next Thursday evening?" he asked.

"No idea right now."

"I would like to buy you all dinner at Alphonso's. My treat."

"Oh wow, that would be great," replied Jeff instantly. Then he remembered Kate.

"Kate is invited too..." Alan had read his mind. "As are all those who have worked on the project."

The Dinner

After Friday's excitement the following week seemed rather quiet. Alan had postponed the Friday session until he had met with Bill; they had not spoken very much during the week so it was almost a surprise when Thursday came around. Alan had been very cryptic about who was attending the dinner.

Sue was exhilarated when he had extended the invitation to Barry. "That's so kind of you Alan, but I don't understand why?"

"Well he was a great contributor to the 11 Rules of Email and he has also borne the brunt of me keeping you late on so many occasions. It would be great for you both to come on an evening out."

"Well in that case we would be delighted."

In fact Sam was the only noticeable absentee from inside the company: Ben, Kate, Jeff, Barbara all trooped in. Jeff was delighted to find Rufus and Peter had been invited as well. He wondered how for a minute and then remembered that Kate would have had their contact details. Even John Abercrombie had made it much to Alan's surprise. "Delighted old boy, fantastic success, pleased for you."

They assembled on a long table down one side of the restaurant. Just as they were settling down and the waiter was taking their orders, there was a commotion at the entrance of the restaurant as another party arrived. Sue looked up and there suddenly was Rafaella right in the middle of things wearing another very elegant black number, swept back hair and a pair of huge diamond earrings. Without thinking Sue called out: "Hi Rafaella!"

This time there was no scowl just curiosity as Rafaella peered across the restaurant to see who was calling her name. "Sue? Oh I don't believe it!" The heels "click clacked" across the wooden floor as Rafaella flew across the restaurant in a waft of perfume and embraced Sue warmly. Sue introduced her to Barry and suddenly the whole table was in uproar as they were all introduced. Sue felt a little sheepish as she had neither meant to drag Rafaella away from her party or disrupt her own table.

"Oh Barbara!" The Rafaella charm was clearly in full flow, as she enveloped Barbara in a flamboyant embrace. After a minute or two, Rafaella finished greeting everyone and departed to her table. "Thank you Sue. Lovely to see you and meet Barry." Sue watched Rafaella return to her table of five and quickly pick up some easy banter with her dining companions. Sue wondered if she had decided to turn over a new leaf.

The evening was very successful. After the main course had been completed, Alan stood up and rapped his spoon against an empty wine glass until the table fell silent. Heads tuned in other corners of the restaurant. "Thank you all so much for coming this evening," he began and before he could continue the compliments flooded in:

"No thank you…"

"Lovely food!"

"What a fantastic restaurant!"

Alan held up his hand in acknowledgement. "I really wanted to thank you all so very much," he continued. "Only a few months ago I was seriously contemplating retirement from the company, and now with all of your help, I find myself – indeed ourselves – back at the heart of what is going on. It has been a fantastic few months, you have all been so helpful and a number of you have worked tirelessly to create a new programme, which is now known as 'The Leopard'," at which the table broke into spontaneous applause.

Alan waited for the noise to die down. "I particularly wanted to thank Jeff and Sue for all the long hours they have put into this, but Ben, Kate, and Barbara you have all been brilliant." There was another round of applause on the table. The mood was decidedly jovial.

"I have some news to share with you but before I do so I wanted to ask you each individually what you had got out of the Leopard programme so far..."

"The Leopard?" asked Barry.

"This is the programme I have been working on," explained Sue. "You know – the email?"

"The email indeed," replied Barry, "well that's been a bit of magic, that has..."

"I'm sorry Barry," asked Alan, "can you enlighten us?"

"Sue gave me that 11 Rules of Email sheet and I have to say it has transformed my life in the office. It took me two days but I am now totally on top of my emails, something I never thought possible. I even managed to get home on time for most of last week."

Alan was dumbstruck. "Really?"

"Yes really." Barry beamed back at him. "And you keep my wife employed too!" He continued.

"Stop it Barry." Sue was becoming embarrassed.

"Why should I? The work your team have done is fantastic," he exclaimed. He picked his wine glass up off the table. "Alan, a toast to all of you on the Leopard I say," he continued.

Alan was taken aback for a second and then everyone else did the same.

"Cheers! Cheers! The Leopard!"

After the hubbub had died down, Alan continued "Thank you Barry, that is very kind of you," he looked around the table. "So would anyone else like to share?"

"Well since Barry has set the ball rolling, I might as well add my part," Sue began. "The whole Leopard project has been a whirl ever since I started working for you Alan. I have to say I have loved every minute of it but in particular the whole Creative versus Functionality thinking has been my real win, especially when it comes to balancing home life and work, which I am now so much better at. Thank you." She finished.

"Sue, I am very pleased to hear that," replied Alan. "Thank you for all your insight also. OK who else?"

Ben put his hand up. "I know you lot are a bit cynical about me, and that's fine. Personally I think the Leopard concept is brilliant and although I know I don't always show it, I really value being a part of it. The best part of it has been Sue's lesson on the value of relationships."

"Well I never," said Alan.

"I went to see Bennett a few days ago," continued Ben. "He's still very upset about the embarrassment he caused last Friday, and I finally understood how highly he values the relationship he has with me. I apologised. There. Said it."

"Ben, thank you for your candour," said Alan. "And for all you contributions too."

"You're welcome," Ben had gone all quiet now, Sue looked at him closely – was he, perhaps, a little emotional?

"I'll go next," ventured Barbara. "Aside from the email, which is I will agree with Barry is great by the way, the best part from my perspective has been the Teamwork session which you did with Sam. It had never occurred to me that you could use these ideas to change the way we all work together. So thank you Alan and I really mean that."

"Alan, I have to say thanks to you, Jeff and the Leopard because saved my career," said Peter quietly.

"I am sorry, I didn't hear that?"

"The whole Creative versus Functional approach saved my career," said Peter clearly. "I am serious. I had screwed up a big project at work and if I hadn't understood that was why we had gone wrong, I would be unemployed right now. As it stands, we rescued the project, so I am very grateful."

"Thank you," said Alan, slightly bemused.

"Rescued me also," said John, not to be outdone. He smiled at Alan. "You and the Leopard have given me both the enthusiasm and the ammunition to challenge the young bucks," John said, slightly cryptically.

"Thank you all," said Alan, trying to draw the discussion to a close. He caught Jeff's eye.

"Jeff?"

Jeff smiled. "You remember I asked you to mentor me?"

"Yes."

"Well I have learnt more than I imagined possible in the last few months. The session on Meetings with John was brilliant, as was the Networking session," Jeff continued. "But I feel that I can take on anything now." He glanced at Kate. "What about you?"

"The hierarchy of communications was my favourite," she said self-consciously. "But it has been a journey."

"What about you Alan?" asked Jeff.

"So I met with Bill today," Alan said quietly, and suddenly there was complete hush around the table.

"And what did he say?" asked Jeff softly and unnecessarily.

"The big news is that the Leopard Programme starts with immediate effect and will be fully funded and rolled out across the entire company."

Pandemonium almost broke out at this point as most of the table made their enthusiasm known.

"Oh and one further thing," added Alan. "We are going to open up the Leopard Programme outside the company, so Rufus, Peter, and John will also be able to participate if they want to."

"What are you going to do?" asked Sue quietly.

Alan pretended not to hear her.

"Alan, I asked you what you are going to do?" said Sue firmly.

He looked at her directly. "I'm still involved," he muttered quietly.

Sue couldn't understand why he was being so evasive. "Come on, Alan!"

He sighed. "I really didn't want to talk about it this evening."

Sue was suddenly mortified. "Oh boy, please tell me you are not retiring. Are you?"

Alan smiled. "Actually I have been appointed to the main board as Director of Development, but I didn't want to make a big deal out of it."

There was stunned silence for a second followed suddenly by a huge cheer around the table and several cries of "congratulations". With impeccable timing typical of Alphonso's the waiter chose that moment to pop the champagne cork so the noisy celebrations continued on for several minutes as glasses of champagne were poured.

"Alan!" John proposed a toast.

After the toast, the table fragmented for a few minutes as people stood up to chat in small groups. Sue and Barry sat quietly by themselves for a few minutes.

"Well you seem to have landed on your feet then," said Barry.

"I never imagined that I would be doing something as big as this," admitted Sue. "What do you think about it all?"

"I'm really pleased for you. I must say I do think Alan is a super bloke to work for."

"I'm really loving it," said Sue. "I do hope it's not wiping you out."

"Oh I'm managing fine," relied Barry cheerfully. "It would be great to see more of you but with this project it will get better."

"Thank you," she said simply. "You are a rock."

They were rudely interrupted by Ben who had clearly had a couple of drinks. "Hiya!" he said flopping into the chair next to them carrying a half full champagne glass.

"Hello Ben," replied Sue neutrally, she was curious to see where this was going.

He leaned over conspiratorially. "That Rafaella bird," he began. "You know the spectacular one with the large," Ben paused. "You know?"

"Yes I know Rafaella," replied Sue, wondering if she was going to have to call a taxi to take Ben home.

"Well Rafaella and Barbara, you know her. There's something going on there!" He looked around the table for more champagne.

"What exactly do you mean by that?"

"I saw them! I did! Out by the cloakrooms!" Ben poured himself another glass. At least one too many thought Sue.

At that moment Barbara and Rafaella walked back into the restaurant and over to the table. "See? Told you!" Ben got up and staggered past them heading for the gents.

"Do you mind if Rafaella joins us for a minute or two?" Barbara asked Alan diplomatically.

"She would be very welcome," responded Alan, ever the diplomat. Much to Sue's alarm, they sat down right next to her. Common sense told her to say nothing. In fact it was sitting on her shoulder screaming, "Leave it! Leave it!" But it was bothering her. What with a social oaf like Ben now involved, she couldn't just leave it.

Rafaella was now chatting to Alan, so Sue seized her moment. "Barbara," she began.

"Hi Sue," in an instant Barbara gave Sue her full attention and for a moment Sue wavered.

"I don't quite know how to say this, but there has been some idle speculation on your relationship with Rafaella."

"Really?" Barbara suddenly went all cold on her.

"Yes really." Sue recovered her confidence and she met Barbara's gaze full on. Barbara peered at Sue for a moment and decided Sue was an ally, so she dropped the chill and grinned. "That's hilarious who was it? No let me guess." she looked round. "One of the young ones I'm guessing?" she ventured.

"Actually I'm not sure it matters," observed Sue.

"Probably not, but it is very funny."

"Really?" Sue was curious.

"There are so many rumours about Rafaella at our company, I am astonished but delighted to find myself the subject of one." She paused for a second. "Was it Ben?"

"I err…" Sue couldn't quite respond quickly enough.

"So let's have a bit of fun." She leaned over and whispered in Rafaella's ear.

Rafaella nodded several times and then laughed hysterically.

Everyone continued chatting until Ben returned from the gents. He wandered over to the table and just as he was about to sit down, Barbara stood up. Sue had a sudden sense of anticipation. "As many of you know I have been single for many years," declared Barbara with a straight face. "So while we are on the good news this evening, I wanted to announce that I am getting engaged."

"Barbara! That's fantastic news, congratulations" interjected Alan.

"Thanks Alan you are so very kind."

"Who's the lucky person?" Sue thought she better steer this in the right direction.

"I thought my chance had passed," continued Barbara, hamming up the acting something rotten. "But when I met Rafaella I knew that I had finally found true love." She turned and gazed longingly at Rafaella and they held hands. Sue was struggling to contain her mirth. The rest of the table weren't in on the joke and there was a stunned silence.

"Err, many congratulations," ventured John politely.

Ben's eyes were on stalks.

"Hey Ben, aren't you pleased for us?" asked Barbara pointedly.

"Oh… err… I… delighted…" he stammered.

It was too much for Barbara and Rafaella. They burst out laughing simultaneously.

"So sorry, Alan, John…" wheezed Barbara. Sue was in bits also.

Alan was perplexed. "Sorry for what?"

"We are not really getting married, it was just a joke."

"Oh. I am not sure I get it."

Rafaella and Barbara were still having hysterics. Alan was completely bewildered.

Sue wiped away her tears of mirth and leaned over to Barbara. "I think you need to let Alan in on the joke," she said.

"Right!" said Barbara, with tears of laughter flowing down her face.

"Sorry Alan," she said. "Let's just say that a certain someone was making comments about Rafaella and I, and I thought that was the best way of winding them up was to pretend we are getting married."

"Well you had John and I fooled," smiled Alan.

"Sorry again!"

Ben still hadn't worked out the joke and was sitting in stunned silence.

"Come on Barry, time for home," said Sue. "Alan - thank you so much for a wonderful evening." As they wandered out, Barbara came after them.

"Sue I just wanted to say thank you."

"What for? It was a pretty good wind up."

"No I wanted to thank you for raising the topic with me. I know that took some courage and you were conflicted." Barbara reached out and gave Sue a big hug. She whispered into Sue's ear.

"Everybody does think I'm single but you should know I have actually lived with a female partner for a number of years."

Sue moved so she could look directly into Barbara eyes. "Seriously? Not a wind up?"

"No. Not a wind up. And you are the only person at the company who knows."

"Well blow me down. No wonder you gave that look when first I told you."

"Generally I protect my privacy like crazy, I guess I just got a little careless chatting with Rafaella this evening – I mean we have become very good friends. But nothing more."

"Well I must say I thought it was very funny, even though Alan and John had no idea what was going on."

"Good. And thanks again for telling me."

Jeff was still sitting at the table and Kate slid up alongside him. "I lied earlier," she said simply.

"You lied? What about?"

"The Leopard project."

"Oh really?"

"Yes. The best part about the Leopard project has been that you and I finally ended up getting together."

Jeff looked at her quizzically, his instinct for discretion forgotten for a second. "It has nothing to do with the Leopard project," he said. "I don't know what I was doing at business school for a whole year, but you are definitely the best thing that happened to me full stop."

"Let's get out of here?" she suggested. And they slipped off into the night.

Escape to France

Alan heaved a big sigh of relief as he climbed into the taxi at Bordeaux airport. "One more leg to go," he thought. "Domme here we come."

His family had all gone on holiday a few days ahead of him as he had been delayed by a Board Meeting which he simply could not miss as it was his first. He dozed gently as the taxi made its way through the valleys of the Dordogne, and before he knew it the taxi driver was shaking him awake. "Monsieur! Monsieur!"

He looked out and realised that they were in the town square in Domme, as he had forgotten to give the final directions to the taxi driver. "Merci, monsieur!" He paid the taxi driver and got out. It was a lovely evening. He didn't have much luggage and it was not far to walk.

As he strolled through the narrow streets he felt himself begin to unwind. He took in the wonderful climbing roses, the lavender and unmistakable smell of plane trees. It was great to be back in France!

As he walked through the town gate down the hill he stopped for a minute to enjoy the spectacular views across the valley. The ding-ding-ding of a passing scooter roused him from his trance and he walked down the hill towards Casternou where they were all staying. The shadows were beginning to lengthen as he reached the sign that marked the house; he turned off the road and began to walk down the long driveway alongside the cliff face.

As he a turned a corner in the drive he suddenly stopped dead. Sitting in front of him in the middle of the drive was a full-grown male leopard. Its tail swished from side to side.

For a brief moment Alan wasn't sure whether he was dreaming or not. Then he remembered the cat.

"Hi, how are you?" he said confidently, hoping that this wasn't a specimen that had escaped from a zoo.

"Well done," said the Leopard. "You made it."

"Yes, I suppose I did."

"Me too," said the Leopard. It stood, turned and then suddenly vanished.

"Thank you for everything!" Alan called after it.

He smiled and walked on through the rays of the setting sun.

FINIS

Chapter Notes

Proper Presentation

Audience – understand the context of the presentation, who your audience is and their expectations. This will fully drive both your preparation and timing.

Timing – unless you are making a depth presentation with detailed information, shortness and punctuality are paramount.

- *7 minutes and 20 minutes are good starting points.*

- *More than 40 minutes requires a break to maintain attention.*

- *Allow for questions either at the end or as you go along.*

Preparation – balance your knowledge of the topic, preparation of the content and rehearsal of the performance.

Three Typical Types of Presentation – Show, Know and Go

Show Presentation – to bring an audience up to speed on a topic with which they are not that familiar. Think of these as an advertising agency pitch. They should tell a story, be engaging and compelling to the audience if possible.

Know Presentation – to provide detailed and in depth knowledge on a topic to an audience that has some context but needs to understand the detail. This would cover financial briefings, operational updates and board reports. These presentations are all about detail and order, it is vital to make sure that the presenter knows the topic intimately.

Go Presentation – a presentation to motivate the troops and stir people into action. There are great military and political leadership examples, but above all this is about firing up the people in the room.

Getting the message across

- *First you must tell the audience what you are going to tell them.*

- *Then tell them.*

- *And finally – tell them what you have told them.*

The Golden Rules

- *Make sure you understand your audience and the context.*

- *Do your preparation thoroughly and above all make sure you are mentally ready.*

- *Aim to get over no more than 3 key points that the audience will take away.*

QUID FACERE DEINDE?

In a rather poetic way, it all started in Africa as many of the best things in life do. On a game drive with our ranger Phil, we were following some leopard tracks. He said he thought there were four leopards on the property but you could never be sure. On another property, he said, they also thought they had four so they set some traps and caught seventeen.

So there are all these Leopards around, being successful doing their thing and nobody knows! How interesting! Could the characteristics of a Leopard help individuals become more successful?

The Leopard in a Pinstripe Suit is about helping you – The Individual – to become more successful and retain some control of your life. Even if one small nugget works that's great or better still you might decide you want to become a Leopard.

My personal goal is to create one day of "Unallocated Time" a week. I am not there yet but I am getting close.

I would love to know how you are getting on, whether you have decided to become a Leopard or if you just need some help.

Visit the website or email me to let me know what you have decided to do. You never know, you might find more than you bargained for!

www.theleopardinapinstripesuit.com

tony@leopardtalk.com

ABOUT THE AUTHOR

Tony Henderson has worked in music, television and technology industries for many years before running a CEO leadership network (which was a lot of fun).

Tony has now returned to work in the technology industry (which he really loves), and lives in Oxfordshire, England.

In his spare time he runs, cooks, drinks and writes but not always exactly in that order.

Lightning Source UK Ltd.
Milton Keynes UK
UKOW031445171212

203760UK00001B/214/P